THE GRIEF NURSE

ANGIE SPOTO

ISBN: 9781914518003

#TheGriefNurse
@SandstonePress

SANDSTONE PRESS

First published in Great Britain in 2022 by
Sandstone Press Ltd
PO Box 41
Muir of Ord
IV6 7YX
Scotland

www.sandstonepress.com

Copyright © Angie Spoto 2022
Editor: K.A. Farrell

ISBN: 978-1-914518-17-1
ISBNe: 978-1-914518-18-8

Sandstone Press is committed to a sustainable future. This book is made from Forest Stewardship Council ® certified paper.

Cover design by David Wardle
Printed in the UK by Severn, Gloucester

CHAPTER 1

Lynx was warm with grief and more was in her grasp. She held a pocket watch, smooth and well-used, worried over by a restless thumb. She kept it firmly in her fist, protected from the snow.

'Lynx,' said Mr. Aster. He sat at the far end of the garden bench. Behind him, the last-remaining leaves of a pruned rose bush shivered. 'Take it.' His shoulders curled and his hands clutched at his chest as if he could tear the grief from his heart with his own hands. 'Please, take it from me.'

He had removed his hat and set it upside down between them on the bench, where it was collecting snow. His black hair was shot through with strands of beryl. From the neck of his coat gleamed a gold tie, a flash of expensive suit. She guessed at what he was thinking: how could he be here, while his eldest son was nothing but dust?

He looked up at Lynx, his gaze fixated on the watch in her hand. 'What are you waiting for?' he asked, voice pleading.

Her heart beat to the rhythm of the watch in her hand. She could nearly taste the Sorrow, could almost feel the buzz of it against her lips.

'My boy's dead,' said Mr. Aster. 'My dear Sculptor is dead.'

The watch was like a heart in her fist. Take it. Take it. Take it.

The garden smelled of roses, though all the roses here were dead.

She closed her eyes and imagined her mind growing white fingers like tendrils of her hair caught in the wind. She unbound the fingers of her mind, letting them shoot forward toward Mr. Aster. His Sorrow was a rose, lovelier than any that grew from the earth. At the sensation of it, her mouth watered. Her nails dug into her skin as she held the watch tighter.

'How could he?' said Mr. Aster, his voice distant now.

The fingers of her mind wrapped themselves around the rose and its thorns. There it was, the taste of rosewater candy, sweet and musky on her tongue. She urged her mind forward, focused on the velvet petals of Mr. Aster's Sorrow—and she plucked it from him.

Relief softened her bones and her eyes fluttered open. Her fist throbbed, and her mouth tasted of salt. She'd bitten her tongue, but she felt light, buoyant now that the grief was settling within her. Mr. Aster's grief was pleasant and untroubled, unlike that of his dead son.

Mr. Aster turned his head. Tears still darkened his lashes, but he smiled. 'Sculptor's dead.' He nodded. 'Yes, my son is dead.' He pressed a hand to his heart. The Sorrow, of course, was no longer there. 'Well, I suppose we have a party to get to.'

As Lynx followed Mr. Aster from the gardens the grief she'd taken eased until it was only a pulsing memory, a cloying aftertaste on the back of her tongue. Now the job was done, an emptiness bloomed inside her. She worried what might rush in. Lynx drew her teeth across her tongue until she felt the jolt of pain from where she'd bitten it.

For a flash of a moment, she imagined a different life. She imagined leaving this island, riding the ferry to the mainland, starting anew, being someone else. But then what? She needed the Asters as much as they needed her. If she left them, she left the protection and comforts of Mount Sorcha. As a grief nurse, she would be vulnerable without them so she didn't let herself dwell on daydreams. She was a grief nurse, there couldn't be any other life but this.

'A shame about the hat,' said Mr. Aster. He'd been holding it down at his side as he walked, and he shook it, scattering snowflakes. 'Such a damp snow we're getting. Now I must get the lining replaced. What strange things grief makes us do.'

She reminded herself how lucky she was. This was a beautiful island, a beautiful place to live, and the Asters treated her well. And she had Andromeda. She swallowed the thought that sprung to mind – of Andromeda last night, before the news of Sculptor's death arrived, appearing at her bedroom door with a shard of bottle-green sea glass held aloft. Look what I found. It must be a good omen. At the time, the sight of Andromeda made her feel foolish and happy. Now, she was afraid of what the Aster's youngest daughter might ask her to do. Lynx bit down hard against the cut in her tongue.

As they left the gardens behind, Mount Sorcha rose into view. The house stood in the centre of a lush lawn, which spread out around it like a picnic blanket. It was made of colourful bricks, the pigments mixed in with the brickwork so the colours would never fade. Blues, greens, purples, oranges. Gables with bronze caps. Wide doors of gold. It was the crown jewel of the island, whose forests and hills, crags and stone beaches all belonged to the Asters.

Outside, servants were lighting the lamps that lined the drive. Soon guests would arrive, stepping from motorcars and brandishing umbrellas, filling the air with the scent of gasoline and perfume. For now, the drive was empty save for the servants and she and Mr. Aster.

The front door opened, and a woman stepped through. She wore a beaded gold dress, and her hair was dyed plum for the occasion.

'There you are.' Ms. Aster swept up to them, arms outstretched and a smile on her face. She bent close to Lynx, feigning a kiss beside her cheek. She would never touch her, never truly brush her lips against Lynx's skin or even press her hand. No one of any respectability touched a grief nurse.

Only an hour earlier, Ms. Aster had been furious. When Lynx had entered Ms. Aster's room, the contents of her jewellery box had been scattered across the carpet, gold chains and jewels flashing amongst the broken shards of whatever it was Ms. Aster had just thrown against the wall. Something had crunched beneath Lynx's feet. It had taken her a moment to realize that Ms. Aster's wailing contained words: the same phrase, how dare he, repeated again and again. Anger was the way of Ms. Aster's Sorrow, Lynx knew, but the words had chilled her.

Now free of grief, Ms. Aster was the woman everyone strove to be. Happy. Content. Bright.

'Lynx works miracles, doesn't she?' Mr. Aster placed his hand on his heart.

'You didn't think to wear your hat in the snow?' Ms. Aster ran her fingers along her husband's hairline.

Lynx stepped aside. She wanted to dissolve into the walls and be forgotten. She'd done her job, and usually that would have been enough. But Sculptor's death party was today. The house would be filled with grief, and the Asters would be showing her off to all the guests. She hated being the centre of attention and much preferred her usual position as the silent observer.

'It's only a light dusting,' said Mr. Aster, smiling.

An upstairs servant dressed in a suit with an emerald waistcoat and matching bowtie appeared in the doorway. His buttons gleamed; the Asters' crest was stamped into every one.

'Have you found Andromeda?' Ms. Aster asked. She spun her bracelets, making them chime. Her wrists were slim like a knotted young branch and they reminded Lynx of Andromeda's wrists. Lynx pressed her teeth against her tongue again, but the pain was nothing more than a dull throbbing now.

'No, madam,' said the servant.

'I can only hope our daughter is not knee-deep in mud somewhere, galivanting around the hills or wherever it is she goes.'

The sea, Lynx thought. If Andromeda is anywhere, it's in the sea. She imagined a girl standing in the waves, the fabric of her dress clinging to her knees. She was looking out across the water as if daring it to drag her under.

Ms. Aster turned to her husband. 'She's doing this to me deliberately. She thinks because she is the youngest she can act like a child forever.'

'She's only lost track of time.' Mr. Aster nodded toward the servant. 'Keep looking.'

The servant nodded once and turned on his heel.

'I suppose none of it will matter if Lynx's dress isn't done in time. We can start without Andromeda, but we cannot start without our grief nurse.'

Mr. Aster opened his mouth to say more, but a commotion made them all turn. A motorcar was rumbling down the drive, and already a team of servants were advancing. The car's tires were still rolling when the door burst open.

A man wearing a blue woollen coat unbuttoned to reveal a patterned cravat stepped from the motorcar. Crater, the youngest son. He bounded up the steps toward his parents. 'You're looking gorgeous, Mother.' He plucked off his hat and handed it to a servant.

Ms. Aster beamed. So freshly unburdened from Sorrow, she looked far younger than she was. Her skin was dewy, her lips parted in child-like anticipation. Only her hands, spidered with blue veins, betrayed her.

'Crater, love. You're looking Bright,' she said, giving her son a kiss.

'Of course,' said Crater. He spun his diamond earring with a gloved hand. Mr. Aster swept him up into a hug before he could say more. Another car began making its way down the brick drive, diverting everyone's attention once again. Lynx considered slipping away but knew it would be pointless. If a guest was arriving, Ms. Aster would want her nearby.

'A guest so early?' said Mr. Aster. 'Was there anyone else on the ferry with you, Crater?'

'Not that I noticed.' Crater stared at the motorcar that replaced the one he'd arrived in. 'No one important anyway.'

Drops of melted snow slid down the cobalt surface of

the motorcar, and its gold trimming shone despite the gloomy weather. The chauffer emerged and opened the passenger door. A man ducked from the car, keeping his face turned away. He was tall and thin, and his coat was worn at the shoulders.

'Eridanus?' said Mr. Aster, his voice rising in a question. His voice was heavy with hope, tempered by apprehension.

'Really?' said Crater at the very same time.

Ms. Aster never looked Brighter. 'It's almost as if Sculptor knew,' she said, and she took her husband's arm. 'That this would be the only way to bring everyone home again.' She shook her head, the beads of her dress clinking delicately. 'All my children back under one roof at last.'

'Not all your children,' said Eridanus, finally looking up at his family clustered at the top step. He slid off his gloves and placed them in a pocket.

Ms. Aster smiled wide and shook her head. 'Sculptor is here in spirit, darling. Death is just another journey for him. You know how much he loved traveling.' Her voice was loud and floating, as if she were an actress on a stage. In a way, she was. She hadn't seen Eridanus for three years. None of them had.

He looked much the same. Thin as a rod, a lugubriousness about his deep-set eyes. The only difference Lynx could see was the streak of grey in his hair that he'd made no attempt to hide. Ms. Aster noticed it too, but she smiled through it.

'Yes, and catching diseases in foreign countries.' Eridanus's voice was liquid with sarcasm. That was the official story, what the Asters had leaked to the gossip newspapers, what would be written on his death certificate. Lynx knew it wouldn't stop the rumours from flying.

'Come inside, all of you,' said Ms. Aster, turning into the house. Her husband and sons followed her, but Lynx hesitated at the threshold. She usually entered the house through the servants' entrance. She wasn't a servant though, she was something else entirely, and after a moment she stepped through the gold doors.

In the vestibule, the men shook off their sodden hats while servants flickered around them, collecting their umbrellas and coats. As a servant slid the coat from his shoulders, Eridanus stared longingly at the fire crackling in the vestibule fireplace. Crater chattered beside him. The diamond in his ear caught the light as his head moved along with his words.

Lynx stood apart, glad that the commotion of Eridanus's return kept the attention off her. Until Crater's eyes met hers.

'There she is.' Crater pressed his hand against the small of his mother's back, making her turn away from Eridanus. 'My little mistress of misery, what are you doing hiding in the shadows? Come out and play. I haven't seen you in ages.'

Lynx plastered a smile on her face. She felt as if she were treading water, just waiting for something to wrap itself around her ankles and pull her under. Was it the party she was worried about, or was it seeing Andromeda, who would be laden with Sorrow?

Crater cocked his head and clucked. 'You don't look ready for a party.'

'This isn't—' she said just as Ms. Aster spoke over her.

'Of course she's not ready. Do you think I'd have her

dressed in her usual uniform? I've had a dress rushed in from the mainland. A seamstress has been working all day to have it ready in time for the party. You won't be able to take your eyes off her.'

'You stick with me then,' Crater said to Lynx. 'I want everyone to know who has the best grief nurse.' He straightened his vest, pulling himself up a little higher. He raised his eyebrows too so that he looked like a marionette, all limbs connected with strings. 'I intend to be prosperous tonight, one way or another.'

'That's the only reason you're here, is it?' said Eridanus.

'What is a party except an opportunity to make a name for yourself?' Crater cocked his head at his older brother. 'And what exactly are you doing here, Dani? What else could possibly bring the prodigal son back home?'

'Oh, but this is perfect.' Ms. Aster took Eridanus's hand. He jerked back, but he didn't pull away. Crater hovered beside them both, his thumb and forefinger twirling his diamond earring. 'We can find you a proper match. There must be a dozen eligible men on their way this very moment.'

Crater's Brightness dimmed when Ms. Aster playfully slapped Eridanus's lapel. Eridanus looked as if someone had just punched him in the throat.

'Have you truly gone and done it, then?' said Crater. 'How does it feel to be a free man? You must be dying for a grief nurse.'

'I've not divorced Syril.' Eridanus looked at his brother. 'I have no more intention to than the day I married him. I'm here because my brother is dead and I came to pay my respects.' His voice faltered, and Lynx sensed something he wasn't saying.

'Pay your respects. Well, now you've certainly gone middle-class,' said Crater with a snort.

Ms. Aster's smile flattened. She pulled her hand away from her son's. 'You did not come here to pay your respects. You came to rip out your mother's heart. Apparently, the first time wasn't enough.'

Eridanus laughed, hollow and low. 'You haven't met him. You won't let him into this house. Who do you think is doing the heart-rending?'

'You need Lynx, Eridanus. You're hurting,' said Mr. Aster, coming between them all. He laid a hand on Eridanus's shoulder. 'It's been too long. We'll all be calmer once the grief is gone from this house.'

'There's always grief in this house,' said Eridanus, but Mr. Aster had a way of defusing any situation, and it was clear Eridanus would relent.

'We're glad you're here,' said Mr. Aster. 'Even if—'

'I'm still married to a poor man. I know.' Eridanus squeezed his father's arm once and pulled away.

'What a day, and the party hasn't even started.' Crater straightened his cravat. 'I'm glad you're here, too. It was a lot of pressure, assuming I'd be the only son now that Sculptor is dead.'

Eridanus made a throaty sound of disapproval. 'Come with me, Lynx.'

Crater turned to Lynx, his big teeth on full display as he smiled. 'Find me when you're done, my duchess of despair.'

Lynx followed Eridanus past the fireplace and into the upper vestibule. The great hall stretched before them, a vast expanse of marble floor and walls covered in colourful tapestries. The hall was airy and made even more so for the balcony that wound above it, making visible the rooms of the upper floor. All the important rooms were there – the drawing room, the dining room, the guest rooms, and each of the family bedrooms.

They took the grand staircase, Eridanus walking in front of her. She watched the back of him. His shoulders drooped, the symptom of a too-tall person trying to fit into a smaller world.

As they walked down the upper corridor, the painted glass skylights above them threw coloured light across Lynx's body. She was speckled green then purple then blue. For once she was more vibrant than the Asters, the blank white canvas of her hair and clothes reflecting the colours in saturated hues. Servants skittered here and there, in too much of a rush to stay invisible, but of course they managed to give her a wide berth, making sure none of them so much as brushed her sleeve.

She followed Eridanus down the winter wing, the skylights painted in cool jewel tones, and turned the corner toward the burgundies and reds of autumn. Eridanus's hair, like all the Aster children's, was dark, but as the colours of the corridor shifted, it was set momentarily alight.

Eridanus looked once quickly to his left, the colour sliding off him like oil, and Lynx's heart scrambled into her throat. Sculptor's bedroom. The door was ajar and there was movement from inside and for one panicked moment, Lynx thought Sculptor would open it, returned from death. She again tasted blood.

The door opened, but it was a round, pale face that appeared. 'Apologies, sir,' the maid stuttered. 'We're cleaning...' She dropped her gaze, never once looking at Lynx, and backed into the room. She shut the door with a snap.

'She didn't recognize me,' said Eridanus, his mouth twitching into a frown. He continued down the hall, but Lynx lingered. The doorknob was brass, forged in the shape of an oak leaf, another indication they were in the autumn wing. She remembered the way it felt in her hand, the ridges of the leaves pressing into her palm, a plump acorn resting just beneath her thumb. She followed Eridanus, glad to be leaving that room behind.

Eridanus's room was in the summer wing, the length of which blushed with pinks and purples. She caught up with him just as he was opening the door. A row of fuchsia tiles, each lined with a thin gold border of paint, marked the threshold of his room. He stepped inside and caught the door with his foot to hold it open for her. He didn't look at her, only slid his hands into his pockets and began to pace.

Lynx watched Eridanus's shoes crush the thick pile of the carpet. She pressed closed the door with her back and waited. She tried to ignore the Sorrow that burned in his heart, but Sorrow was the strongest kind of grief, and the hardest to resist. Eventually, he tugged at the chain around his neck, dredging up a small gold locket from beneath the folds of his shirt. 'My token. Here.' He slipped the chain over his head and practically threw it at her.

Lynx looped the chain around her fingers. Already the tang of smoke bit her tongue.

'I hate that I need this.' Eridanus slid his hands in and out of his pockets. He looked her in the eyes for the first time in years. 'It feels like a betrayal.'

'I'm sure Sculptor won't mind.'

'When you die, do you want everyone to go their merry

way as if you never existed?' He turned and began to pace again. 'Do you want to be forgotten?'

'Where did you get that idea?' Lynx moved farther into the room. She thought she might sit in one of the armchairs by the fire but then remembered how Eridanus's grief would feel, and she moved closer to the window instead. 'You haven't been drinking, have you?'

'Of course I've been drinking. My brother's dead.'

He didn't say anything more to fill the silence, so she dropped her gaze to the token wound round her fingers.

'Don't.' Eridanus's voice made her step back, and her spine juddered against the windowsill.

'Don't?'

'Don't take my Sorrow.' He looked directly at her, then at the locket resting in her palm. 'Say that you have, but don't take it really. I need it.'

'What do you mean don't take it?' Lynx asked, unsure if she had heard him correctly. *I need it. Why would anyone, beside a grief nurse, need grief?*

'I mean just that.'

'I don't understand,' she said, shaking her head. 'They'll notice. Even if I tell them I took it, they'll be able to tell.'

'Oh, that is the least of my worries.'

'Is it? This may be all your mother needs to cut you off. Your father is sending you money, and for now she's pretending not to notice.'

Eridanus smiled thinly. 'Well, good. I don't need her money.'

'Yes, you do.'

Eridanus laughed. Lynx smiled back. She couldn't help it. Eridanus had a smile that drew you in and kept you there. She often wondered what his husband was like.

Did he smile like Eridanus or was he dour and dull, like Crater claimed? She couldn't imagine Eridanus with someone dull, but his husband didn't have a grief nurse. He wasn't Bright. He couldn't be. Then again, Eridanus had never been Bright, not properly, and perhaps that was why his smile was so potent. It was real.

'You're the only one in this house who tells the truth.' He looked again at his token in her hand. 'So tell me truthfully: is there any good in grief?'

No, she thought. Nothing. 'If there was, no one would need a grief nurse.'

Eridanus considered this. 'That's what I always thought.'

'But?'

'So many people don't use grief nurses.'

'You mean the poor,' said Lynx. 'You want to be like them?'

'No, I just—' He shook his head.

'It's not the done thing to keep your grief,' she said, although she could tell from the look in Eridanus's eyes he wasn't listening. A log in the fireplace collapsed, and she tensed, nearly jumping. It had turned almost completely to white ash and crumbled under the weight of the log above. Tiny orange sparks leapt from the flames.

'Give me three days,' said Eridanus. He paused, probably expecting her to protest but she didn't. She was curious.

'Three days?'

'Yes, and if I can bear it that long, you may take it.'

His grief was a fire, a dying fire with black choking smoke that sputtered upward. She stepped backwards, and the cold seeping from the windowsill nipped her back. The heat of his grief burned and tightened her throat but there was a sweetness there too, a little like cinnamon. With the token in her hand, it took all her effort not to take it.

Lynx turned to look out the window. She sought the sapphire line of the sea, but of course she couldn't see far beyond the snowflakes illuminated in the yellow lights of the house. What could compel anyone with a grief nurse to want to endure grief? As her guardians, the Asters were entitled to have their grief removed at even the slightest glimmer of its presence. Theirs was an elite position and a coveted one; few even among the wealthy were allowed a grief nurse.

She turned when she heard movement. Eridanus now sat in the armchair beside the fire. He leaned his head back, and his gold-brown eyes watched her.

'Here.' Lynx dropped the locket into his upturned palm. 'You must like pain.'

Eridanus laughed. His mouth was wide when he smiled, lighting up all his features. 'Thank you for indulging me.' A pause. 'Would you let me explain? I'm not mad, I swear.'

'That may be up for debate.'

'Yes.' His smile fell away. 'We don't have a nurse at home.' He turned the locket around in his fingers. 'My husband – Syril – he wasn't raised as we were, in a big house with a grief nurse to keep us Bright. He lost his brother when he was young. His twin brother. They were very close, and when his brother died, there was no one to remove the Sorrow.'

'I could take it,' said Lynx. 'If you somehow—'

Eridanus shook his head, impatient. 'I know. He doesn't want you to. He doesn't want anyone to. He won't even let me put us on a waitlist.'

'He wants the Sorrow?'

'Yes. He can't look in a mirror without seeing his brother, but he wants it still. Even though it's…' Eridanus shook his head. 'He says he needs his Sorrow.'

'You think there's something good about that?'

'No.' Eridanus sat up. 'Of course not, but Syril is convinced. He says removing the Sorrow would be like cutting away the memory of his brother. I say what Father has always told us, it's like cutting away the rot of an apple. Why let a spot destroy the whole fruit?'

'But you aren't sure?'

Eridanus sank back into the chair. 'No, I'm not sure of anything. Syril says I don't know grief, not really. I haven't seen a grief nurse in three years. The Dread is bearable – you grow accustomed to the fear. It's only intolerable at night, when your head is spinning. Heartache you can largely ignore, if you keep yourself busy. But I know little about Sorrow. Sorrow is the difference between Syril and me.' He held the locket by its chain and let the gold pendant swing. 'If I let myself feel Sorrow, I can prove there is nothing good in it. Syril will relent. We'll get a grief nurse. Perhaps—' He shook his head. 'I don't want to lose him. Do you see what I mean?' He cleared his throat before she could respond. He slid to standing. He dipped his head and returned the locket to its place beneath his shirt. 'Avoid Crater if you can. He's practically high on happiness. I don't think he ever liked Sculptor.'

'Neither did you,' Lynx pointed out.

'Yes, but I never pretended to.' Eridanus held the door open for her. 'And I loved him.' He pressed a hand to his chest. 'I still do. Perhaps thanks to you.'

CHAPTER 2

The hallway was unexpectedly empty when she emerged from Eridanus's room. There were still hours yet before the party, and if she was lucky, she could sneak away unnoticed. She craved the cool sea air. As she hurried down the summer wing toward the autumn, making her way to the servants' stairwell, she passed Sculptor's bedroom door again

A memory rose to the surface. Sculptor was gone, and she wanted to forget. She wanted to look forward, but memories have minds of their own.

It had been two in the morning. She was used to the bell's sound, but Andromeda had startled. The deck of cards she'd been holding tumbled into her lap. 'What was that?' Andromeda had whispered, looking around. 'I've never heard anything so eerie.'

'The signal box,' said Lynx. Andromeda looked up at her, and she pointed to the box above the door. Ten small windows in two neat rows, each housing a tiny bell, a name or place scrolled in gold ink above it. Lady Aster, Sir Aster, Master Sculptor, Master Eridanus, Master Crater, Miss Andromeda, the drawing room, the dining room, the morning room, the upper vestibule.

The bell in Sculptor's window was still trembling.

'Why have I never noticed that before?' Andromeda scowled at the box and turned back to her cards. She swept them back into a neat deck and tapped them against the cold ground. She leaned over the three cards laid out in front of her. She waved at Lynx without looking up. 'Come here, and let's see what they have to say.'

Lynx watched the bell shiver, the sound now just an echo in her ears. 'I have to go.'

'The cards are laid. You're not going anywhere until I read them.' Andromeda still didn't look up, but she tapped the edge of the first card impatiently. Lynx slid off her bed and sat in front of the spread. Her knees nearly touched the cards, and she was aware of how close Andromeda was. She could smell the oil in her hair. Her mouth watered at the taste of saltwater, a hint of Andromeda's grief. She pressed her hands against her knees, letting her hair fall around her face as she leaned forward.

Andromeda's slim fingers turned the first card.

A woman with white hair, tendrils rearing up like snakes, stood holding a silver orb in her hands. It was a moon, and more moons were drawn around the card's border. The woman was dressed in white, and her eyes were white discs.

'Shut up, Lynx,' Andromeda said.

Lynx looked up, catching Andromeda's golden eyes. 'I didn't say anything.'

'You were thinking very loudly.' Andromeda's lips drew into a line. 'As you know, this is the Grief Nurse.' She tapped the card and before Lynx could object, she turned the next one.

A man and a woman, arms entwined in an embrace. A radiant sun shown above them, and at their feet were stars. 'The Lovers.' Andromeda's gaze flickered upward for a moment before she turned the next card.

It was simpler than the others, devoid of any border or decoration. A tree, roots twisting into invisible earth and branches reaching for the sky. Its branches were gnarled, and its bark was lined like an old woman's skin. The card was reversed. 'The Life Tree.' Andromeda leaned back and puffed out her cheeks.

Lynx's stomach twisted. Andromeda didn't know what these images meant to Lynx. She didn't know of the tree growing at the centre of Lynx's being. All grief nurses had trees within. Their roots and branches were the source of the white tendrils of a grief nurse's mind.

The cards seemed to be mocking her, a sly reminder of the distance between her and Andromeda. She wanted to sweep the cards away, rip each one of them to pieces and scatter them into the sea. Why had she agreed to let Andromeda read her fortune? She didn't believe in this sort of thing anyway.

'I have to go.' Lynx stood up. Her foot disturbed the first card, sending it sliding atop the Lovers.

'It was a mistake.' Andromeda looked behind her at the signal box. 'Sculptor isn't home tonight. He returned to the mainland.'

'He must have come back.'

Andromeda's lips were pressed together, just barely holding in the questions Lynx knew danced on the tip of her tongue. Andromeda plucked each of the cards from the ground and added them to the deck. She turned the deck around and around in her hands as if she were thinking of what to say.

Lynx didn't want to look at Andromeda. Alone together as the house slept, playing silly card games, she could forget they were from different worlds, but when she was called upon to be a grief nurse, the space between them was uncrossable. When Lynx first arrived at Mount Sorcha at ten years old, Andromeda had just turned eight. They grew up together, were taught by the same governess, played among the same forests and hillsides, lived in the same cavernous mansion on a lone island, but their futures were vastly different. Andromeda had choices – who to marry, where to live, what to do – while Lynx's path was already set before her, unchanging.

When she went to leave, Andromeda was there beside her. She tugged the sleeves of her pyjamas over her fingertips, releasing the scent of bergamot oil from the silk. Lynx opened the door and Andromeda cautiously followed her into the hall. 'I'm coming with you,' Andromeda said.

Lynx pretended she hadn't heard.

'Who do you think is dead?' Andromeda was two steps behind her as they climbed the servants' stairwell. Her whisper vibrated with excitement.

'No one.' Please, Meda, just go.

'Someone must have died. Why else call the grief nurse in the middle of the night?'

Lynx's shoulders stiffened. She hated when Andromeda called her the grief nurse. 'It must be Heartache.'

'Really, can you imagine Sculptor ever having Heartache? You took our Dread just last week, so it can't be that.'

'It was probably a mistake.'

'But you still have to check?'

It's my job, she wanted to say, but that didn't feel right. Being a grief nurse was more than a job. It was who she was, and it was the reason she didn't need a card reading to know her future. It was already determined: this was the best her life could be.

She knew what would happen if she left the Aster's island. Grief nurses were vulnerable without the protection of their guardians, subject to violence and exploitation by those desperate to be free of grief. Life here was far better than the alternative.

The two emerged into the upper corridor of the main house, the one that looked down onto the great hall below. All at once Andromeda said, 'Lynx, really, who do you think is dead?'

Lynx thought she smelled seawater, a riptide tug of Dread, and she stepped away. 'No one.'

Andromeda looked toward Sculptor's bedroom door. Her expression was closed-off, unreadable. 'Fine. Good night, then.'

'Good night,' said Lynx, but Andromeda's lips only twitched, and she turned away.

The sea was gone, replaced by a new temptation.

Lynx didn't bother to knock on the door. She grasped the awkward handle and slipped inside. Moonlight flooded the room, casting everything in blue. A warm summer air filled the place, making the curtains dance. Sculptor sat in bed, his back against the headboard, his legs stretched out and crossed at the ankles. He was fully dressed, and the heels of his shoes sunk deeply into the duvet. Even as she entered, he continued looking straight ahead, out the window across the room.

'Just the usual, please.' He tapped the crook of his elbow. His familiar joke. Better than drugs.

'Does it have to be at two in the morning?' She stood at the foot of his bed, blocking his view of the window. He was forced to look at her.

'My apologies. Did I wake you?' Sculptor slid the watch from his wrist and tossed it to the end of the bed. 'Take it.'

She stared at the gold watch nestled in the duvet, a snake in the grass, waiting to bite. Stronger than the desire to snatch up the token, to reach inside him and wrap her fingers around his grief was a hatred so clear and uncompromising she was afraid of it. She would not pick up the token. She did not want a grief like Sculptor Aster's inside her.

The second before Sculptor scrambled across the bed toward her, she sensed his grief flare. Silver. Blood. A blossoming of pain. He seized her hand and thrust the watch into her palm. He held it there, its clasp cutting into her skin, and twisted her wrist.

'Take it.'

The watch ticked against her palm, sending tiny vibrations into the bones of her hand. Take it. Take it. Take it.

She thought of the cards Andromeda had revealed on the floor of her bedroom. What was the point of reading a grief nurse's fortune? There was never any different path, no surprise ending. She was tethered to Mount Sorcha, but she couldn't be with Andromeda. They could be nothing other than friends.

He forced her hand against her heart, the token beating against her chest. She hated it. She wanted it, she was afraid, and he knew.

'Take it.'

Sculptor's grief was a knife, polished enough to make a reflection, sharp enough to cut the fingers that reached for it.

The longer she held the token, the stronger the blade called to her. She ground her teeth, and her mind's fingers stretched forward, touching, not taking, making sense of what she was feeling. Mostly common Heartache, the lightest grief, edged with Dread, that tenacious, fearful grief that clung to her fingers. She wasn't surprised to find no Sorrow – she hadn't lied when she told Andromeda that no one Sculptor loved had died. But what Andromeda didn't know was that no one was ever completely free of grief. There was always something lingering. For Sculptor, this was truer than for most.

'You like it just as much as I do.'

She hated that he was right. She wanted even Sculptor's bitter grief.

She closed her eyes. Her mind's fingers played across the blade. Beneath the flickering white tendrils, the knife began to change. Its surface shivered. The once-solid blade rippled as if it were now made of molten metal. A single silver drop fell from the tip.

Sculptor drew a sharp breath.

Another drop off the blade, and Sculptor's fingers clawed tighter around her wrist Another drop and she felt his breath on her face, pulling her close. Take it. Take it. Take it. Her mind shifted, tumbling forward, finally releasing, and for a moment she was no longer a grief nurse. No longer a white-haired girl but a young man with too much grief and too much money, too much time and too many opportunities to let the loneliness become him. She twisted, her mind's fingers curling like claws, anger and want boiling up inside, the urge to take and take until the world took shape in her hands. She knew how easy it would be, how easy—

'That's enough,' Sculptor said, his voice creaking.

The sensation flickered, and she was back inside herself, her mind's fingers still playing across Sculptor's blade. She let another drop fall, enjoying, despite herself, the way it made Sculptor flinch. She took the grief and pulled it inside her. The pain was sweet.

Sculptor released her. Her wrist ached, was wet and cool from his sweat. His scent, tobacco and mint, still lingered in her nostrils. She pulled away and settled into the armchair beside the window. She tucked her legs up against her chest and sank into the velvet. She still clutched his token, and with her free hand she reached out and felt the warm air from the window. Her body hummed.

Sculptor knelt at the edge of his bed. He tilted his head back and looked up at the painted ceiling. It was covered in images of planets and stars. A sun burst just above the bed's centre with the Asters' crest painted inside its golden heart.

'It will come back tomorrow,' he said eventually. When she didn't respond, he pulled himself forward, clutching the foot board. 'It's too difficult to lie. I can't spend my entire life pretending I'm Bright. I can't—' His voice broke. 'Lynx, don't leave.'

'I won't.' She turned her head to look out the window.

'You're the only good thing in my life.'

Piss off, she wanted to say but let the silence speak for her.

After a long while, he said, 'One more time. Make me Bright again.' Reluctantly, she reached inside him. Grief was there, faint but growing, just as she expected. She snapped the blade cleanly from his heart and pulled it into her own. The thrill dissipated immediately. She was left feeling empty again and worse, unclean.

It was one memory among dozens. The closed door loomed before her. It was a just a room now, as insignificant as any other. Lynx drew her hair up and let the cool air kiss her neck.

Sculptor was dead. She'd never have to go in there again.

CHAPTER 3

The petals of the gorse were shivering. The air here always had a bite to it, but now it felt electrified, ominous. Lynx watched the yellow lipped flowers until her legs, folded beneath her, grew numb. When she stood, the wind was stronger without the shelter of the bush, and her hair was tugged out of its hold and thrashed around her face, catching in her lips and eyelashes. She lifted it back up and twisted it into a knot. She had wandered far from Mount Sorcha, to the western shore of the island, where the sea churned against crags whose slopes and summits sprouted angry bushes. The grass was long and pressed flat, exposing the earth like bald spots. She looked out to the sea, at the sodden clouds in the distance. For now, the snow was holding, though it was clear it would only be a short respite. The sun was gone, if you could say it had ever even arrived, and the water was whipped up into metallic swells. It was late afternoon, but already the moon was rising, a thin waxing crescent.

A dark spot broke the surface of the water, and Lynx wondered what bird it could be. The gannets that divebombed into the water, dropping like stones straight into the sea from impressive heights, were white with black-tipped wings. The spot disappeared and reappeared again closer to the shore. It was the crown of a head, slick and black. A seal?

Lynx watched as a tall figure pulled itself onto the rocks. A curve of a bare waist, a long arm. Andromeda was almost unrecognizable without her dress, with her hair tamed by water, with her long legs bare, but Lynx knew her immediately.

She felt fuzzy with guilt. She was an accidental voyeur, watching as Andromeda turned and looked out over the sea.

The air was cold. She could hardly imagine how the water must feel.

Another gust of wind made Lynx step back. Certainly, Andromeda could see the dark clouds, feel the threat of a storm in the air, but she didn't turn away from the water. She took one step back then ran, throwing herself into the sea. Once again, she was only a dark shape bobbing in the water.

Lynx held her breath as the dark spot slipped beneath the waves. She picked her way through the bushes toward the shore, which was covered in slick sea-worn rocks. She stayed behind a boulder that was covered with lichen, vibrant in the grey afternoon.

It was a long time before Andromeda returned. This time, she knelt on the shore, the water licking her knees, and took gasping breaths. Lynx thought she had swallowed water but soon realized she was sobbing. Lynx couldn't resist. She reached forward, searching for Andromeda's grief. What she found made her sit back, rocks sliding away beneath her, and she fell hard on her tailbone. Her hair came undone again.

When she finally had it tamed, Andromeda was no longer crying. She was striding toward Lynx's hiding space, the water sluicing off her skin.

'Lynx!' she called. 'What are you doing here?'

Lynx tried not to let her eyes wander over Andromeda's body. So close, she could see the twist of her bellybutton, the groove of her clavicle. She was dizzy with the nearness of Andromeda, her body – but, even more potently, her grief.

There was nothing that physically marked a Fader, nothing like grief nurses' white hair. Only a grief nurse could sense the difference in a Fader's grief. It was impossible not to. A Fader's grief wasn't an object to be plucked. It was a place to step into, to be devoured by. She could taste and smell and touch a normal person's grief, but a Fader's grief gave her something more. The sensation of someone's fingertips against her skin. A tightening between her legs. A desire that made her want to pluck the hairs from her head or bite her lip until it bled. Something painful and delicious.

That was how she felt now, standing in the rising tide of Andromeda's Sorrow.

She could swallow the temptation of Mr. Aster's grief. She could pretend she hadn't enjoyed the way Eridanus's fire burned her throat. But she couldn't ignore Andromeda's ocean. She knew Andromeda felt the same attraction. There was a mutual hunger between a Fader and a grief nurse. To admit to it would be to admit a gross sexual deviance, a fetish that broke every social taboo: to Andromeda, grief-taking wasn't just a pleasant thrill.

'I don't like being underfoot,' Lynx said, biting back the impulse to let her knees buckle. She turned her head in the direction of Mount Sorcha. 'They're looking for you.' Waves rose and fell. A dark, berry-rich colour threaded with white veins as they peaked. They were wild, cresting and crashing, flinging water into the sky as if they wanted to drench the moon.

Andromeda twisted her hair into a rope and pulled her hand down its length. A snake of water flicked off the tip. 'I'm sure Mother's furious.'

'Not as much as you might think. She's very Bright.'

Andromeda snorted. 'Of course.'

'Andromeda—' Lynx sought the familiar flash of gold in Andromeda's hair. A pin in the shape of a sand star, encrusted with diamonds. Her token. She wanted to take it into her palm and close her fingers around it. She wanted to draw her thumb across the diamonds, and with just as much effort, smooth away the waves of Andromeda's Sorrow until the sea was as flat and still as glass.

But there was no pin in Andromeda's hair.

'She said now that he's dead, it's my responsibility to marry well and save the estate.' Andromeda's fingers clawed at one another, tearing at the skin around her nails. 'I'm not going to sell myself to the highest bidder. If Mother wants to save the house, she can find another way.'

Lynx heard the words Andromeda spoke, and she knew the ones she didn't. Andromeda couldn't be the one to save Mount Sorcha. What was worse than the attraction Faders had for grief nurses and the thrill they felt at grief-taking was what they had the potential to do.

As a Fader, Andromeda might have a grief nurse child. Only Faders could bear grief nurse children; grief nurses themselves were barren. The Aster's reputation would not survive the birth of a grief nurse into the family. Oh, among the lower classes, grief nurse children were seen as opportunities – a means to a generous stipend from the government in exchange for giving up the child. But in a family like the Asters, where status was far greater than money, a grief nurse child was a curse, a reputational disaster. A secret like Andromeda's would not only get her sent to a madhouse, it would destroy her family's good name – and it was nearly all they had left.

'As if she isn't the real reason he's dead. As if she didn't force him into the arms of that witless Vela Deleporte. As if she didn't pretend our whole lives that he was just like everyone else. When he's—' Her voice caught. She pressed the heels of her hands against her eyes, clawing her fingers into her hair. 'He was my brother. He was my selfish, reckless, stupid brother.'

If Lynx weren't a grief nurse, she would have taken Andromeda's restless fingers into her own. Instead, she could only watch as Andromeda angrily wiped away her tears.

'Will you take it now?' Andromeda asked, her voice dropping low so it was nearly lost in the wind. Her gaze darted toward a nearby rock.

Lynx stepped back. Of course Andromeda would want her to take her Sorrow. She was her grief nurse, after all. But somehow, Lynx was caught off guard. She had tried to avoid thinking of Andromeda all day, of the sweetness of that Sorrow and how it would taste when she took it. Now that she had felt it, she was afraid.

'I can't,' she said. 'Not now.' Lynx bit her tongue and ignored the way her stomach felt – as if she had swallowed stones.

'What do you mean? Why not?'

'This isn't Heartache, Meda. This is Sorrow. This is

different than any kind of grief you've had before.'

'I know that.'

'So you know that if I take it, you might— you might do something you regret.'

She didn't have to say more for Andromeda to know what she meant. Lynx had been taking Andromeda's grief all her life, but she'd never taken her Sorrow. With Heartache and Dread, it was easy to pretend there was no shared hunger between them. It was easy to pretend that everything that wasn't said didn't hang between them like ghosts.

"Then take it quickly,' said Andromeda. 'Just don't linger.'

'We should wait. It's too strong right now, but it'll lessen given time.'

She wasn't lying, but neither was she being truly honest. She was not afraid to take Andromeda's Sorrow because she feared Andromeda's reaction – she was afraid of herself and what a taste of that grief could make her do.

'Oh, really?' said Andromeda, crossing her arms, her growing anger so palpable, Lynx could nearly see it like sparks flickering across her skin. 'I suppose I'll just pretend I'm Bright all evening. I'll certainly fail spectacularly, and Mother will be furious, but, really, you'd be only doing me a favour then, wouldn't you?' She turned around again and began wading into the water. She said over her shoulder. 'In fact, I'll just wait forever, if that would suit you better. If you really don't trust me enough.'

'You need to be careful, Meda.'

Andromeda froze. For a nauseating moment, Lynx saw two oceans. The one that churned beneath a darkening sky and another one – with a full moon high above its waters. Andromeda's grief was so strong, it was difficult to know what was real and what was Sorrow.

'Why is everyone always telling me that?' Andromeda said.

'Because we're worried for you.'

Andromeda spun around. Lynx felt her anger like lightning. 'I won't end up like my grandmother, locked away in a madhouse just for being who I am. I won't.'

'But that's why you need to be careful. Just wait until after the party, please, Meda.' By then perhaps Andromeda's Sorrow really would have lessened, and she could take it as Andromeda said, quickly and without lingering. It had to work. She couldn't entertain the alternative. 'It's just the way things are,' she said, hating the words that left her mouth all the more for knowing they were true.

'I hate the way things are.' Andromeda bit out the words.

Me too, Lynx wanted to say, but what did it matter?

Andromeda' gaze once again lingered on that rock, and then she turned back to the sea.

'Meda, don't go back in. There's a storm coming. The currents—'

'I don't care about the currents.' Andromeda's voice was low.

'I'm sorry—'

'Save your breath, Lynx.' The waning grey light of the sky illuminated the edges and curves of her. Andromeda was alight and she was beautiful. 'I wish you weren't a grief nurse,' she said. Whatever Lynx was going to reply caught in her throat, and Andromeda turned and ran into the sea. White spray flew up around her as she dove back in.

The cut on Lynx's tongue had opened. She pressed a fingertip to it. It was scarlet only for a second before the blood was whisked away in the wind. When she couldn't see Andromeda anymore, she turned to the rock that had drawn Andromeda's gaze.

The pin was tucked into a nook in the rock. Its tiny diamonds and gold filigree gave it away. It wasn't a real sand star, only a glittering, expensive imitation. A heavy snowflake melted against her cheek and rolled down her jaw. She couldn't see Andromeda in the water nor any evidence that she was there at all.

Lynx crouched, bending her head toward the token. Even in the grey light, it sparkled. The wind blew her hair around her face, white tendrils cutting across her vision, and a violent desperation rose inside her – to cut it all off, to become someone else, to fight instead of letting herself be held under. If she didn't fight she would drown. Without thinking, without trying to resist, she reached for Andromeda's token.

As soon as her fingers brushed its surface, she was overcome with the force of Andromeda's Sorrow. A tidal wave that made her gasp, as if the sea really were crashing against her body, dragging her under. Take it. Take it. Take it.

With the token clenched in her fist, she slipped off her shoes and bounded across the rocks. A length of bladderwrack wrapped around her shin, its flesh cool and rubbery. She shook it off and waded until the water was above the knots of her anklebones. She closed her eyes, her hand squeezing tighter around the token. She reached out with her mind and pushed through the disorientation, the mixing of grief-sense and the physical world, until she found the waters of Andromeda's Sorrow. She wanted to peel the clothes from her skin, to submerge herself in a darkness so complete not even the glowing whiteness of her hair could be seen. She wanted to feel the severity of Andromeda's hip bone against her palm, to sink her fingers into the soft flesh of her waist – she wanted to touch Andromeda, skin against skin, until there was no space between them.

She threw herself into the waves of grief, letting the waters close over her. There was darkness and muted sounds, until she realized what she was doing, how far she could go, and she pulled herself, gasping, from Andromeda's grief. She turned and ran to the shore, falling on her knees beside the rock where Andromeda's token had lain. She set the token back in place before grasping her arms and taking a shuddering breath. How could she lose control like that? How close had she been? She tried to focus on the wind against her skin, the snowflakes speckling the rocks around her, the crashing of the waves against the shore – anything but that memory she'd buried long ago.

Eventually, she rose and turned to look out at the sea. Great wet snowflakes were splashing into the water. She searched for Andromeda's dark head but saw only the swell of the waves, the seaweed tumbling against the rocks to be sucked back out a moment later.

Take it. Take it. Take it, the voice still urged, but she refused to listen.

CHAPTER 4

The servants' quarters were immaculate. The walls were tiled in stripes of indigo and gold, and while the floors were wooden, at least they were polished. All the rooms, including the kitchen and the butler's pantry and the bedrooms and the laundry cupboard, were strung along a single corridor. Looping archways gave the hall a tunnel-like effect. Lynx often imagined the whole thing filling up with water like a sea cave at high tide.

She stepped into her room and began to shut the door, but it was too late.

'Lynx?' said Solina. She knocked on the door while pushing it open. 'You can't hide away all night.'

Lynx knew there wasn't any point in picking a fight. Solina was right. She had been hiding, from Andromeda or everyone else, she wasn't sure.

Solina was an upper servant, dressed in a simple emerald wrap dress with a gold silk apron. Her hair was twisted up in a gold scarf, and the sparkles dusting her eyelids flashed. She picked at Lynx's plain white shirt with the tips of her nails. Draped over her other arm was a white cascade of fabric. 'Take this old thing off.'

Lynx undressed without arguing. Her usual uniform, white from collar to trouser hems, she tossed onto the bed where it lay there, forlorn. Lynx could never escape the loneliness of the colour white.

The dress rustled as Solina dropped it onto the bed beside the discarded uniform. The maid crossed her arms and waited. She begrudged having to always be the one to get Lynx ready, but Lynx was too important to be left to the other servants. As the lady's maid, Solina needed to ensure Ms. Aster looked her best, and that meant ensuring the grief nurse did too. Solina always performed these duties with an angry twist of her lip and breathy huffs of irritation.

Lynx picked up the dress with deliberate slowness. It was made of silk. As she took it in her arms, a long-sleeved lace jacket parted from the dress and fell to the floor. It was just as long as the dress, which most certainly would drag across the floor in a train of several feet. Ms. Aster's intentions were clearly to make Lynx look mysterious and otherworldly. The shoulders of the jacket were capped with strings of pearls, looped like flower petals. A loose strand slipped through Lynx's fingers and fell to the floor with a rattle. Lynx thought at first she'd broken it, and her heart leapt in both shock and pleasure. But Solina only stared at the coiled string of pearls and said, 'For your hair.'

Lynx stepped into the dress and pressed it against herself to keep it in place. She raised her eyebrows at Solina and waited. The maid came up behind her and with quick movements began to button the dress's back. Solina was so close, Lynx could smell her perfume and underneath it the harsh, cool scent of her grief. She felt Solina's fingers pulling and adjusting the gown and imagined her pursed lips, her flaring nostrils.

Lynx had once seen a sliver of Solina, a slice of her naked body through Sculptor's bedroom door. She had cleaned up the teacup Solina had shattered the day the news arrived of Sculptor's engagement.

Solina's grief was sharp stalactites of ice.

'Do you need me?' Lynx asked. She kept her voice quiet. It was a stupid thing to say, but there was something in the sensation of Solina's fingers tying up her dress that made her heart yearn.

'Pardon?' Solina's voice was stiff.

'I'd be discreet.' She was taught, as all grief nurses were, the rules and regulations of the use of her skills. She was not to take the grief of anyone who was not a member of her guardian's family unless expressly granted permission. Ms. Aster had never allowed Lynx to take the grief of the servants, and she undoubtably never would.

Lynx didn't know why she was taking such a risk, but now she'd sensed Solina's Sorrow, she wanted it. Or she wanted to help, she wasn't sure. Maybe it was both: a perverse desire to feel grief again, the gratifying snap as she pulled it from someone's body, and a desire to see Solina smile for once. Sculptor wasn't worth grieving over.

'Do you hear yourself?' Solina asked, suddenly releasing Lynx and stepping away as if Lynx was a wild animal, claws out. 'Do you think I feel Sorrow for Sculptor? That I care at all that he's dead? I ought to tell Ms. Aster what you've said. I could do that. I could get you out of this house in a heartbeat. Grief nurses don't survive on the streets.'

Solina's grief flared along with her anger, and Lynx had to dig her nails into her palms to resist it. 'Forget I said anything.' Lynx stepped forward and lifted her hair away from her neck. She felt hot and uncomfortable already, and she still had an entire evening to get through.

'Keep your hair down.' Solina snatched Lynx's hand and forced it away. Immediately, Solina realized what she'd done and wrapped her hand in her apron, rubbing it furiously until it was scarlet. 'You can braid it yourself. Just at the top, two fishtail plaits. String the pearls through them.' Solina smoothed down her apron. 'Keep your mouth shut about Sculptor. He died on holiday, that's all.'

'Of course,' said Lynx. 'How else could it have happened?'

Solina huffed. 'Don't ruin this for Ms. Aster. She's just lost a son. Think how she must feel.'

Happy. Content. As Bright as the sun. 'I can't imagine.'

'No,' said Solina. 'You can't.' The sharp crack of the door slamming shut made Lynx flinch, hot blood pulsing in her temples.

Lynx felt more conspicuous than usual as she ascended the servants' stairwell to the main house. Servants passed her, and she had to scoop up her skirts and press herself against the wall to let them by. None of them spoke to her, although some eyed her dress and hair with fear. She understood why it made them nervous. It was a reminder that someone was dead. She took the stairwell to the grand corridor that wound above the great hall and emerged into the blue lights of the winter wing. The house was lively now, less than half a day after she'd taken Mr. Aster's grief. Voices rose up from the hall, and there was laughter and exclamations of greetings.

Lynx peered over the edge of the balcony railing. Already a cluster of people stood in the vestibule, where servants unburdened them of their winter coats. A valet carried a voluminous bouquet of pink roses. Another carried a pointedly smaller bunch of red ones. Lynx watched as a woman approached the valet with the scarlet roses only to be directed toward the other man. Her pinched lips were visible even from Lynx's distance.

She had heard all about the roses. It seemed as soon as Ms. Aster announced the idea, the servants were already placing bets on which guests would be granted which colour. Red roses for the important guests, the ones who were closest to Sculptor– and people the family wanted most to impress. Pink for all the others. Only red roses would be invited to the private dinner in the dining room and drinks in the drawing room after.

Lynx stepped back into the shadows of the corridor. She didn't want to think of what awaited her, but when she tried to think of something else, all she could think of was Andromeda and the token nestled in the rocks.

'Lynx.' She turned to see the butler, Orion, coming down the hall toward her. His face was obscured by the shivering vase of fern leaves he carried. 'Help me for a moment.' He made no indication that he'd stop, so she stepped in line with him, matching his rapid march down the hall toward the dining room. He looked at her from between the bowed leaves of two bracken. 'I nearly didn't recognize you.'

Lynx looked down at her dress. The fabric rippled as she walked, as though she was underwater. 'It's awful.'

'Not for me to judge,' said Orion, but his eyebrows touched briefly in a commiserating look of distaste. They reached the dining room, its door propped open by a golden weight. He set the vase on the buffet. 'Since you're here, I could use your help.' He nodded to the long dining table, already set with everything but the first course. 'We need another place at the table. Ms. Aster has decided to pretend Miss Deleporte will arrive after all.' He turned away and began arranging items on the buffet.

Only Orion wouldn't balk at her touching the place settings, getting grief all over the goldware.

She remembered meeting Orion when she was ten years old, when she first arrived at Mount Sorcha. She remembered the rolling ferry that made her ill, the lushness of the grounds and the gardens, and the towering mansion home that was waiting for her. She remembered the smell of shoe polish and the roses on the windowsills and the wax that gave the marble floors their watery shine. There to get her settled was a man with a back so straight and clothing so immaculately pressed, she would have believed he was an automaton had she not sensed a twinge of his grief, the fleeting scent of an animal. Dirt and the musk of fur.

'Welcome to Mount Sorcha.' His accent was clipped and formal, and she was afraid, but he had her sit at the long table in the servants' hall. He shooed away the other servants, craning their necks through the door trying to get a look at her, and he made her a cup of tea. It all felt unreal, as fleeting as the wisps of steam that rose from the cup before her.

As he held his hands behind his back and looked down at her, she thought she knew him in that instant. The stoic butler, ruled by custom and tradition. A grandfather clock of a man who knew his place in the household and enjoyed keeping everyone else in theirs.

But then he did the unexpected. He held out his hand. She had taken it and pulled away almost immediately, feeling like she didn't deserve it. She was a grief nurse; a handshake was beyond the pale.

A pin on his lapel glinted. It was a little golden arrow. He wore the arrow still, nearly twenty years later. It was his token, even though as a servant he wasn't entitled to a grief nurse. Unlike the other servants, he was permitted to wear it openly.

'Miss Deleporte hasn't RSVP'd?' she asked. She watched Orion carefully as he appraised the dining table. He was never flustered. As the butler, he had more responsibility than anyone in the house but he bore the weight easily, like a jacket he'd worn all his life.

'Not a word,' he replied.

She began to arrange the table as Orion carried over another chair. 'That's unexpected, even for her, isn't it?' she asked. It was no secret that Miss Deleporte and Sculptor's engagement, as short as it had been, was tumultuous. They hated each other one moment, were desperately in love the next. They were a dangerous combination – she an heiress without a name, he a name in need of an inheritance.

'Her reputation precedes her,' said Orion. 'She certainly has an ulterior motive. She's the only one who's seen the will.'

'Everyone wants to know who will become the guardian of Sculptor's grief nurse,' said Lynx, saying what Orion was too polite to mention. 'There,' Lynx stepped away from the table. There was another place now, for the guest who may not come.

'Ms. Aster will want you downstairs any moment now,' Orion said, and she realized he had asked for help not because he needed it but because he knew Lynx dreaded what would come next. 'You should go.'

Lynx shrugged. 'I'd rather not.'

Orion looked up, his eyes green and piercing. 'You have to.'

Lynx tapped the handle of an appetizer fork with her fingertips. 'Maybe she will come.'

'Either way,' said Orion, reaching up and adjusting the token on his lapel. 'There will be trouble.'

CHAPTER 5

Crater found her after she'd taken no more than three steps into the hall. 'My duchess of despair,' he called. It seemed he was always shouting, his voice a register louder than everyone else's. 'What were you doing in the dining room?' he asked as his gaze skimmed over her. 'Never mind, we're going down.' He turned and she followed. 'The dress is perfect.' He led her out of the winter wing and into the spring, the lights above them shifting from blue to green. 'Mother, did you hear what I said? The dress is perfect.'

Ms. Aster was standing at the balcony railing beside the staircase that led down to the great hall. Her husband was beside her and Eridanus was hovering behind them, his hands in his pockets. The men wore red roses pinned to their lapels. Ms. Aster wore hers tucked into her hair.

'She still hasn't arrived,' Ms. Aster said.

'Andromeda is always late,' said Crater. Eridanus had been right: he did seem high on happiness. He looked as eager as one of his hounds before a hunt.

'Not Andromeda, darling. Vela.' Ms. Aster turned and looked down into the hall. 'She should be making her entrance with us.'

'More importantly, won't she be bringing the will, if she does arrive?' Crater asked.

'Yes, I expect she would,' said Ms. Aster, clearly trying

not to look displeased. She pressed her lips together and turned to her husband. 'She's making a fool of me.'

'I've never seen you be made a fool of, Cassiopeia.'

Ms. Aster gripped the balcony railing and looked down again. 'Then I won't let today be the day.' She looked at Lynx. 'Our grief nurse is perfect. All of us are Bright.' If she saw Eridanus shift, she ignored it. 'If Vela chooses to arrive, then we will graciously offer her a red rose.'

'Perfectly said, my love,' said Mr. Aster.

Ms. Aster took Mr. Aster's arm and they began to descend the staircase to the great hall.

'Shouldn't we wait for Andromeda?' Eridanus asked. He glanced at Lynx, but she kept her expression blank.

Ms. Aster looked over her shoulder. 'We don't have time to wait for her to grow up. If she cares about this family, she'll arrive. Crater, don't stand too close to Lynx, you'll look desperate.' Crater allowed his smile to dip for only a moment as he adjusted his cravat and followed Eridanus.

The noise of the party grew with every step. They turned the bend of the staircase and all the majesty of the great hall was suddenly upon them. The marble arches and pillars, wound with coloured ribbons, flowers tucked in between the folds. The woven tapestries hung on the walls. The floor so polished, it was like a mirror. And above it all, Mount Sorcha's own sky. The ceiling of the great hall was painted the colour of midnight, constellations of stars drawn in gold, positioned to match their respective seasons. Lynx rarely experienced the great hall from this angle, from the position of a guest standing at the foot of the grand staircase. When she had first arrived at Mount Sorcha, she had entered through the servants' door. Now, it was like entering a new, glittering world.

For a breathless moment, she forgot who she was.

Over a hundred guests stood waiting in their finest evening dress, most wearing pink roses, a lucky few with scarlet blooms. A buzz crackled throughout the room, that rainbow thrill only a grand party could ignite. Like a wedding but headier, the flush of a fresh death making everything seem more dangerous, more illicit, more fragile.

Bells began to chime, cutting through the sounds of conversation and laughter until the hall miraculously fell silent. Gazes shifted. Bodies turned. Every pair of eyes watched the Asters. And her.

'Come,' whispered Crater, and he nodded for her to follow him as he moved to stand beside his mother.

Ms. Aster was smiling now, her palms open, her chin raised. 'Welcome to Mount Sorcha.' Her voice carried throughout the hall, and there wasn't any doubt that this house belonged to her, was built on her family's money. 'Each and every one of you is a cherished guest, and we are delighted to open our doors to you this evening, to celebrate our dear son Sculptor, who left us far too soon. We were devastated to learn of his death – it surprised us all – but the fog of grief has been lifted. Our minds are clear and our hearts are Bright.' As she swept her gaze across the hall, she gestured toward Lynx. She need not have. As soon as Lynx had stepped out to stand beside the family, the guests had seen her. Heads leaned together, sharing whispers, eyes taking in her white hair, the white dress trailing its hem across the ground. She felt their gazes like scum clinging to her skin.

'Grief is fleeting in Mount Sorcha, and we hope you

leave here Brighter than you arrived.' Ms. Aster nodded once, looking off to the edge of the room where a footman waited for the cue. 'Now, let us all share a toast.'

At these words, servants stepped away from the walls and spun toward the guests, trays of drinks in their hands. Everyone was distracted for a moment as they reached for drinks, and Lynx felt the lifting of their gazes with relief.

A footman kept his distance from Lynx as he handed each of the Asters a drink. Lynx tried to glare at him as she sometimes did when a servant was making a point of avoiding her, but he looked down at his feet. He nearly tripped over a guest trying to get away.

Ms. Aster raised her glass. Another bell chimed, but it took longer this time for the hall to fall silent. Ms. Aster pressed her lips together, and Lynx saw Mr. Aster hold his palm against the small of her back. 'To my beautiful son, Sculptor,' she said, when the room was silent once again.

'To Sculptor,' the guests replied. Glasses clinked. Someone whistled. The party broke open, conversations burgeoning, music striking up. Ms. Aster sighed and leaned into her husband's shoulder. 'I'm glad she isn't here. It's perfect just the way it is.'

Guests began to wander Lynx's way. First the brave. The ones who might have snuck in hipflasks and drank them empty. The kind of people who made a point of being the first at anything, just to prove they could. They leaned close to see how pale her eyes were – the paler the eyes, the better the nurse, wasn't that the common opinion? One woman blew across her cheek to see her hair move, as if that was proof enough it was real.

Then the jealous came. The ones who plucked a few

petals from their pink roses to make them smaller, easier to hide behind crossed arms and drinks. They called her dress garish, the pearls wound in her hair too ostentatious for a grief nurse. They compared her to other grief nurses in veiled language that suggested they had nurses of their own.

Finally, the curious and the frightened. They flitted around her like moths, whispers escaping from behind fluttering hands. These were the worst, the ones who thought her more monster than human.

Hungry eyes, all of them. Whether they were brazen or jealous or afraid, they still wanted her. They wanted to be as Bright as the Asters. She made them beautiful and happy and loved.

'Lynx.' Ms. Aster had moved beside her again. A man was walking toward them, his confident stride parting the small crowd around her. 'Come closer. This man's important.' He wore an elderberry suit and tie and a pair of thick square glasses. He carried a drink – something pink sloshing in a fluted glass. A red rose was pinned to his lapel.

'Your grief nurse,' he said in a voice to rival Crater's. 'She is marvellous. Cassiopeia, why did Sculptor never tell me of this – the beautiful creature of Mount Sorcha?' Gold glinted in the man's teeth as he spoke. 'How could you have kept her hidden from me for so long?'

Lynx reached with her mind, not expecting to find much of interest, but… She squeezed her hands into fists, hiding them in the flowing fabric of her dress.

If he had been like the others – Mr. Aster with his grief like a rose, Ms. Aster with her snake that turned itself in knots, Crater with his black-eyed corvid – his grief would have been an orange, perhaps, or cluster of berries. But he was a Fader and his grief was a grove filled with an impossible array of fruit.

Ms. Aster took the man's hand and kissed the air beside his cheek. 'Mr. Mensa. I'm ashamed Sculptor never offered you our grief nurse.' Her cheeks were tinged pink. 'I thought I raised him better.'

'Oh, but he was generous, I assure you.' He made a point of looking around. 'Tell me, is your daughter-in-law here or have I missed her?'

'She wasn't quite yet my daughter-in-law. It's a shame about the wedding. I've been planning it for months and now it will all go to waste.' Ms. Aster took the man's arm and pulled him closer to Lynx. She couldn't ignore him now. The scent of overripe fruits, berries plump with sugar turning bitter with the taste of spirits, the room filling to bursting with the arms of trees, the green crush of leaves. Lynx's lips tingled at the anticipation of breathing in that grief. It was layered, thick enough to sink into, rich, like syrup sliding down the curve of a glass jar. 'But tell me more about my grief nurse,' said Ms. Aster. 'Will you use her this evening?'

The man drew his fingers along his tie and looked at Lynx. 'I think I must.' He looked at Ms. Aster. 'Sculptor was my dear friend. I feel the Sorrow already returning.' From the way he spoke, the performance of his gestures, Lynx expected him to be lying. But he wasn't. There was Sorrow amongst the orchard.

'He would be glad you're here.'

'Yes, and I am certain his fiancée won't be, if she does arrive.' He laughed, and Ms. Aster tried to smile. He saw her look waver and leaned towards her, lowering his voice, as if telling a secret. 'You look astonishingly Bright this evening, Cassiopeia. Your grief nurse truly must be impeccable. But the rumours fly, as you knew they would.' He looked over his shoulder at the expanse of the great hall, the chittering guests. 'I will be on the hunt for any naughty gossips, and I will rid them personally of their roses and see them out the door.' He nodded once. 'Sculptor died abroad. Let no one question you on it. Not even Miss Deleporte.'

'Thank you, Mr. Mensa.' Ms. Aster adjusted the red rose in his lapel. 'Laurient,' she said affectionately. 'I'm very pleased to have you here with us.'

'As am I.' A glint of gold. A flash of a look toward Lynx. The rising scent of oranges.

'Will you excuse me?' said Ms. Aster, and she was swept away by another guest. When she was gone, the man stayed. He sipped his drink, one elbow propped up on his knuckles, and watched her.

'You,' he said, and that single word made her mind's fingers flex. She looked him in the eyes, but he didn't flinch. She had never met this man, but there was something familiar in the breath of his grief.

'Mr. Mensa. I see you've already found our grief nurse,' said Crater.

'How could I not?' Mensa turned to Crater as he approached.

'She's tempting, isn't she?' Crater smiled.

'Necessities, these days,' said Mensa, not rising to the bait. He took a sip from his glass. 'Yet far too difficult to acquire.'

'I couldn't agree more.' Crater's eyes lit up. 'Dreadful waitlists. There should be preferences for a good name. For legacies. If you've grown up with a nurse, it stands to reason you ought to have one, and not spend your days withering away on a waitlist for goodness sake.' Crater's voice rose as he spoke, acquiring a tinny anger.

Mensa nodded and murmured agreement. 'I've always said so. The old families are accustomed to the necessities of guardianship. They know how to care for nurses, and have the means to keep them.' He drank from his glass, shot another glance at Lynx. 'I'm drafting a bill at the moment. To, among other things, raise the income threshold for grief nurse guardians. It will protect the nurses, ensure they are well provided for.'

'Of course,' said Crater. 'I've been following your party's platform for some time, and I couldn't agree more. I have some ideas.'

Mensa smiled. 'I hadn't realized you were politically inclined.'

'Not publicly. Not yet.'

Lynx could sense Crater bluffing, could tell by the cadence of his voice that he was testing to see if Mensa believed him.

'Well then.' Mensa looked right at Lynx, and his grief flared. A hot burst of energy. A beckoning. 'Perhaps we may be of use to each other, Mr. Aster. The night is young. I'm certain I'll see you – and your lovely nurse – again, soon.'

Mensa turned away. Lynx willed herself not to look at him again.

Crater huffed, looking for a moment like his little sister when she'd just gotten away with something. 'My new project, Lynx,' he said in her ear. 'Mensa is the shadow minister – leader of the opposition. And I know his preferences. I know what he likes. I have a plan to fix everything.'

Lynx's hackles raised at the implication of Crater's words.

A servant glided by, and Crater snatched a drink from his tray. He pressed it into Lynx's hand, careful not to touch her fingers. 'But if Miss Deleporte doesn't arrive with the will, I may as well be wearing a pink rose tonight. I'll have no influence. No one here of import will take me seriously.' Crater kept a smile frozen on his face as he talked, but his fingers tapped impatiently against the side of his drink, clicking and clacking as his rings rapped the glass. 'She hasn't even RSVP'd. I suppose she has no more time for us now that Sculptor is dead.'

The alcohol made her head spin. Someone had released floating lanterns that bobbed against the ceiling, knocking into one another like awkward lovers, and they were dizzying to look at. She thought of the three Aster brothers, gathered in the drawing room one evening years ago. Years before Eridanus's marriage, before Sculptor left Mount Sorcha to live with his fiancée on the mainland, when they were just boys desperate to fly the nest.

As usual, they hadn't seen her standing in the shadows of the drawing room's doorway. It was so easy to make herself invisible, even dressed in all white, and she preferred it this way. She liked to watch them, their lives so vastly different than her own.

Sculptor was pacing, hands stuffed in pockets, a scowl on his face. Eridanus was leaning against the windowsill, watching something outside. Crater sat on the settee, spinning his earring.

'What's taking them so long?' burst Sculptor. 'I'm tired of this.'

'You're next,' said Crater. 'At least you can get it over with sooner than us.'

Sculptor rounded on him, all that energy hurtling toward Crater. Always Crater. 'What do you mean get it over with? Are you afraid?' He smiled, not a Bright smile. Sculptor hardly ever had those.

'No.'

'Yes, you are. You look green.' Sculptor nudged Eridanus. 'Crater's afraid of the grief nurse. She's just a girl. She can't do anything to you.'

'I just don't like it.' Crater shivered. 'Her touching my grief. It feels wrong.'

Sculptor snorted. 'Good thing Mother isn't counting on you for anything. You'd be quite the disappointment.'

A swath of lanterns shifted across the ceiling, as if chased by a gust of wind, and Lynx realized Crater had been talking to her as she'd lost herself in the memory. He was saying something and holding out another drink. The one in her hand was empty.

'Sculptor was supposed to be Prime Minister one day, but he never got further than the back benches. He was supposed to save Mount Sorcha with Miss Deleporte's money.' Crater chuckled as he raised his drink to his lips. 'But he got himself killed before the wedding.' His gaze had wandered toward his mother. 'Let's be honest, "died abroad" is as thin as water. My brother was a failure. The only successful thing he did was find himself a grief nurse.' She tasted his grief then, a mouth full of feathers. A crow sat on his shoulder. It cocked its head at her and blinked its black, glassy eyes. A challenge, but she took another drink, and when the warmth rolled down her throat and she looked up, the crow was gone.

'I don't know how he did it. He knew someone or – somehow he jumped to the top of the waitlist.'

Lynx looked toward the door, a small part of her thinking Sculptor might walk through at any moment.

'It doesn't matter. I'm going to get that grief nurse, no matter what the will says.'

Lynx took a large gulp of her drink. It burned, and she pressed a hand to her mouth to keep from coughing it up.

'No offence, my princess of pain. You're perfect, but you're not mine. I want to make a name for myself, and for that I need one of my own.' Crater threw his head back and polished off his drink. He snapped his fingers at a servant and took another cocktail from the man's tray as he approached.

'Luckily, I know everything about everyone.' Crater grinned at her, but his gaze wandered. He gave a short shout, and in a flash, he was gone, attaching himself to a more desirable circle of guests. Without him there, she felt exposed.

Lynx looked down into the pink, bubbling liquid in her glass. She felt suspended, outside of time. She wanted to stretch out this moment forever, just her and the rosy depths of the cocktail, the bitter tang of cordial and the tiny bubbles popping against her cheeks. She wanted to forget she was a grief nurse, forget the tug of Mensa's Fader grief, forget the taste of Andromeda's Sorrow before all her spooled regrets came undone.

'Announcing Miss Vela Deleporte,' Orion's voice broke through the sounds of conversation. Lynx looked up. Everyone fell silent. Beneath the arched entrance of the great hall stood Sculptor's fiancée, dressed like a bride.

CHAPTER 6

Vela Deleporte was small and clear-eyed with dark hair flawlessly straight and cut along her jawline, the tips of her hair dyed red. She was dressed in wedding scarlet, her dress barely reaching below her knees, and on her head she wore a gold coronet. Snowflakes dusted her hair like little white jewels.

'It seems I'm late,' she said as she plucked off her gloves. 'I hope this doesn't mean I'm getting a pink rose now.' She smiled, and laughter crackled throughout the great hall. Lynx wondered what Vela's grief felt like. She tasted brass and felt the edge of something cold and hard.

Crater appeared again at Lynx's elbow. 'Miss Vela Deleporte,' he whispered to her. 'She's an absolute eyeful, isn't she?'

Crater wasn't wrong, Vela certainly was an eyeful. She slid a fur stole from her shoulders, baring a long neck, begging to be kissed—or bruised.

Lynx blinked. Crater looked as if he were thinking the same.

'Certainly not,' said Ms. Aster. 'You're family.' She leaned forward to kiss the air beside Vela's cheek.

'You'll have to blame the weather for my late arrival, Ms. Aster.' Vela accepted a red rose from a valet. 'It's dreadful out there.'

The heiress looked out of place in the grand building,

beside Ms. Aster in her floor-length gown. Her dress was too short, too stylish, her gaze too brazen. She was a product of the mainland, and Lynx could almost smell Ms. Aster's distrust.

'Please, you must call me Cassiopeia,' said Ms. Aster. She looked Vela up and down. 'Is this your wedding dress?'

Vela touched the circlet in her hair. 'Yes, I thought I may as well wear it tonight, since I won't get another chance. Do you like it?'

'It's certainly modern,' said Ms. Aster. She touched Vela's arm. 'Let me offer you our grief nurse. You must have had a terribly long journey.'

'No, thank you,' said Vela, accepting a drink and stepping into the hall.

Lynx tensed, preparing for more stares, but those that did look her way seemed to be looking beyond her. A murmur rose up. Then Orion appeared, the tight line of his mouth betraying the tiniest hint of anger. Vela smiled.

'Pardon me,' he said, bending to speak to Ms. Aster. The nearest guests hushed themselves. 'Where shall I put the grief nurse?'

Ms. Aster looked toward Lynx. 'She's already here.'

'Pardon, madam, but I mean the other grief nurse.'

Ms. Aster's jaw tightened. 'The other grief nurse?'

'Well, well,' Crater said in a husky whisper. 'This got interesting.'

'Yes, madam.'

Lynx pressed a fingernail into the soft flesh of her thumb. Another grief nurse, here under Mount Sorcha's roof? The room seemed to shrink around her, the guests pressing close to catch a glimpse of what couldn't possibly be. The servants in the vestibule were in confusion, footmen frozen in indecision, housemaids tugging smooth their aprons, and Orion waiting for orders with his hands behind his back. A footman raised his eyes and seemed to realize that everyone in the great hall, all hundred guests, esteemed and otherwise, were looking in his direction. His neck flushed right up to his ears. He stepped aside, and there she was. A figure in white.

Lynx hadn't seen another grief nurse in fifteen years, not since she'd come to Mount Sorcha. Her eyes were as pale as Lynx's, bold beneath white brows. She wore trousers and a waistcoat, a jacket with a high collar. Her white hair fell around her shoulders in a hundred small braids. Sculptor's grief nurse was nothing at all like Lynx expected, and she realized why. The grief nurses of her memory were children, no more than ten years old, waiting to be assigned guardians. It must have been a trick of the light because it looked as if she were smiling.

Mr. Aster knew that not even he could provide succour to his wife in her plight. He stood to the side, running his thumb over his pocket watch. Ms. Aster looked once at him, and he clutched the watch in his fist. She smiled, not even enough to show her teeth, and turned to Vela. 'What is this?'

'Your son's grief nurse. Someone in this house is going to inherit her guardianship. I thought I may as well bring her along.' Vela took a tiny sip of her pink cocktail and looked around casually, as if the whole room wasn't staring in her direction. Crater finally caught her eye and winked. She raised an eyebrow in return.

In that moment, Ms. Aster looked very much like her daughter. She seemed ready to grab Vela by the scarlet tips of her hair and drag her out into the snow.

Then, by some miracle – or more likely Orion's quick thinking – the dinner bell rang.

The long dining table was decorated with ferns and flowers, tiered trays of fruit, napkins twisted into the shape of peacocks. Lynx imagined how much Sculptor would have hated it all, how he'd have shaken out the napkin in disgust and plucked an apple from a tray, biting into it with a great crunch that would make his mother wince.

Lynx wasn't supposed to be here in the dining room as the red rose guests were directed to their seats. But when the dinner bell had chimed, and Vela climbed the stairs to the upper floor, Sculptor's grief nurse had followed. Without a word, Ms. Aster had flicked her fingers at Lynx, and she, too, trailed after the others

Lynx braced her hand against her chair's back. The wood was smooth, curved, and for a moment, she was holding Sculptor's blade in her palm. She swallowed and sat.

The other grief nurse was seated at the opposite end of the table. She sat with a straight back, her hands folded in her lap. Though she looked to be older than any of the Aster siblings, perhaps several years shy of forty, she gazed about the room with an open expression that made her seem younger than any of them. She looked self-assured and certain in a way Lynx admired.

'I hope the snow doesn't last,' said Mr. Aster, as he took his seat. He looked over his shoulder at the window behind him, at the heavy flakes of snow, then at his wife. 'You don't suppose they'll stop the ferry, do you?'

Ms. Aster pressed her lips together. She looked toward Orion, as if he had all the answers. 'I'm sure it will be fine.' The room once again fell silent. The space sparked with unasked questions.

Servants streamed into the room carrying the first course, filling the room with the scent of fennel and lime. Little flags of steam hovered over each bowl of soup as they were placed before the diners.

'Everything served today was grown on the estate,' said Mr. Aster in the wake of the obligatory admirations of the first course. 'We have three glasshouses in the garden.'

Vela's nose wrinkled as she looked down into her soup.

'Our gardener devised an ingenious system for keeping the plants warm in the winter,' he added between mouthfuls of soup. 'The houses are lined with pipes pumped with hot water. It works brilliantly for vegetables, but I've been trying unsuccessfully to grow orchids. If your gardener is cleverer than ours, Miss Deleporte, you will have to bring them next time you come to Mount Sorcha.'

'I wouldn't know.' Vela dipped her spoon into her soup and swirled it around. 'I don't engage with the gardeners. I don't find plants very inspiring.'

'I agree. Dreadfully boring.' Crater tapped his glass, and a servant poured in more wine. 'Eridanus's husband is an academic. Perhaps he knows about the ideal growing conditions of orchids?'

'Syril isn't a botanist,' said Eridanus.

'Well, then, what does he study?' Vela asked.

'I wouldn't want to bore you.'

'Can we stop talking about orchids?' said Ms. Aster, dropping her spoon into her soup. She looked across the table at Vela. 'You've read the will.'

Vela licked her spoon clean. 'I haven't. That would be a breach of your trust. And legally circumspect, I suppose.'

'Then why did you bring the nurse?'

Vela shrugged. 'Why not?' She paused, making a show of deliberating if she'd go on. 'Well, I couldn't be sure your nurse was as good as Karina. She can be an alternate, if your nurse proves to be inferior.'

Mr. Aster spoke before Lynx could decide if she was offended or merely annoyed. 'Lynx is the finest nurse I've ever come across.' He patted his chest. 'She is very thorough. I wouldn't expect her to be inferior in any circumstance. You're welcome to her, Miss Deleporte, if you feel your grief return.'

'Shall we have a contest then?' said Vela. 'My grief nurse against yours?'

'Aren't you being a bit hasty?' said Laurient Mensa, who had been watching the family with interest. 'She isn't your grief nurse.'

Vela flicked her eyes to the ceiling. 'Aren't you being pedantic?'

'I don't think so. Is it pedantry to point out the obvious? She was Sculptor's grief nurse. I would be astonished if he bequeathed her guardianship to you.'

Vela straightened her shoulders and her eyes sparkled in the light from the chandelier. 'I suppose we'll find out soon. We could perhaps open the will over dessert?'

'But the cook has made treacle tart,' said Crater.

'And?'

'We wouldn't want to spoil it for anyone.'

Vela laughed. 'Oh, I don't know. I think treacle tart would taste lovely with a side of disappointment.'

'Isn't disappointment much like Heartache?' said Eridanus. 'If that's the case, then you have nothing to worry about.'

'Yes, this is perhaps the safest room in all the country,' declared Mensa. 'We're protected on all sides from grief.' He looked from Lynx to the other nurse and back again. The other nurse caught Lynx's eye. Lynx immediately looked away and then felt foolish for doing so. She wasn't sure how to feel. She had never prepared herself for meeting another grief nurse and Karina's presence was both intriguing and disconcerting; Lynx was curious and hesitant in turn.

'Some people believe one oughtn't spend too much time around a grief nurse, in case the grief they take rubs off on you,' said Vela. 'Maybe we're actually in quite a lot of danger.' She smiled and shivered.

'I respectfully disagree, Miss Deleporte,' said Crater. Vela cocked her head at him. 'I enjoy having our nurse nearby. Grief has never rubbed off on me. I'm always Bright.'

'It's true,' said Mr. Aster. 'Crater is always the Brightest.'

'So there you have it.'

Vela shook her napkin and placed it again in her lap. 'Don't you think it would be interesting to use two grief nurses at once?' Her smile suggested she knew she was dragging the conversation into a territory bordering on taboo. No one ever talked about what happened when a grief nurse held your token in their hand and freed you of your Sorrow or Dread or Heartache. Certainly no one ever talked about what else a grief nurse could do, not in a setting like this.

'Certainly not. It seems... invasive,' said Crater.

'And that's a bad thing?' Vela retorted.

Crater looked puzzled. Lynx could practically see his mind working, trying to decide how to please her.

'Why not try it now, Miss Deleporte?' said Mensa. 'You can report back to us what you've learned.'

'I'm afraid Karina has already taken my Sorrow.'

'You do know that everyone has a trace of grief about them always,' said Mensa.

'I don't think that's true.' Crater leaned forward. 'I feel fantastic.'

'Oh, it is true,' said Mensa.

'We have two grief nurses here,' said Eridanus. 'We could ask them.'

'I didn't know you were a prolocutor for grief nurses, Mr. Aster,' said Mensa.

'It's Mr. Deimos.'

'Oh.' Mensa raised an eyebrow. 'I didn't realize.'

'Well,' said Vela. 'What's the answer then?' She looked at the other grief nurse. 'Karina?'

Karina looked at Mensa, who leaned his elbows against the table and waited. 'Mr. Mensa is correct. There is always grief inside a person.' Her voice surprised Lynx. It was warm and low, and unexpectedly lovely.

Crater grimaced. 'That can't be right.'

'Do you want to know something else fascinating?' said Mensa.

'No, I'd like to enjoy my dinner,' said Eridanus.

'Grief nurses can sense your grief without a token. They're likely touching our grief right now. I've heard you can tell by a lightening of the eyes, but I've never been able to verify it myself.'

A rustling as the diners shifted uncomfortably.

Mensa sipped his wine. Lynx tried to imagine she was somewhere else. On the hillside with the nutty scent of gorse, a fresh rain settling on her skin. Not in the dining room with another grief nurse.

'That's terrifying,' said Vela. 'This whole time your grief nurse could be playing with my grief, and I wouldn't have the faintest idea.' She looked intently at Lynx, apparently trying to see if her eyes had turned even paler.

'Aren't you open to an invasion?' said Mensa.

'Not like this.'

'I'm not playing.' Lynx's chair squealed as she pushed herself backwards, almost standing up.

'Be quiet, Lynx,' said Ms. Aster. She looked to Orion. 'We should take the grief nurses from the room. This was a mistake. They're spoiling the dinner.'

'I don't want Karina to leave my sight,' said Vela. 'Not until I know who her guardian will be.'

'They both should stay. It's quite the entertainment.' Mensa turned toward Lynx. 'Touch her grief. Tell us what you see.' He smiled and rose an eyebrow at Vela. 'If that's okay with you, Miss Deleporte?'

Vela shrugged. 'Well, since I've already been invaded.'

Lynx looked around at the faces staring at her. She could feel her heart beating in the vein along her temple. She pressed her palms against her thighs. If they wanted a show, that's what they'd get.

'Everyone's grief is different,' said Lynx. 'I can tell you that Mr. Aster's grief takes the form of a rose. Crater's is a crow.' Crater slouched in his seat, looking uncomfortable. 'Miss Deleporte's—' She held Vela's gaze for a long time, surprised at how long the woman returned her stare unflinchingly, but eventually Vela broke and that's when

Lynx closed her eyes.

Her mind reached toward Vela's heart, where her grief gleamed. She saw a mirror, so dark it was almost black. Lynx drew toward it, her mouth filling with a strange syrupy sensation. The grief was sour, reminding her of Sculptor's bitter blade. The fingers of Lynx's mind danced around the edges of the mirror, like smoke rolling off still, black water. Her limbs ached for it.

She opened her eyes. Someone gasped.

'What is it?' Mensa asked, looking hungry.

'It's a mirror.'

Lynx had expected Vela to be pleased, or to at least feign interest, but she was frowning. 'How much of it is there?' she asked.

'I didn't—'

Vela stood suddenly and slid the bracelet from her wrist. 'Take it then, whatever it is. I want to be Bright.' The bracelet dangled over the centre of the table. It was made of pink glass beads secured by golden links.

'Vela, darling, if you would like to use Lynx, your bedroom has been made up,' Ms. Aster began.

'Well, why not do it here? I want to see how good your grief nurse really is.' Vela was still standing, and she looked around at everyone at the table. A challenge. 'It's part of the fun. Tonight's entertainment, isn't that right, Mr. Mensa?'

'I'm game, certainly,' said Mensa.

'I'm not,' said Crater. 'It's inappropriate.'

'Then Sculptor was right about you,' said Vela, cutting him a look. Crater gripped his cravat and for once had nothing to say. 'Don't be prudish. Have some fun.' Lynx held out her palm, and Vela dropped the bracelet into it.

63

Lynx curled her fingers around it. 'Go on.' Vela settled into her seat, crossed her legs and leaned back, a small smile on her lips. Everyone else was silent. Lynx glanced at Ms. Aster, who seemed displeased, but she nodded once.

Lynx closed her eyes.

There it was. A dark mirror framed in gold. As she approached it, she could see the reflection of her fingers in the glass. She sucked in a long breath. A cool fragrance, almost the absence of scent. She could pluck this and take it for herself. She imagined how it would feel, vibrating through her body.

She wrapped her fingers around it, ready to pull, but – she felt the presence of something else there. She snatched her fingers away from the mirror, and white tendrils, not her own, slithered across the glass. They were like hers but different, moving swiftly and with confidence, but of course they could not take the grief. Lynx squeezed Vela's token in her fist. She reached forward again, uncertainty battling with desire. When she tapped the glass, the other fingers slid away.

Just as she moved to pluck the grief, the other fingers shot forward, entangling with hers, and in that moment, the world fell away.

CHAPTER 7

When Lynx opened her eyes, she was in the great hall. No lanterns obscured the ceiling, no ribbons in garish hues wound round the marble pillars. No music, no guests, only a cool breeze and the scent of pine.

Rising from the centre of the hall, expanding to fill the ceiling with its branches, was a yew tree. Its branches were twisted, the bark rough, the trunk corrugated with thick striations. Red berries dazzled among the needles.

The wind was stronger here, and as Lynx tipped her head back, she realized why. The ceiling of the great hall, which should have been painted with constellations, sparkling with gold stars, was torn completely away. The true sky shown above her, an unabashedly silver moon hanging among a smattering of stars. She was held captive by it all: the creaking of the yew tree in the breeze, the salt air on her tongue, the glow of the moon.

If she listened close enough, she could hear the yew tree singing. It was a quiet, almost imperceptible hum. It felt like a whisper.

The white fingers she had seen flitting across Vela's grief had grasped her own and pulled her here – beneath an ancient tree, bursting from the marble floor of Mount Sorcha. This was a place like Mensa's orchard – a place where grief grew – but it didn't belong to a Fader. It belonged to a grief nurse.

Among the tree's roots sprouted impossible things: a cluster of goldenrod flowers, crowns nodding as bees flitted among them. A carousel horse grinning with its head thrown back, umber mane flowing across its jet-black withers. Autumn leaves that twisted through the air as the wind blew. Grief. Taken by a grief nurse, pulled inside herself and kept here in the roots and branches of the tree that made her what she was. Every grief nurse's tree was different, as different as each person's grief.

Lynx had a tree, of course, but she didn't want to think of it.

She reached her hand out to run her fingers through the goldenrod, feeling as she did so the soft skin of a baby as she pressed her cheek against her neck, the child's soft breath, and the absolute conviction that she would do everything in her power to keep her. When she pulled her hand away, she was herself again, only a tingling sensation in the back of her mind a reminder that for a moment, as the petals of the flowers tickled her fingertips, she'd been privy to the heart of a stranger.

She curled her fingers into a fist. Why had Sculptor's grief nurse brought her here? She hadn't been to a place like this for years, not one belonging to another grief nurse, not since before she came to Mount Sorcha.

She was careful as she walked to step over roots while avoiding the many objects of grief among them. Her feet slid on the carpet of needles on the floor, her dress catching around her legs, and she threw her hands out to keep from falling. Her palms pressed against the trunk of the yew, the bark so close the grooves and ridges looked like canyons. For a single disorientating moment, she wasn't herself. She remembered things she'd never seen –

66

oily canals cutting through cobbled streets, a letter made from paper soft as linen, a the scent of anise and wine.

She straightened, yanking her hand away. What she saw then made the blood rush to her head, her fingertips going numb. Embedded in the trunk of the tree nearly up to its hilt was a knife. Her heart hitched, but she reached for it anyway, her fingers hovering over the smooth wooden handle. She couldn't bring herself to touch it.

'I wouldn't,' said a voice, and Lynx spun around. Sculptor's grief nurse stood watching her. Her irises were so pale, her eyes were like white discs. 'You're welcome to,' the other nurse added. 'But that is a bitter grief, and I prefer mine sweet.'

'It's Sculptor's grief.'

'I'm sure you know it as well as I,' said the other nurse. 'A grief like that, that won't stop growing no matter how much you take, there's something different in it.' She reached up and tapped her fingernails against a windchime made of cockles and sea glass. A look of pleasure passed across her features, and Lynx instinctively looked away.

'Why did you bring me here?'

'I'm sorry to be so forthright. I wanted to introduce myself. Properly, away from the others.' The other nurse stood easily, at home beneath the branches of the yew, her feet among its roots. A wave of yearning swept over Lynx. She felt the presence of the tree beside her, as if it had a heartbeat. 'I'm Karina.'

'Lynx.' She wanted to put her hands in her pockets, but she had none. She hid them in the folds of her dress instead.

'We're in a rare and unexpected position, aren't we? We're lucky Miss Deleporte likes to make a scene whenever she gets the chance.'

Lynx bit her tongue, trying to think of what to say. All she could think about was the beauty of this place, how welcoming and unexpected it was. 'Did you play games as well?' Lynx asked eventually. 'Before?'

She remembered the years she had before Mount Sorcha, when she knew other children like her with white hair and pale eyes. At a place called a school, where grief nurse children were trained on how to use their skills. They learned to never take grief by touch but through a token. They learned how to take discretely and what to say and how to keep a mild expression. They were taught all manner of things so they could slip easily into their guardian's lives. Music, languages, the domestic arts, card games and lawn games and the proper forms of address.

It wasn't a happy time, not really. There were too many rules, too many mistakes so easily made, too many punishments to endure. But at night they would climb into each other's beds, legs intertwined, hands grasping hands, cheeks pressing against bellies or nestled in the crook of arms, and they would go to each other's places. They hadn't known they were different, that it wasn't normal to pull each other into their grief places and play among their trees. They would play for ages in these places where everything was theirs and they were kings and queens.

It was the only time in her life she hadn't felt alone. Hadn't felt as if she were the only one. Until now, she thought she'd never see another grief nurse again.

'We'd spend all our time in each other's places, even though there was hardly any grief there yet, until they kept us apart.' Lynx wanted to take her words back as soon as she'd said them. She never to spoke to anyone about her life before.

'I still play games,' said Karina with a smile.

The wind blew harder, shaking the nearest branch so that it dipped down and brushed through Lynx's hair. She stepped back, suddenly feeling self-conscious. Karina's tree was beautiful. Strong, vigorous and wild. Something in her gut made her look up, toward the balcony above. Creeping black tendrils were spilling across the railing, dropping down the balcony like vines. She knew those roots.

Suddenly, she was afraid – at the strength of that yew tree, how it seemed to radiate power. It felt too much. And she was ashamed, too, to think of what a grief nurse like Karina would think of her if she saw her own ugly, little oak. 'I need to go,' Lynx said. The world was spinning. She wanted to throw herself from this place, taking those black roots with her, before Karina could see her for what she really was.

Karina was beside her. She wasn't looking toward the railing only at Lynx's face, her own eyes creased with worry. 'It's okay,' said Karina, and she took Lynx's hand.

As she was pulled from that place, Lynx felt the cool rush of Vela's grief, as dark as midnight, edged in gold, and saw her mind's fingers still playing across its surface, poised to snatch it. She took it almost absent-mindedly, as the sensation of Karina's fingers in hers lingered.

And then she was back. When she opened her eyes, everyone looked as she had left them, leaning toward her, waiting. Karina was watching her, too, her brow still furrowed. Lynx wished she could disappear completely.

'Well, your verdict?' said Mensa to Vela.

Vela's cheeks were flushed. She took the bracelet from Lynx and settled into her seat. 'It's a draw,' she said, her voice springy. She smiled, her eyes shining, her skin glowing. A servant placed a slice of treacle tart before her. 'Is it that time already?'

'I thought you promised a will reading over dessert,' said Crater.

'I entrusted it to your butler,' replied Vela.

Everyone looked toward where Orion had been standing all night. He was gone. Ms. Aster exchanged a look with her husband, who started to stand, but then the door opened. Orion strode through, a letter balanced on a tray atop his open palm.

'There we are,' said Vela, but it was clear as Orion set the paper before Ms. Aster that it wasn't the will. It was a single paper folded once to hide its contents, too small and insubstantial to be the document everyone was waiting for.

'A telegram,' Orion said. 'From your solicitor.'

Silence as Ms. Aster unfolded the paper. She read it, eyes darting across the page, and she seemed to read it again and again until Crater broke.

'Well, what does it say?' he asked.

Her nostrils flared as she looked up. 'Nothing of interest,' she said, her gaze not meeting anyone's as she returned the paper to the tray Orion still held upright beside her. 'Estate business.'

Ms. Aster's grief was showing: a black snake with a scarlet stripe down its back wound round her arm, raised its head and flicked its tongue towards Lynx. She was lying.

Orion turned away and began to make his way across the room, the letter sitting exposed atop the tray he carried. Lynx sensed the other eyes watching it, wondering the very same thing as she. What did it really say?

'Well, where's the will then?' Crater asked.

Just then, Andromeda appeared in the doorway of the dining room. She was no longer the girl at the sea's edge. She wore a dress of blue and green silk, plunging at the neck, patterned like a peacock's feathers around her feet. Her chin was raised, her shoulders back, but even though she was composed and elegant, she wasn't Bright.

She stared intently at her mother, seeming to understand that something had happened, something was wrong. 'Wait,' Andromeda said, and she pressed her hand against Orion's arm, stopping him. She glanced down at the paper, and something on it caught her, her expression flattening. 'Nothing of interest,' she said slowly, and she must have heard, she must have seen her mother's face as she read the letter.

Ms. Aster rose just slightly in her seat. Dread clung to her, was building. 'Andromeda—'

'This is nothing of interest?' Andromeda plucked the paper from Orion's tray, held it up. The sound of paper moving through air was unnaturally loud. Everyone was silent.

A current of anger ran between Ms. Aster and her daughter. Nothing good could come of this, Lynx knew. It never did.

'Aren't you tired of lying?' Andromeda said, at first looking only at her mother, then turning her gaze on everyone else.

'This is a private matter, Andromeda. Put that down.'

'I think he would want them to know,' Andromeda said.

'Know what?' asked Crater, sounding exhausted, tired of being left out of the conversation.

'How Sculptor really died.'

Andromeda finally did as her mother said. She placed the letter back onto Orion's tray.

'Suicide.'

CHAPTER 8

Seawater rushed down Lynx's throat, burning it raw as she plunged beneath the waves. Moonlight, dragging currents, a chill that made her bones ache. She blinked the world back into place. Andromeda's grief was flaring, calling to her.

'Are you certain?' someone asked, and it might have been Crater but all sounds were distorted and dull. Only her heartbeat was clear.

Sculptor's death was a suicide. She tried not to think of how, and fought down all the images that arose, bobbing up in her mind like flotsam. It didn't help that everyone's grief was flaring, Mensa and Andromeda's so strong, she had to grip the table to stay tethered to the present.

'Was it madness?' someone asked, and at that word, Lynx felt an old wound opening. She felt as if she were falling, and even though she scrambled to stay in the current moment, she was dragged into the past—

She loved the way her scalp tingled, as her hair was worked into a braid. She looked at the wall before her, on which was painted a menagerie of animals, and searched for her favourite bird – a blue bird with a yellow belly. It was smaller than the other birds – a seagull, a starling, a regal heron standing in the rushes – but it was the most joyful. It looked as if it was the happiest creature in the world. She imagined that this, this moment, was what it felt like to fly.

'I do apologize for my daughter's antics,' Ms. Aster said, her voice yanking Lynx thankfully from the memory. 'I didn't want to make a fuss, but here we are.' Her voice was level, controlled. She had taken the power back from her daughter, who had wielded it for only a single, potent moment. 'There was an investigation. The death was ruled a suicide, and so the will is void.' She said all this matter-of-factly, as if it didn't change everything.

'According to the law then, he died intestate,' said Vela, the only one in the room whose grief wasn't threatening to overwhelm Lynx. 'That means Karina's guardianship belongs to you now, Cassiopeia.'

Ms. Aster shook her head. 'No, we won't keep her. She will go to one of my children.'

'Which one?' asked Mensa.

'I will decide this evening.'

Eridanus looked down at his dessert. 'If that's the case, would anyone fancy something stronger?'

They left shortly after for the drawing room, lured by the promise of drink and the desire to break into groups, to scatter gossip like pebbles. No one said much until they stood beneath the golden lights, and then with the thin stems of cocktail glasses between eager fingers, the conversations began.

Lynx made herself invisible. She moved to the edge of the room, a curtain woven with bronze threads shimmering beside her, and watched them. The memory still ached at the back of her mind, and she feared that at any moment it might reach out and grasp her again. She focused on the Asters and their guests, hoping they would be enough of a distraction.

Eridanus stood beside the glossy piano, his fingers resting against the closed lid. 'Do you remember how Sculptor would play the piano at midnight?' he said to Crater, who grimaced and took a sip of his drink. 'You'd be lying in bed, drifting off to sleep, when there'd come a great crash, and it was Sculptor bashing away at the keys. Everyone else be damned.'

'Yes, he always was a selfish prick, wasn't he?' said Crater.

'It's strange,' said Eridanus, staring at the piano. 'How it's out in the open now, no longer the secret we all keep.' He chuckled. 'He killed himself.'

'It's no longer a secret, but you don't have to shout it across the room,' mumbled Crater. He looked as if he wanted desperately to leave but Vela was making her way toward them.

'Mr. Aster, we hardly had the chance to speak at dinner,' she said, but she wasn't speaking to Crater. She caught Eridanus by the elbow and smiled.

'It's Mr. Deimos,' he said, frowning.

'Oh, you did say that didn't you?' She swirled her glass. There was a great gold-framed mirror hanging behind them, and through it Lynx could see all three of them reflected. Both Crater and Eridanus looked uncomfortable, and Vela seemed to know this and revel in it. 'You took your husband's name. I've never heard of Deimos.'

'No reason you would have.'

'He's not one of us, then?' she said with a whip of a smile.

'Not at all.'

'You said he was an academic. What is his research?'

'He studies grief.'

She laughed. 'Oh, he must know all the secrets to being Bright.'

'Being Bright doesn't concern him. He is interested in Sorrow.'

'Really? How awful.'

'Is it?' Eridanus looked down at the piano for a moment, as if he were contemplating playing. 'Imagine if we knew about grief instead of always having a grief nurse take it. Perhaps my brother wouldn't be dead.'

Now Vela looked uncomfortable, as if she felt the heat radiating from Eridanus's skin, smoke clawing at her throat. Vela glanced up at the mirror behind them and looked quickly away.

'Would you shut up about Sculptor, Dani,' said Crater. He turned to Vela with a smile. 'Miss Deleporte, I must apologize on behalf of my brother.' He was making an effort, showing off his teeth and puffing out his chest. 'You must excuse him. I think his Sorrow is showing.' He put a hand on his brother's shoulder. 'You should go to Lynx.'

'I've already seen her,' said Eridanus. He shifted his shoulder, so his brother's hand fell away.

'It shows that you don't have a grief nurse. I hope you've finally put yourself on a waitlist,' Crater said. He gave Eridanus a satisfied look before turning to Vela. 'I don't know how Eridanus goes without a grief nurse. What did you think of Lynx? Isn't she magnificent?'

'Of course, she is.' Vela pressed a hand to her heart. 'Don't tell me I don't look Bright, Mr. Aster. It is Mr. Aster, isn't it? You're not married to a professor, too, are you?'

Crater laughed. 'My poor mother if I were. Please, call me Crater.'

She lifted one finger away from her glass. 'Crater, tell me I wasn't your first?'

Crater's smile faltered. 'Pardon?'

'Have you never seen anyone's grief being taken before?'

He tightened his cravat and looked at his brother, who took a long drink. 'Why would I have?'

'You make me feel like such a daredevil. I find it so endearing.' She looked to the taller brother. 'Now, I feel like you, Mr. Deimos, have tried some things.'

He smiled for the first time, more of a smirk, really. 'I don't see the allure of grief play.'

'Why would you? When you lie in bed with Sorrow every night.' Crater looked into his glass as he spoke.

'But tell me at least that you've tried it.' Vela finished her drink and set it atop the piano. Eridanus watched without a word, as condensation slid down the glass' stem to settle in a tiny puddle. He swept his sleeve across it. 'Well?' She took Eridanus's drink and sipped it, not breaking his gaze.

'I don't believe that's any of your business, Miss Deleporte.' He pulled the glass from her fingers, and as he did so, he let it go. The glass shattered at Eridanus's feet, the liquid dappling his shoes like dew drops. Two servants were upon him immediately, and Vela hurried backwards. Eridanus stood in the centre of the small storm, looking satisfied. 'My apologies.'

'Here.' Crater swept in with a new drink, which he pressed into Vela's hands.

Vela smiled as their fingers brushed. 'Don't you think

all this is a bit dull?'

'Dull? We've just learned our brother killed himself.' Eridanus glanced toward his mother. 'And now our loving mother gets to decide our fate.'

'You want the grief nurse?' said Crater, raising both eyebrows. 'I thought you loved living like a poor boy.'

Eridanus let out a long breath and ignored him. 'I wouldn't call this evening dull, Miss Deleporte.'

'I mean all of this.' Vela waved her hand around the room. 'The dinner. The drawing room. All the other guests are dancing in the great hall, drinking themselves insensible.' She looked up at him from beneath her eyelashes. 'Aren't we the red rose guests? Doesn't that mean we get to have more fun?'

'No,' said Eridanus. 'It means we're trapped with the same handful of people all evening, telling the same stories, bragging about our lives, trying to outdo each other with how Bright we look.'

'Well, all the more reason to make some fun of it. Anyway, you two need a distraction from your fate, as you put it.' Vela clicked open the clasp of her bracelet and unwound it from her wrist. Both brothers looked taken-aback as she held her token toward them. 'Here's what we do. Everyone hands in their token.' She looked toward Karina. 'We'll give them to the grief nurse, and she'll pick out two. Have you ever played mixing before?'

'Mixing?' Crater asked.

Vela tried to look shocked. 'You haven't heard of it? Imagine feeling someone else's grief inside you, yours filling them up. It's more intimate than fucking.'

Crater choked on his drink.

She waggled her token. 'Shall we try it?'

'I think you're mistaken,' said Eridanus. 'This isn't that kind of party.'

'If it were, everything would be so much more exciting.' Vela dropped her bracelet into her palm. She sighed and looked at Crater. 'Who do you think your mother will give Karina to?'

Crater's eyes lit up. 'I have some theories.'

'You think it'll be you,' said Eridanus without inflection.

Crater shrugged. 'Well, it won't be you, will it?'

'Maybe Mother thinks a grief nurse can fix me,' said Eridanus. He seemed to consider his own words for a moment. 'Maybe that's true.'

'What about Andromeda?' Vela asked. 'She's quite eligible.'

'She's quite incorrigible,' countered Crater. 'I'd make the most of a grief nurse. I think that's obvious.' Crater pressed his palm against Vela's back, leading her away from Eridanus. He leaned his head close to hers as he said, 'Would you like to hear my ideas?'

Eridanus watched his brother walk away. He tapped the top of the piano, looking as if he were considering opening it, and looked about the room. He spotted Lynx and came toward her.

'You must be dying of boredom,' he said. He stood beside her in silence for a moment. 'He's a Fader, isn't he?' Eridanus looked from her to Mensa. She said nothing, only parted her lips, but she couldn't bring herself to answer. 'Well, everyone knows. It's an open secret.' Eridanus shrugged. 'It's ironic, since he's the champion of that anti-Fader bill, the one that requires Faders to register their status. Syril was outraged it was even being considered.' He fiddled with the chain around his neck, and Lynx knew there was something else on his mind. 'Lynx, I need your help.'

She sensed the heat of his Sorrow. 'Eridanus—'

'It's the remembering.' He pressed two fingers against his temple. 'Every little thing reminds me of him. I'll be perfectly fine one moment, and then I'll see the light shining a certain way in the autumn wing or hear glasses clinking together, like the sound of a piano key, and suddenly I'm dragged into a memory I didn't even know I had.' He looked at her. 'It's the Sorrow, isn't it?'

'Yes,' she said. Grief was full of memories.

'Well, then how can I dispose of them?'

'The memories?'

'Yes. Not the Sorrow, not yet. Just the memories. They're the worst part.'

She hesitated. 'You can't. There isn't – when I take your grief, the memories are there, but they're not separate. They're part of the Sorrow itself.'

Eridanus nodded, but he was frowning. 'I don't understand why he would do it.' He paused. 'I should say, I understand why he would want to, but I don't understand how he could bring himself to, knowing he'd leave us all behind.'

'He didn't expect you to have Sorrow for more than a day,' said Lynx, looking up at him.

'Even a day is long enough,' said Eridanus, looking out at the guests, at his family among them. 'Is it possible for Sorrow to get stronger over time?'

Lynx considered this, but even her understanding of grief was limited. 'I haven't had much experience with Sorrow, but I've never known anyone to keep it on purpose.'

'You'll have to meet Syril then.' He looked over at her. 'He'd have much to say to you.'

'I would love to meet him,' Lynx said, genuinely.

'If my mother ever deigns to let him into this house.' He looked at Ms. Aster, who was talking with a small group of guests, Mensa among them. Her bracelets flashed, and she appeared Bright, but Lynx could still see the snake of her grief coiled around her wrist, watching everything. 'I know I have perhaps the smallest chance of Mother giving me that nurse, but a growing part of me wishes she'll take pity on me.'

Her name is Karina, Lynx wanted to say. She resisted the urge to seek out Karina in the room. She was still embarrassed about leaving Karina's place so abruptly, but at least she believed now that Karina hadn't seen those black roots. If she had, she probably wouldn't have taken Lynx's hand with such compassion.

Just then someone laughed, a thundercrack of a sound that knocked a pause in everyone's conversations. A gaggle of guests surrounded Vela and Crater beside her. It was clear that Vela was trying to liven things up, although apparently through more conventional means than grief play. She was contorting her face and wagging her fingers as she impersonated someone. The thunderous laugh cracked again.

In the pause that followed, Lynx heard Mensa's voice, and she looked to where he stood beside Ms. Aster. Andromeda was there now, drink in hand, looking as elegant as usual, but her lips were parted, and Lynx knew she was up to something. Solina was nearby, standing quietly with her hands folded in front of her apron. Lynx looked for Orion, but he was not there. She noticed how

Solina and Vela's gazes each wandered toward the other, never once catching.

'I will refrain from giving my condolences,' Mensa said. 'I know if anyone can take news like that and transform it into something productive, it is you, Cassiopeia.'

Ms. Aster shook her head and pressed a hand to her heart. 'I'm utterly surprised. Of course we'll be doing our own investigation. Sculptor had a grief nurse, after all, and that is motivation enough for someone to influence the findings.' She seemed unable to help herself and flashed a look toward Vela.

Mensa nodded. 'Good. Good, it heartens me to hear you say that. Your son was different, I'll grant that, but he would never murder himself. He had too much to live for. Let me know if I can assist you in any way.'

'Thank you,' she smiled and touched his elbow. 'There is another matter I could use your help with. You know my predicament, Laurient.' She looked at Andromeda, who was taking long sips of her drink.

'Me in general?' said Andromeda. 'Or that we're going to lose the house if one of us doesn't marry rich quick?'

Ms. Aster's nostrils flared, and she ignored her daughter, turning back to Mensa. 'Andromeda is looking to marry. I expect she will find someone here at the party. Someone who has a particular interest in Mount Sorcha.'

He nodded sagely. 'A financial interest. I may know someone.'

Ms. Aster somehow beamed even Brighter. 'Lovely.' She glanced toward Vela. 'We gratefully no longer have to attach ourselves to Miss Deleporte. That girl is a scandal waiting to happen.'

Mensa raised his eyebrows in Vela's direction. 'I would

say she is the product of a scandal that already has.'

The scent of pepper made Lynx's nose itch, and she looked away from Mensa to see Karina standing beside her.

'How are you?' said Karina, and even though Lynx had heard her speak before, she was reminded how warm her voice was. How the rise and dip of it seemed to cradle her.

'I didn't mean to throw myself away from your place like that.'

Karina shrugged. 'It was forthright of me to drag you into it in the first place.'

Lynx wanted to say that she would go back. That she'd love to stand beneath that great yew and breathe in its scent, listen to its singing, but she wouldn't. Karina would want to go to Lynx's place, in turn, and Lynx couldn't allow that.

They stood for a while in companionable silence, watching the guests flit about the room, their gestures expanding, their bodies swaying, their fingers more prone to grasp a shoulder, brush a hand. The drinks were flowing. Lynx felt ease settle into her body. She realized that while standing beside Karina, she felt neither invisible nor alone. It was a completely unexpected and unfamiliar sensation.

Karina nodded toward Andromeda, who was standing beside a woman with hair dyed half purple, whose grief was an orchid. Presumably someone eligible that Mensa had found for her. 'She's doing well to make herself undesirable,' Karina said.

'What's your general opinion about madness?' Andromeda was asking the woman. 'I've been told it's a hereditary predilection. You don't suppose that's true, do you?'

The woman looked uncomfortable and at an utter loss for words. Andromeda looked pleased.

Karina was smiling as she watched her, and Lynx had to ignore a twinge of jealousy. 'I don't blame her,' said Karina. 'If I had a mother like hers, I'd have run away years ago.'

'She's tried,' said Lynx, smiling at the memories of Andromeda throughout the years. When she was only nine, wearing a puffy blue dress and shoes that clacked when she knocked the heels together, dragging a suitcase almost bigger than herself across the lawn. She'd only made it to the swirling yellow border of daffodils before Orion found her and scooped her up. There were other attempts when she was older. Some careless dashes into the night, some meticulously planned. One time, she even managed to escape on the ferry and spent a night on the mainland. But she always came back.

As if she sensed them looking at her, Andromeda turned her gaze toward Lynx and Karina. She assessed them both, her expression unreadable, before stepping away from the stalled conversation, leaving the other woman looking relieved, and exchanged her nearly empty drink for a full one. She plucked the pin from her hair and rapped it against the glass. The room took a long moment to quiet itself, but once it did, Andromeda was standing centre stage, her pin now sparkling in her hair, her feathered gown rustling softly around her feet.

'I never properly gave a toast to my brother,' said Andromeda, raising her glass. Several guests mirrored her but let their hands drop when they saw Ms. Aster wasn't reciprocating. 'I'm certain that only a rare few of you here liked him. His company was at times difficult to endure, but I loved him. I loved him when he was Bright, and I loved him when he wasn't.' Her gaze wavered. She shot a glance toward the window. 'He called me Little Fish, even though I was taller than him. He saved me from drowning once, and after that he taught me how to swim. He said that one day I would be strong enough to swim away from this island. He told me that I should do what I wanted, even if that meant someone else got hurt. He told me to fuck propriety.' Someone muttered an objection.

'I take it she doesn't want me?' said Karina with a smile.

'She doesn't want a grief nurse, full stop,' said Lynx.

Karina nodded. 'She doesn't want to keep a grief nurse, but I wouldn't say she doesn't want one.'

Lynx looked at Karina, who had a small smile on her lips, but Karina was still watching the room.

'It was the best advice I've ever been given,' continued Andromeda. She raised her glass higher and said, 'To Sculptor.' She took a sip and looked around at the speechless guests watching her.

'Thank you, darling,' said Ms. Aster, swooping in with a smile. She rested her arm gently around her daughter's shoulders. They looked alike then. The resemblance was clear in their set jaws, the determination in their eyes. They were both unrelentingly stubborn, and with a dawning fear, Lynx realized what was about to come next. 'This is the perfect time for me to announce that I have chosen which of my children shall become the guardian of Sculptor's grief nurse.'

Everyone was watching her. Even Eridanus wasn't

pretending to be disinterested.

'As you all know, guardianship is a great responsibility. It is a promise to protect and care for a grief nurse, who will in turn protect you and those you love from grief. There is power in what grief nurses give. A clearness of mind, an unburdened heart. To be always Bright is an honour only a very few are afforded.' She looked at her daughter triumphantly. Andromeda no longer looked pleased with herself. She looked at Lynx, who felt her growing Dread. It seemed to echo in Lynx's heart. 'Guardians must be a model to others, and that is a burden that you must bear, my dear. The grief nurse is yours.'

Time seemed to stop then. Lynx had to remind herself that this was real. The golden lights of the drawing room. Karina beside her. Her own body. The flowing dress that hid her feet. It was all real. Andromeda had a grief nurse, and it wasn't her.

The room was silent save for the mournful cawing of a crow.

CHAPTER 9

Lynx stepped from the drawing room, hoping to stay in the shadows of the corridor and slip away unnoticed to her room. But the hall was filled with light, and music rose up from the great hall, plucky fiddle sounds and stomping feet, drunken shouts and the ocean-burr of conversation. She wanted to shut it all out, all the carefree people, whose lives hadn't been shattered in a single moment. A single sentence changing her life irrevocably. The grief nurse is yours.

Ms. Aster's declaration had shifted the mood in the drawing room. It was the catalyst the guests had been looking for to tip them over the edge of propriety, the stimulus they needed to loosen their ties and speak in louder voices. After that moment, the guests began to slip away, lured by the music and dancing in the great hall. Eventually, only Lynx and Mr. Aster remained. He'd sat content on the settee, sipping an amber drink and watching the flames in the fireplace.

'You should go to bed, Lynx,' he said after a while. 'I think drink has taken your place, though I expect there will be much regret in the morning.' He smiled and looked toward her. 'Much better to trust your emotions to a grief nurse. One suffers no consequences that way.'

She said nothing, only nodded.

Mr. Aster's smile flickered. Something like

understanding shone in his eyes. 'We're very lucky to have you,' he said. 'She doesn't know it, but Andromeda is spoiled to have grown up with a grief nurse like you.'

His words left her feeling even emptier, despite the attempt at kindness. 'Good night,' she said. She heard his echoed reply as she left, leaving the faint smell of roses behind her.

As she made her way down the corridor, questions rose up behind her, beating their wings, swooping and diving at her back. Now that she had her own grief nurse, would Andromeda do as her mother wished and find a match, marry and move away, leaving Lynx alone? Now that she had Karina, would she ever come to Lynx again?

She imagined spinning around and shooing them away, but questions weren't birds, and she couldn't scare them off with a fluttering of her fingers. Instead, she continued down the hall, focusing on the lights, on the sound of music drifting from the great hall.

All she wanted was to go to bed, to start a new day and forget the party ever happened. She lifted her skirts and made her way down the corridor.

A door opened. A square of golden light illuminated the floor at the far end of the hall. Solina appeared in the doorway of the antechamber in the corner between the winter and autumn wings. She had a small smile on her face, and she looked more content than Lynx had seen her since Sculptor had left. She moved down the hall as if it were rolling beneath her, her steps light. Lynx drew back into the shadows, but Solina wasn't looking around. She seemed set in her direction, toward Ms. Aster's room. She didn't notice Lynx as she passed.

The stairwell down to the servants' quarters was

blessedly empty. When she finally reached her room, the exhaustion hit her. She was already undoing her hair, fingers clawing through the braids, as she opened the door. She imagined stripping off the dress and falling into bed. But when she kicked the door closed behind her, she realized she wasn't alone.

Mensa stood with his back to her, his hands in his pockets. He was looking at her dresser, the row of sea glass atop it. If she could, she would have thrown him aside and swept the softly rounded shards into her open palm. Each was a moment: Andromeda swooping unexpectedly to snatch a jade piece from amongst a pile of salt-crisp bladderwrack, holding it up to the sunlight so Lynx had noticed for the first time how long and slender her fingers were. The burnt orange shard that had washed up against her toes the day Andromeda taught her how to swim. The white one that was hardly worn away, its edges still hard enough in places to nick the skin, sitting like a queen in the centre of the small circle of cockles Andromeda had placed outside her door one day.

Mensa picked one up and she wanted to scream. Her body was heavy, her mind addled as if her skull were stuffed with velvet. She wanted to close out the world. She wanted to be alone.

'I've met many grief nurses, but never one like you.' His stance was relaxed. His grief, on the other hand, was wild. She could sense it craving her. Craving to be plucked. It unfurled around him, a creeping sweep of vines laden with fruit, impossibly clustered together: oranges, pears, plums, and blackberries.

'What do you mean?'

'You're not beautiful.' He turned his gaze to her hair. Mensa slid the glasses from his nose and cleaned them with a handkerchief pulled from his pocket. 'None of you are. But you are memorable. There is something about you that will not let me be. You are the model grief nurse, but I am certain you are full of secrets.'

'I'm not.' She swallowed the lie, banishing the twist of worry she felt at the mention of secrets.

'I saw something in you this evening. A hunger. You're looking for more.' Something shivered at the back of her mind, trembling in agreement. She did want more. She wanted to be satisfied. To be free.

Mensa lunged toward her, faster than she could react. His words had distracted her, and now he grasped her by the wrist, hovered his lips beside her ear. 'Play with it.' He pressed something into her hand.

'I can't.' Lynx pulled away, but he clung on. When she uncurled her fingers, she saw his token: a brass thimble.

'You can. You're feeling it right now. And you want it.'

She did want it. She was always wanting. Always hungry. She wanted to be surrounded by it. She wanted to take and take until it filled her up.

The thimble was a hot coal in her palm. She thought of Andromeda's cool grief, and she turned her hand over and flung the token away.

It clattered to the ground, and Mensa bounded to pick it up.

'How dare you.' He held the thimble in his fist. 'He said I could have you.'

The bitter scent of oranges bloomed around her. 'I'll take your grief. Nothing more.'

'You'll do what I ask.' He came closer. She imagined

the friendship between this man and Sculptor Aster. They had the same desires, the same needs, although for different reasons. And both of them were certain of their right to get what they wanted.

'I was promised you tonight,' he said. 'I can do whatever I want.'

Crater, it must have been. 'What did you promise him in exchange?'

'To introduce him to some friends of mine. An invitation to the club I frequent. And perhaps I may have a way of acquiring him a grief nurse, if I'm feeling so inclined.' He licked his lips, and she imagined him partaking of his own grief. She could taste it, too. The velvet skin of a grape breaking against her tongue, bursting sweet juices.

Mensa pressed the token into her palm. This time, she acted without thinking. She was too tired to resist, too tired to fight. She closed her eyes and was at once surrounded by his grief. Her mind's tendrils uncurled, entwining themselves with the vines and roots of Mensa's orchard.

Lynx was only half aware of Mensa pulling her toward him, the hard edge of his glasses as he drew his lips along her neck, his fingers tugging through her hair. She devoured a peach, and then she picked another, while all around her, the white fingers flitted among the orchard.

'Don't stop,' he said, and she felt him move behind her, his fingers plucking at the buttons of her dress. Distantly, she urged her body to protest, but her mind was absorbed in the grief, too focused on its hunger. Lynx would do anything as long as she could stay inside Mena's orchard. She stretched her fingers as she walked among the rows of trees, brushing bark and flesh and leaves.

She held a peach in her hand, the curve of it fitting perfectly in her palm. It fell away from its tree easily, and in the next moment, her teeth were breaking through its flesh, juice on her lips, on her chin.

It did not smell of peach. It smelled of oranges.

She knew this grief. She knew its scent.

Several months earlier, she had woken in the early hours of the morning from a dream. As she lay in bed, she tried to cling to its memory. Of trees rising around her. Of sweet-smelling fruits dangling from branches, of bushes bursting with berries. She had walked down the corridor of trees, drawn toward something glinting in a tree at the very end of the row. An orange tree, bejewelled with fruit. Not until she stood beneath its branches did she realize what she was looking at. A knife thrust into its bark. She had reached out to touch it, but then she'd woken.

Sleep wouldn't return, and since it was too early for even the kitchen maid to be awake, she snuck away upstairs. She loved the feeling of being the only one awake in all the vastness of the house, to stand alone at the balcony and watch the twinkling of the stars on the ceiling of the great hall, as moonlight filtered in through the long, painted windows. As she leaned her arms against the railing, she caught the unexpected scent of oranges. She ignored it at first, but there it was again. She stepped back

She followed it to the autumn wing, and when it led her to Sculptor's door, she knew she ought to walk away. Just turn and go back to bed. But excitement was rare. A new grief even rarer. She couldn't help herself, as she pressed her palm against the door and stretched out her mind.

It was a Fader's grief, an orchard like the one that had drifted into her dreams. It was no wonder she had sensed it from such a distance. Through the haze of grief, she heard voices.

'What do you think? Will she suit?' A man's voice, one she had never heard before.

Sculptor's voice, replying, 'You've outdone yourself...' and fading away as he moved about the room. He must have been visiting from the mainland, where he now lived with Vela Deleporte. He was often coming back to partake is Lynx's skills. This time, though, he had not called on her.

She could feel Sculptor's grief, but the unmistakable metallic tang was distant. It was muted beneath the Fader's grief, but even so it was weaker than usual. As if he'd had it removed. Not days ago, not even hours, but just then. She drew away from the door. Her mouth was filled with the bitter taste of oranges.

Only now, as she sunk her teeth into that very grief did she realize what she had discovered.

Sculptor did not suddenly move to the top of the waitlist. His mother's influence had been worthless. It was Mensa who had procured him a grief nurse. He had given him Karina's guardianship. And that night she had sensed them mixing – Sculptor's grief and Mensa's combining. A knife in the trunk of an orange tree.

She pulled away from him. The fingers of her mind raked against the ground of the orchard, dragging vines and branches toward her.

'What are you doing? Grief nurse—'

'Lynx,' she said.

'What? What are you saying?' Mensa's voice was desperate. He knew she was taking his grief.

'That's my name. Lynx.'

Lynx opened her eyes just as she untangled herself from Mensa's grief. She let his token fall to the floor, where it rolled beside his shoe. He stooped to pick it up, and when he looked at her, his eyes were wet and bloodshot. He grabbed her by the shoulders, and she could feel his entire body vibrating with anger.

'I was not done,' he said.

'I took your grief, as is expected of a grief nurse.'

She felt how much he hated and wanted her in that moment. 'We're done when I say we're done. This is on my terms.'

'Is it?' she asked.

She felt him tense, ready to strike her, but he froze.

'Laurient,' said a woman's voice, low and firm.

Cool air rushed across Lynx's skin as Mensa pulled away from her. He seemed captured by something which she had to turn to see.

Karina stood in the doorway. 'That's enough,' she said in the same firm way which left no room for uncertainty.

Mensa scowled. 'I don't take orders from a grief nurse.'

Lynx knew Karina's fingers were pushing forward, finding Mensa's orchard, exploring its fruits. Her right hand was down at her side, but Lynx could see her forefinger rubbing circles atop her thumbnail. She was focused on him. Mensa relaxed beside her, and his grief grew sweeter.

'Come with me instead,' Karina said.

'She was promised to me,' said Mensa, but his voice had lost conviction. He stared at Karina as she tilted her head, revealing the curve of her neck.

'I know you, Laurient. She doesn't know what you like.' Karina held out her palm, and like a man entranced, Mensa placed his token into it. 'Good,' she said, as she curled her fingers around it.

'Karina—' started Lynx.

Karina put a finger to her lips and shook her head. 'Good night, Lynx.' She turned and led Mensa into the hall.

Lynx stood in the empty room, her body buzzing, unsure of what to think or feel except that without a doubt she was no longer tired.

CHAPTER 10

Lynx watched Orion, who held one hand behind his back, his shoulders squared. If it hadn't been for the cigarette in his hand, he would have looked as though he was still on duty. He leaned his head back and blew a perfect ring of white smoke against the indigo sky. They stood outside the servants' door. The ground here was packed dirt, and the threshold of the door was flanked by empty crates waiting to be picked up when the next delivery arrived. The night was quiet, only the distant muffled sounds of music could be heard, from the party that never seemed to end. The air smelled of snow and cigarettes.

'How was your evening?' Orion held the cigarette out for her, and she moved beside him and took it.

'I'm relieved it's over,' said Lynx, the smoke curling out from between her lips.

'It's not over, I'm afraid. They're hunting tomorrow if the weather holds, and Cook is frantic, preparing another dinner. Ms. Aster wants to keep the guests here for as long as she can.'

They were both silent.

Their fingers brushed as she handed the cigarette back to him, but Orion did not flinch from her touch. They said nothing for a long moment, the length of two deep drags. Lynx looked up. Pale clumps of cloud drifted across a smattering of stars.

She felt his anger before he said another word. She looked down. At his feet sat a mountain hare, narrow face alert, completely still save for its flickering ears. Orion himself was motionless.

'I don't like any of it,' he said eventually, and the hare looked up at her, its eyes catching in the light of the stars. 'I've never liked it.'

She could stroke the soft fur of that grief, feel the beating muscled energy of the hare's body beneath her fingers. She could do it, but she knew she wouldn't. She'd only touched Orion's grief one time, and afterwards he'd told her to never touch it again.

In the fifteen years she'd been at Mount Sorcha, Orion had forgone his duties only once. He'd received a letter, which she'd seen him read silently before folding it crisply and slipping it into his pocket. Within an hour, he was gone. The thumping of a hare's feet beat in time with her blood as she watched him stride across the lawn, a case in one hand and a hat on his head.

The house had felt bereft without its butler.

His sister's son was dead. The servants spoke of it in murmured voices, casting their eyes away from her as she passed. She could feel their hatred like heat, but she didn't begrudge them. She was a reminder of the great distance between themselves and the Asters. Orion lived under the same roof as a grief nurse, yet still he must grieve.

Unlike the servants, the Asters spoke of Orion's loss freely. Lynx was called to them as they sat together in the drawing room, Mr. Aster on the settee with a cup of tea, Ms. Aster standing beside her desk flipping through the papers atop it. The three brothers were there, trying to play a game of cards, and Andromeda was sitting in an armchair, sketching a still life composed of a small collection of bric-a-brac she'd arranged on the nearby table.

'I'm astounded he would just take off like that. That's a bit inconsiderate, isn't it?' said Crater as he flipped a card. 'Not very professional.'

'Orion is the epitome of professional,' said Eridanus. 'I think we should trust his judgement.'

'We don't want grief here anyway. It was good of him to leave.' Ms. Aster didn't look up from her papers. 'Let him do what he needs to start thinking straight again.'

'He didn't say how long he'd be gone?' Crater asked.

'He said he would return as soon as he was able,' said Mr. Aster.

'Whatever that means.' Sculptor slapped down a card and smirked at Crater. 'Sorry, brother. Your mistake.'

Crater's brow furrowed, but then he saw Lynx waiting at the threshold. 'Ah, the angel of agony has arrived!'

'Who called her?' Sculptor said, only glancing at her quickly.

'I did,' said his mother. 'I wanted to remind her that no matter what the servants are twittering about downstairs she is not, under any circumstances, permitted to touch anyone's grief outside this family unless I've explicitly approved it.'

Ms. Aster didn't look at her, so Lynx was not obliged to nod or say a word in acknowledgement. She stood beside the window and waited for them to send her away.

'Orion was a part of this house before I was,' said Andromeda. 'Don't you think he ought to count as family?'

'You're being absurd,' said Ms. Aster.

'Who does it hurt, to let him go with Lynx just this once?' Andromeda looked out the window, toward where Orion would be stepping onto the ferry for the mainland. She caught Lynx's gaze for a moment before looking again at her mother.

'Us.' Ms. Aster turned a page decisively. 'There is an order to the world, and it is our responsibility to uphold it. If we are seen to compromise, we are failing ourselves and everything we stand for.'

'We stand for something?' Sculptor snorted.

'We stand for civility,' said Ms. Aster. 'We are models of propriety. They are always watching what we do, and we cannot slip up, not once.'

Sculptor prodded Eridanus in the arm. 'Did you hear that, Dani?'

'Orion must endure his grief,' said Mr. Aster, taking a sip of tea. He looked regretful. 'Grief is what separates them from us.'

The next day, when she saw Orion striding back across the lawn, she waited for him in the butler's pantry. He stepped into the small room, hat in hand, and she knew he'd take her offer. The hare cowered between his legs, ears pressed flat against its back. He gave her his token, and she closed her eyes, took the hare into her arms, pressed her nose into its fur.

When she opened her eyes, he took back his token without a word. She thought he'd say nothing, but as she went to leave, he caught her by the arm. 'Don't ever do that again,' he said, and it wasn't anger that made him say it. 'You do not deserve it, but if they hear of this, they will send you away. They will not hesitate.'

Orion had not known the consequences could be far

greater than exile from the Aster's protection.

Now Lynx's cigarette had gone out, and Orion re-lit it for her. She looked at him, and realized she felt the same. She didn't like any of it either. That she couldn't take the servants' grief, that she was complicit in the Asters' hoarding of her skills, that even though she could take without limit, she was allowed to take for only a few. She hated, too, how they had spoken of Karina all evening, like a thing to be inherited, not a person with her own free will.

She felt the looming presence of Mount Sorcha behind her. She wanted to see the coloured skylights shattered, the paintings ripped from the walls, the lights gone dark. If she could, she would burn the whole house down. And as the anger rose and grew within her, she was only half-aware of her mind's fingers flexing. Not until she felt a prickle of coarse fur did realize that she was stroking the hare's back

Lynx pulled herself away, reeling in her anger until it was safely dulled, safely stored away. Her heart was in her throat, her pulse throbbing, but she'd done nothing, only touch the hare. She'd done nothing. She'd done no harm.

'It's okay,' she said. 'It's just the way things are.'

Orion didn't nod or agree. He looked at her and said nothing. A moment passed, the opportunity to tell him how she really felt slipping away.

'Mr. Aster is worried the grief will come back,' Orion said, looking out into the night. 'I can see it in the way he holds his hands.' Orion crossed his arms. 'He doesn't know what to do with them.'

'If it does come back, I'll take it. He knows I do good work.'

Orion tapped his temple. 'Up here he does. But not here.' He tapped his chest, above his heart. 'He's frightened. Like a child that fears the monsters in the dark. He's afraid of the unknown. And for him, that is grief.' He paused, didn't look at her. 'What is worse? Grief itself or the anticipation of it?'

'Grief, of course.'

Orion looked at her. Even though it was dark, she could see the green in his eyes.

'Anyway, anticipating grief is pointless when you have a grief nurse. He should know better.' She angled her head back, lost herself in the stars. The clouds were closing in. It would snow again soon.

'You said at dinner that we always have grief, even if our Sorrow is removed,' Orion said.

She didn't want to talk about grief. 'You don't feel it. Vela didn't even know it was there until I told her.'

'Hm.' Orion looked up at the stars. 'I've always wondered – where does it go? The grief after you take it.'

Lynx ran her thumb over the cigarette's filter. She thought of the tree within her and said nothing.

A pause. 'Have a good night, Lynx.'

'Good night,' said Lynx, handing back Orion's cigarette.

He took the final drag and dropped it, crushed it with his boot. He bent to pick it up before heading inside.

The smoke from a fresh cigarette curled up and around her head. She inhaled, filling her lungs, feeling a rush of warmth. She felt hollow, wishing she could have told Orion about all that had happened tonight. Karina's unexpected kindness. Andromeda's Sorrow. The incident with Mensa, which had left her feeling both angry and ashamed. Her fear at what would happen now that Andromeda didn't need her any more. Though she was relieved, too, that she hadn't said anything. Orion wasn't a grief nurse. How could he really understand?

She took the final drag of the cigarette and dropped it into the mud. She looked behind her at the door. She knew Mount Sorcha wasn't yet asleep. She buttoned her jacket and began to walk. The grounds were starkly illuminated by the light of the moon. Every molehill and tuft of grass cast its own black shadow. The lawn was covered in a thin layer of snow, and already stray flakes had begun to fall again, floating and bobbing on the wind. She looked up and considered the moon. For now, it hung unobscured by clouds, as if its light were warding them off.

She walked with a growing sense of urgency, and by the time she was across the lawn, nearly at the line of trees that marked the forest's edge, she was running. The air was cool in her lungs, her breath billowing out in a white cloud before being carried away by the wind. Everything she had been holding in all night came undone. Her anger and desire and fear unravelled, and she was falling away from Mount Sorcha, plunging from the real world into herself, into a place of rolling hills where all the grief she'd ever taken sat among the roots of a barren and ugly tree.

It had not always been ugly. Once, it had been a young but lively oak with vibrant green leaves and little perfect round acorns that she would roll around her in her palms like dice. Once, she had loved to come here and sit beneath its branches, her back against its trunk, listening to its song. The tree was adorned with the grief she'd taken from others and once, she had loved to sit among that grief.

Now she only came here when she could not help herself. When she felt as if she could not bear to be herself a single moment longer. When she could no longer push away the desire to see everything she knew aflame.

She stood back from the tree, not letting its roots touch her, and she clawed the fingers of both hands, lifting them, and with that movement, the roots lifted, too, tearing away from the earth. They whipped through the air to clutch at the branches above, and as the roots tore at the branches and the branches bowed and creaked and broke under the weight, Lynx imagined what her life would be like if she hadn't been born with white hair. She would kiss Andromeda. She would take her hand and pull her into her bed. She would do with her what she'd always wanted, and Andromeda would let her because as Lynx leaned over her to kiss her neck, the hair that fell around her face would be the colour of earth not ice. She would no longer stand against the wall and watch the Asters live their lives. She would go and see the world, get off this island.

As she lost herself in these imaginings, the tree continued to tear itself apart. Branches fell at her feet, making her step back, but she never touched them. She balled her hands into fists and the roots stopped tearing at the branches, instead shooting forward, and she felt a thrill as the tree creaked, the roots closest to the trunk lifting away. If she pulled long enough, if she used all her strength, she could rip the tree from the earth. She could destroy it. She could kill that part of her that made her who she was. What would happen then?

Even as she imagined the tree's trunk slamming into

the earth, its empty branches shivering as they fell, she could hear its singing. She felt it in her body, a vibration that made her teeth ache. Though her mind wanted to tear the tree from the ground, her heart stopped her. Her hands fell slack at her sides. The tree still stood, crooked now, still black, still bare. She didn't dare look at it, and when she fell to her knees, she fell out of that place and onto the lawn of Mount Sorcha.

The snow seeped through her dress. She sat despite the chill until the feeling passed, until she felt in control again. She rose slowly. The moon was gone, covered completely by clouds.

She was nearly across the lawn, when she saw a dark swatch of something against the snow. There was an unnaturalness in the shape that made her quicken her pace toward it. Someone was stretched out on the ground. A stroke of emerald. Lynx stopped, her breath clouding around her, her head pounding. She moved toward the figure.

The wind picked up. The streak of green took shape, revealed itself to be a dress, the same one the upstairs servants wore. There were two pale legs stretched out, a hip, an arm. The woman was lying on her side, one arm beneath her head. Her scarf had slipped from her head, revealing wisps of auburn hair.

Solina looked as if she were only sleeping. The pink veins running through her eyelids were visible even beneath the layer of shimmering makeup. White flecks of ice clung to her eyelashes. Her mouth was parted, her lips frosted.

She wore no jacket, and her feet were bare.

Her skin appeared dappled, pockmarked, and for

a long moment, Lynx looked at it in confusion. She blinked, willing her eyes to adjust better to the darkness. Then she realized that frost covered all of Solina, not just her lips and lashes.

Lynx bent and pressed her fingertips against Solina's wrist. Nothing. She felt for the rise and fall of breath. Nothing. Just the scent of souring grief and a body as cold as ice.

The ground beneath her feet crackled with ice as she backed away, and she felt the world closing in around her. She found Solina's token, a round compact mirror, tucked beside her hip. She picked it up and reached forward with her mind, hating herself for the desire that shivered within her as she found Solina's grief. It was fading fast, dissolving beneath her fingers.

After a moment, it was completely gone.

CHAPTER 11

Lynx stood paralyzed, as the snow began to fall around her. She recalled Solina's fingers tugging at the buttons of her dress, and she thought as she had never allowed herself to of another woman's hands, running through her hair, combing through the knots with gentle persistence. Lynx could almost feel it now, the sensation on her scalp, the scent of the woman's skin.

Lynx stepped back, away from Solina's body. Her mouth tasted of metal, and her heart was in her throat, threatening to cut off her breath. She pressed her hands against her eyes. She wanted to turn inward, to tear at the roots of her own heart, but she didn't dare look inside herself for fear of what she might find.

She turned and ran.

Her mother's hair had been piled atop her head in a sloppy bun, blond strands escaping and floating about her face. She stood at the very top of a wooden ladder, which creaked and groaned as she shifted her weight. She was chewing her lip and staring intently at the wall, as she drew her paintbrush across it. A silvery crescent was taking shape, vibrant against a midnight sky. She was painting the moon, and below it was the beginning of a sea filled with creatures. Already she'd painted a pink conch shell, a starfish clinging to a rock, a rainbow of anemones, arms waving.

Lynx's knees were drawn up to her chest as she watched. The room smelled of shortbread, of butter and sugar. There were biscuits in the oven, for the elderly woman in the basement flat.

As she rested her chin in the dip between her knees, her hair fell around her face. It wasn't blond, although she often imagined it to be, but a shocking white. She hated her hair. It was her hair that caused all their problems. It was her hair that meant the curtains could never be opened, that instead they were punctured with holes no bigger than her little nail, sending spots of light across the ground. It was her hair that kept her from going outside. But it was also because of her hair that she had the pictures on the walls. If she could go outside, she wouldn't have those, and she loved them. Almost the whole room was covered – in a forest, a hillside, and now a sea. A feat, even though the room was tiny. She did love the pictures, but she hated her hair more.

Without thinking, she tugged at it, pulling until her scalp burned.

'Lynx!' her mother said, lifting her paint brush from the wall, a single drop of silver paint falling from its tip to land on the floor below. 'Your poor hair. Let it be.'

'You could paint my hair,' said Lynx holding a clump of it in her fist. 'Then no one would notice.'

As her mother looked at her, she felt something, a familiar wonderful something that made her stomach flutter. She loved these moments, though her mother seemed to find them painful. She closed her eyes, and when she opened them she stood on a hillside, much like the one painted on the wall opposite the incomplete sea. The grass was a vibrant green, the rocks grey and bursting from the earth like fists. The hills were layered, one behind another and another as far as she could see. Some even were crowned in snow.

Lynx stood in a valley between two hills, and she felt safe. She couldn't go outside, but she could go here. It was her favourite place in the world.

'Your hair is beautiful just the way it is,' she heard her mother say, her voice distant. Lynx knew she was lying, but it made her happy anyway.

Orion took the news with composure. He told Lynx to go to bed, he would handle it, and she tried doing as he said. She sat on her bed, her mind spinning, everything in her room reminding her of Solina. There were old memories, of when Solina had first arrived at Mount Sorcha, a young new maid from the mainland whose whiplash personality immediately disproved the downstairs of the notion that she was just a pretty face. New memories, of Solina's grief for Sculptor, the way it had stung when she was alive, how it melted away to nothing as she lay dead in the snow.

Memories of her mother kept mixing among the memories of Solina, mingling among them like an uninvited guest. Those were the worst, the ones she most desperately wanted to ignore. Lynx knew what Eridanus had meant when he'd said the memories were the worst part.

Forcing her mind away from her mother only made Lynx's memories of Solina stronger. One rose up more clearly than the others, from the summer Andromeda turned twenty. The night air was warm, the usually persistent wind no more than a soft breeze.

'Come up,' Andromeda had shouted at her from her perch in her favourite tree. It was the oldest one on the grounds and had been struck by lightning when Lynx was ten years old, the year she'd arrived at Mount Sorcha. Twelve years later, it still stood strong but most of its upper branches had broken away, and a great, pale line of stripped bark ran through its trunk. Lynx's head was tipped back as she watched Andromeda sitting comfortably in the highest branches, her bare feet swinging through the air.

It was late enough that most of the house was asleep but near enough to midsummer that the sky wasn't yet fully darkened. Andromeda was slowly becoming a shadow as the gloaming faded away to true night.

'I'm never going to climb that tree,' Lynx said. 'I don't trust it.'

'Suit yourself,' said Andromeda. 'The view is gorgeous.' She shifted, looking toward the west. 'The sea is calm. It would be a lovely night for a swim.' She sat still for a moment, watching the sea, before looking toward the gardens. 'Oh, look.'

'You'll have to elaborate,' said Lynx, when Andromeda didn't immediately go on.

Already Andromeda was clambering from the tree, a sparkle of excitement in her eyes. 'There's a light on in one of the glasshouses.'

'Is it the new heating system?' Lynx asked.

Andromeda dropped onto the grass in front of her. 'No, that's done through pipes. This is a proper light. Someone's in there.' She was marching in the direction of the gardens before Lynx could respond.

'Maybe it's the gardener,' said Lynx, hurrying to catch up. Everything was darker now, as they made their way onto the forest path that would lead them to the walled gardens and the trio of glasshouses that sat in the centre.

'At midnight?' Andromeda smiled, the gap between her front teeth endearingly obvious. 'I think it must be a rendezvous. Who do you think it might be?'

Lynx tried to think of the most unusual combination. 'Crater and the cook.'

Andromeda snorted. 'Oh, that would be too strange. Perhaps it's Orion with one of the footmen.'

'That seems even more unlikely,' said Lynx, returning Andromeda's smile.

'I hope for unlikely,' she said.

When the garden wall loomed into view, Andromeda held a finger to her lips. They slipped through the gates as quietly as they could. Andromeda had seen true – there was a light on in the smallest glasshouse.

'Lynx,' Andromeda whispered. 'Cover your hair. It's so loud in the moonlight.'

'With what?' Lynx asked, but Andromeda was already unwinding the sash from her dress. She held it out to Lynx. It was soft and thin and when fully unravelled, revealed to be quite significant in size. Lynx wrapped it around her head, tucking in her hair. She was enveloped with Andromeda's scent, bergamot and vanilla. If she could, she would have captured that moment in a glass jar, to return to it time and again.

Andromeda snickered. 'It's really becoming.'

Lynx rolled her eyes. 'This is how you know I'm truly committed to this investigation.'

'Oh, investigation. I like that.'

They crept toward the glasshouse, trying to stay in the shadows. It was impossible to make out anything beyond the many leaves pressed against the glass. They had to come right up to it and peer through the gaps between ferns and flowers to see into the space beyond.

'Look,' Andromeda said after several minutes of no success. Lynx came up beside her, so close their shoulders nearly brushed, and looked inside. She could see shifting shadows, nothing more, until a person came into view. A pair of gold-brown trousers, a not-quite-completely tucked in shirt, a gold watch flashing on a wrist. Sculptor stepped forward then spun to face whoever was behind him. He pressed his hands against a waist. An emerald dress, auburn hair loose and long around her shoulders.

Solina was smiling, and through the glass Lynx could hear her laugh. The sound was so unfamiliar, the look of unbound joy on Solina's face so unexpected, that Lynx had to look twice to be sure it was truly Solina she was seeing.

The two kissed, long and passionately, and when they finally broke away from one another, Sculptor whispered something in Solina's ear that made her laugh again.

'What a rascal,' said Andromeda, shaking her head and smiling. 'Of course, it's Sculptor and Solina. Haven't they been making eyes at each other for months? She's far too pretty for him. I can't believe she would really fall for someone with ears as big as his.' She was still smiling, radiant in the light of the moon, and Lynx wanted more than ever to reach up and brush away the hair that had fallen into her face.

'He does have other redeeming qualities.'

Andromeda raised her eyebrows. 'You find my brother redeeming?'

'I meant his money,' said Lynx.

Andromeda nodded knowingly. 'Yes, I suppose that helps, although there is a lot less of it than most people realize.' She looked back at the couple. 'But I don't think it's that, do you? That's what other girls are interested in, at least all the ones I've seen him with, but this looks real, doesn't it?' Andromeda pressed her palm against the glass. 'I hope it's real. That would be too romantic.'

'I don't think it's romantic,' said Lynx. 'He's going to break her heart. How could there be any other way?'

'What do you mean?' Andromeda looked at her, and there was genuine surprise on her face.

'Sculptor can't be with a servant. Your mother wouldn't allow it.'

Andromeda considered this. 'Maybe they'll run away together.' She began to play with her fingernails. 'He could take a suitcase full of trinkets, some of that useless junk we keep in the attic because we have nowhere for it in the house, and when they arrive on the mainland, he'll sell it all. They'll have enough to live for a year. They'll get a flat in the city, and they won't have much, but they'll be sure the vase on the windowsill is always filled with flowers, no matter the season.' Her eyes were flecked in gold, and they shone as she spoke.

I'd do it, Lynx wanted to say. I'd run away with you.

Instead, she said what she needed to to survive. 'What happens when a year passes, and their money runs out? Everyone knows where they came from. Their reputation is ruined. Eventually, he'll have to come back home, but she won't be coming with him. If she leaves, she can never come back.'

Andromeda pressed her lips together and looked again

at the lovers. Solina had her arms around Sculptor's neck, her face pressed against his collar bone. It did look real, but that didn't mean it would work. It only meant more grief in the end, more pain later.

She and Andromeda stood in silence, unsaid things between them, until she pulled a face. Sculptor had pressed Solina against a tree and was peeling off her dress, while her fingers were unclasping his belt. 'Let's go,' said Andromeda, pulling away. 'Before I see something I can never unsee.' She smiled and Lynx laughed.

But as they made their way across the gardens, back onto the forest path, the unsaid words still hung between them.

Lynx, of course, had been right in the end. Sculptor had broken Solina's heart. He'd loved her for a while, then Vela Deleporte had come along. Just as pretty but with the inheritance his mother needed. There could be no competing with that.

It was hard to believe that the two lovers Lynx had seen in the glasshouse three years ago were both dead.

A worm of misgiving wriggled in her mind. How had Solina really died? She dropped from the bed and strode out into the hall, careless, reckless, not caring if anyone saw her. She went upstairs to the autumn wing to look down at the partygoers below. It was nearly midnight, but still the party went on.

The great hall had been transformed into a dancefloor. The crooning of a squeezebox, a fiddle's twang, laughter that was its own kind of music. It rose up to Lynx, where she stood looking down at it all, trying and failing to make sense of the joy below and the death she knew lurked outside those great double doors.

Everything seemed starkly present, flamboyant and bold in the face of death. The guests downstairs danced as if they would live forever. The clusters of flowers that twirled up the length of each immense pillar in perfectly arranged colour gradients had been crushed by careless bodies. Velvet petals littered the floor alongside trampled sweets and spilled and shattered drinks. Servants were darting here and there, doing their best to avoid stamping feet and recklessly swinging arms, to clean up the messes, but it was in vain. Above it all, skeins of silk in a multitude of colours rippled among a sea of glittering lanterns.

Had Solina really died from the cold?

A man, eyes shining with drink, took a wrong step. He swung desperately, his arms windmilling as he stumbled over his feet. He fell over himself and went sprawling into a group clustered on the edge of the dancefloor. Glasses shattered as they hit the ground, drinks slopping over the floor. There was a great roar of approval from the nearest dancers. The man was hefted by the armpits and thrown back into the dance.

It was at that moment that the doors opened. Orion stepped through, Solina's body in his arms, two footmen at his heels. For a surreal moment, the music continued, the guests danced, the great hall sparkled with colour. Until a woman screamed, and it was as if someone had taken a knife to the night.

Chaos broke out in the vestibule, rippling across the dancefloor until the entire hall was a confusion of screams and exclamations, people turning this way and that, trying to discern what could have caused the music to stop.

The sound of a door slamming shut. She turned to see

114

Eridanus striding toward her, still tying his robe. 'I heard screaming,' he said.

She nodded and looked again toward the vestibule. Orion knelt and gently laid Solina's body onto the rug before the fireplace. Her auburn hair has loosened from its scarf and splayed around her head. Her dress and hair were wet, as if Orion had pulled her from the sea.

'That's Solina,' said Eridanus. 'She's—'

'Dead,' said Lynx. A swell of Dread moved across the guests below like a wave, as they realized what had happened. She gripped the banister.

'How?' he asked, but he didn't wait for an answer. He began to walk down the hall toward the grand staircase. 'You better come,' he added without looking at her, and she followed.

She watched the gold chain around his neck shift and sparkle in the lights as he walked. Why? Why? Why? her mind asked with every footstep. Why had Solina walked out into the night and let it take her?

As Lynx and Eridanus reached the final steps, her presence ignited another flurry of commotion. The guests shrunk away from her, and suddenly Solina's body was in clear and vivid view. She looked different now, no longer embellished with frost. With her wet dress clinging to her skin, her hair unkept, she looked small and insignificant. The force of her was gone. Orion still knelt beside her, the two footmen who had helped him retrieve the body standing humbly beside him.

She sensed their grief without even trying: a spring of holly and an uncut emerald with veins of black. Orion's hare sat at his feet.

'What is this?' Ms. Aster's voice rang out, hushing

115

those nearest. They parted for her too, just as they had parted for Lynx. Lynx wasn't surprised to see a snake twisted around Ms. Aster's wrist, its head reared above her knuckles, black tongue flickering. 'What have you done?' she said, but it was unclear who she was speaking to. She saw Solina's body, and she sucked in a breath. 'Orion, what's happened?'

'We found her on the lawn,' said Orion. 'Her skin was like ice.'

Ms. Aster bent over Solina's body, for a moment looking like a different woman altogether. She took Solina's hand and held it to her lips. A long moment passed. Slowly, the snake's body shifted, muscles flexing. It lifted its head and opened its jaws, its two fangs bared. Lynx stepped back, a second before Ms. Aster stood and spun toward Orion.

'What were you thinking, bringing her in here like this?'

'Apologies, madam,' he said, his head dipping. She felt the coiled energy of the hare at his feet.

'Where's Lynx?' Ms. Aster said, impatient.

'She's here,' Eridanus said.

Ms. Aster glanced at her and then turned to the nearest footman. 'Fetch the other nurse.' The man froze, shot a glance at Solina's body. His throat worked as he swallowed. 'Go!' she shouted, and the man hurried away.

Crater appeared, brushing past Eridanus. 'So it's true. Solina's dead.' He came up short as he saw the body. His face twisted. 'Why is she wet? Did she drown?'

'We found her on the lawn,' said Orion. 'Stretched out as if she were sleeping. She looked peaceful, wholly unharmed.'

'Except that she's dead,' snapped Ms. Aster.

'Who walks outside, in the middle of the night, to fall asleep in the snow?' said Crater.

Someone who's mad with grief, Lynx thought, but while it seemed to be the only logical reason for Solina's death, it didn't feel wholly right. Solina had seemed content, almost happy when Lynx had seen her last, striding down the hall toward Ms. Aster's room. Solina had grief, Lynx had sensed her Sorrow, but there had been nothing unusual about it. All the servants had Sorrow, and they lived with it day-to-day. Solina wasn't like Sculptor, with a grief that grew too fast. Lynx couldn't believe that Solina had chosen to die.

'How exactly did she die?' asked Eridanus.

'I can only think she died of the cold,' said Orion. 'She wasn't wearing a coat. We couldn't find one anywhere near the body. And she's barefoot.'

'As if she just walked into the night,' said Eridanus, and Orion nodded.

Crater held a hand to his mouth. 'The Dread is making me sick. I can hardly breathe.'

'Tell them all to go,' said Ms. Aster to Orion. 'The red roses will have their Dread removed by one of the grief nurses. The others will leave as soon as the ferry is ready. I don't want them in my house. I don't want their grief beneath this roof.'

'Everyone is going to be talking about how the Asters allow dead servants to crash their parties,' said Crater. 'Do you really want them thinking we have no decorum? Can't we do something else instead of send them all away?'

'Enough,' said Ms. Aster, shooting only a glance in her youngest son's direction. 'I didn't ask for your opinion.

Lynx, come with me.'

Lynx stood in the library, waiting as Ms. Aster paced across the room. She picked at her fingernails, the same way Andromeda did when she was struggling to find the right words. Ms. Aster didn't need words. She strode to the nearest bookshelf, slid out a book, cracked it open and peered down at it. She drew in a long breath and clawed the fingers of one hand atop the pages. They crumpled, and she yanked, tossing the ball of paper to the ground. Lynx watched the minutes of the clock tick by as Ms. Aster tore page after page from the book, until her feet were drowned in paper. Eventually she snapped closed the book and looked up at Lynx.

'I should have him dismissed for this,' she said. 'What was he thinking, laying her out in the great hall for everyone to see? I should have hosted an intimate affair with only red roses. Only the best for my Sculptor.' Ms. Aster spun the ring off her smallest finger. She set it on the desk before her, the metal clacking against the polished wood. 'All I want to do is save this house, for my children. For posterity. We're a dying breed.' She looked up at Lynx. 'I've done everything I could, and it is not enough.'

Lynx took the ring into her palm. Ms. Aster drew a shaky breath. Still standing, she braced her hands against the desk and closed her eyes. Her snake watched Lynx, waiting.

She took Ms. Aster's grief, quickly, making a point not to linger. It tasted of grass, of sun-soaked air. While she enjoyed it, she was glad it was a quick extraction. She still couldn't shake the image of Solina's body, the creeping sensation that there was more to her death than appeared. The memory of her mother, too, still snapped at her heels, threatening to return.

'Good,' said Ms. Aster, opening her eyes. Lynx returned the ring to the table, and Ms. Aster slid it back onto her finger. 'I will not be discouraged,' she said. 'I will have Orion send for another girl from the mainland. She won't have worked for a home like Mount Sorcha, but I will train her. I'd always wished Solina was better with hair. Perhaps the new girl will have defter fingers, a more inspired vision.' She turned and looked down at the mess of papers she'd made minutes earlier. She kicked them lightly with the toe of her shoe. 'Nothing is wasted. The red rose guests are staying until tomorrow evening. Surely, long enough for Andromeda to make her choice. In fact, I wouldn't be surprised if we are inundated with offers tomorrow via telegram. She'll be quite eligible now.' She paused, looking uncertain. 'Crater will manage well without a nurse. He always has. Certainly, he'll get one soon. He's been on the waitlist for years.'

She turned and walked back to the desk where she tapped the edge of a stack of paper, righting their edges so they were aligned. 'Am I delusional in thinking I can save Eridanus from ruin?' She looked at Lynx. 'Offer to take his grief more often. Remind him what it feels like to have a grief nurse.' She nodded. 'I'll get my son back eventually. Andromeda will save the Aster legacy. Everything will be perfect.'

Crater was waiting in the hall. 'Good evening, darling,' said his mother, when she saw him.

Crater raised his eyebrows. 'Lynx, you've done well,' he said once Ms. Aster was out of earshot.

The sound of heels striking against the floor made them both turn. Vela was coming toward them. She still wore the scarlet dress, the gold diadem in her hair, and she looked as fresh as the moment she had walked through Mount Sorcha's doors.

'There you are,' she said to Crater. She adjusted his cravat. 'You're in disarray. I take it you haven't seen your nurse yet.' She stepped back, brushing her fingers through her skirt so it fluttered. 'I've just seen Karina. I feel absolutely vibrant. Honestly glowing. And I've had a brilliant idea, now that there are only a few of us left.' She lowered her voice, sent a mock cautious look over her shoulder. 'We can finally have some fun.'

'I thought we were already enjoying ourselves,' said Crater.

Vela laughed. 'Come to my room tonight at the witching hour. Take the nurse with you.' She pointed a finger at him, pressed it into his chest, just above his heart. 'Don't get so jittery. It won't be anything scandalous. I've invited a few others. Andromeda. Your brother. Mr. Mensa. He despises me but he can't resist grief games.' She shrugged. 'Something to take our mind off that dead maid.' She shivered and looked down to the great hall. Already, it was empty, save for servants who were tearing down the ribbons, sweeping up the trampled petals and shattered glasses. Solina's body was gone. 'She was obsessed with Sculptor.' Vela shook her head. 'Poor thing. He shouldn't have let her think he loved her, but he could never resist a bit of adoration.' She stepped away before Crater could respond. 'See you shortly,' she said, as she began to walk away.

Only once the sound of Vela's heels against the floor

had faded away did Crater look at Lynx. His jaw tensed. 'I will need to be Brighter even than Miss Deleporte,' he said. 'Do your very best.'

'Lynx.' Andromeda hurried down the hall toward them. She wasn't fresh and lively like Vela. Her Sorrow was palpable, threaded with Dread that made Lynx dizzy.

'Can it wait, Meda?' said Crater. 'Lynx was just about to take my Dread. I must look a mess.' He brushed his lapels, which were impeccable as always. 'You have your own nurse now, anyway. Use her.' His tone was sharper than usual, and Andromeda seemed to notice because she narrowed her eyes.

'You use her. I want to speak with Lynx.'

'You want to speak with Lynx?' said Crater, raising an eyebrow.

Andromeda huffed. 'Crater, just go to Karina.'

He shrugged and waved his hand dismissively as he turned away. 'Fine. You're the star of the family now. I suppose I ought to listen to you.'

Andromeda played with her fingernails as she watched her brother walk away. 'He is honestly so infuriating,' she said. An awkward silence stretched between them. An upstairs servant walked past. She dipped her head when Andromeda caught her staring and quickened her pace. 'There are too many people,' Andromeda said. She looked down the hall toward the ante-chamber at the end.

Lynx followed Andromeda down the corridor, struggling to keep her mind spooled tight. With Andromeda's Sorrow so near, she felt on the verge of coming undone.

'Is it possible to take my Dread and not my Sorrow?' said Andromeda when the door to the ante-chamber was closed. Lynx pressed her back against the cabinet that stretched the length of one of the tiny room's walls.

'Meda—'

Andromeda was sliding the pin from her hair. 'There is so much I'm afraid of. This morning, I woke up believing that if I could just get through the day, everything would return to normal. I don't want anything to change.' Her eyes were wide. Lynx could see the ghost of herself reflected in them. 'I didn't want the nurse. I still don't. But—' She looked away. 'Maybe I should stop fighting. Maybe I'm only making matters worse by always running away from my life.'

Lynx could tell her to give up Karina. Just bequeath her guardianship to Crater and everything could go back to normal, couldn't it? But there was Solina's death, strange and unexplained, and Lynx knew life couldn't go back to the way it was that morning, when she and Andromeda pretended as if there were nothing between them, as if every time Lynx sunk her fingers into Andromeda's Heartache, her body didn't thrum with desire. Lynx couldn't resist Andromeda's Sorrow forever, and if she tried—she remembered the way her tree's branches bent and creaked, how the roots whipped wild and senseless through the air. She remembered Solina's dying grief.

She could not undo time. Andromeda had her own grief nurse now. Like Solina and Sculptor whose love was fated to end in heartbreak, she and Andromeda could never be together. She felt ashamed for giving up without a fight, but any other choice would lead to misery. Lynx decided to let her go.

'Take it, Lynx.' Andromeda held out her token. It sparkled, a tiny sun. Lynx longed to take it into her fingers, but she shook her head.

'No.'

'They're inseparable then?' said Andromeda.

'No. I could take your Dread and ignore the Sorrow,' said Lynx. 'But I won't.' She looked up into Andromeda's eyes. 'I won't touch your grief again.'

Andromeda's features shifted, as if she would cry, but Andromeda never cried. She was like her mother. Anger was the way of her grief. She clutched her token in her fist. 'You have to. You're my grief nurse.'

'No, I'm not.'

The anger flashing in Andromeda's eyes gave way to surprise. She stepped back, the feathers of her dress catching the light, as brilliant as a peacock.

Lynx slipped from the room before she could take it all back.

CHAPTER 12

Lynx was prepared to claw herself out of her dress. With Solina gone, there was no one to assist her. The kitchen maid would do it if pressed, but the girl was terrified of her, and Lynx didn't want to frighten her just for the sake of a gown she'd never wear again. She had managed only the top three buttons when there was a knock on the door. She glanced at the signal box, wondering if she'd been so absorbed in undressing that she hadn't heard a bell ringing.

When she opened the door, she was surprised to see Karina standing at the threshold.

'Is this a bad time?' Karina asked.

'Not at all. It's just that I don't usually have visitors.' Lynx rubbed her neck. 'Please, come in.' She stepped aside to let Karina pass. She felt her cheeks grow warm, as Karina smiled at her.

'You don't mind an intruder?' Karina asked. She looked about the room, her gaze lingering on the sea glass on Lynx's dresser. Lynx swallowed the urge to scoop them up and drop them into a drawer.

'Do you want a cup of tea? I can fetch you one from the kitchen.'

'No, thank you,' Karina said, flashing her another smile. She cocked her head, appraising Lynx. 'Do you want help with that?'

Lynx looked over her shoulder at the partially undone buttons of her dress. She could think of no good excuse. She did want help, and she was glad for Karina to be the one to provide it. 'If you don't mind.'

'I refuse to wear dresses for this very reason,' said Karina, coming up behind her. Lynx felt the pressure of her fingertips plucking at the top button. She could smell her skin, the warm scent of pepper.

She was overly aware of herself, too. Of her hands. Where should she put them? Of her heartbeat. Could Karina hear how fast it had become?

'You have a choice?' Lynx asked.

'Make them think it's their idea, and you can get what you want most of the time.'

'I've never thought to do that,' said Lynx.

'We were always told that we needed a guardian. That without their protection, we'd be sucked dry by the desperate poor. Did they tell you horror stories, when you were young, of nurses who ran away from their guardians, who were captured on the streets and forced to take grief until they went mad?'

'They did,' Lynx said.

'It's all bollocks. I've been on the streets. I know. We were always made to believe that it was either do what they told us to do or death. But haven't you noticed how they need us just as much as we need them? More, I think.' She laughed. 'Sorry, that's a long way of saying that I decided long ago I was nobody's dress up doll.'

'The party's nearly over now anyway,' said Lynx, too embarrassed to admit that she had still believed it. That nurses without guardians were driven mad in the hands of people desperate to have their grief removed. That there was no other way to live. She felt something that must have been hope open within her. What else didn't she know? 'I can go back to my usual uniform. There are far fewer buttons, and all easily accessible.'

Karina made a frustrated sound. 'These last few are stubborn.' She tugged harder on the buttons. 'I hate silk.'

Lynx looked over her shoulder to see Karina chewing her lip, an expression of intense focus on her face. Lynx couldn't help but smile, and Karina noticed. Their gazes held one another until Lynx broke and looked away.

'I take it you'll be joining the grief games tonight?' said Karina. 'I don't think Miss Deleporte can resist the opportunity to play, not while she has two grief nurses at her disposal. Nor Mensa, even though he's quite capable of procuring two nurses at any time he pleases.'

The ease that had quite unexpectedly settled over her disappeared at the mention of the grief games. She didn't want to admit that she was terrified. She had taken Sculptor's grief when he called her, and that was play of sorts, but Sculptor was always alone. Lynx had never mixed grief before, although she understood conceptually how it was done. Then there was Andromeda's grief to contend with. She would want it. She'd be desperate for it, but she could not take it.

'I'm quite looking forward to it,' Karina continued. 'For a house with two grief nurses, there is an awful lot of grief here.'

'You're familiar with the games? You've played them before?'

'I have. Vela and Sculptor hosted parties. It wasn't uncommon.'

'But—' She thought of Solina's body speckled with

frost. What if... what if? 'But does anyone ever get hurt?'

'Of course. Grief hurts. But, you know, there is a fine line between pleasure and pain.' Karina laughed. 'It's novel to them. When you never suffer, not truly, pain can feel sweet.' There was a pause, and all Lynx could hear was Karina's breath. She felt its warmth against her neck. 'I know you like Andromeda,' said Karina, her voice low. 'But I think you should know that I believe she doesn't deserve you.'

An urgency reverberated through her body, and she turned around just as Karina was undoing the final button. Her lips were inches from Karina's. There were freckles dotting the bridge of her nose, and her irises were not completely white. They were flecked with brown like imperfections in a diamond.

Karina's fingers slid down her arm until she brushed the bare skin of Lynx's knuckles. Before Lynx could stop herself, her mind unfurled, pulling Karina towards her until they were no longer in her room. They were on a hillside, and directly above them stretched the barren branches of a tree.

Karina looked up, her lips parted as she took it all in. The tree's upper branches dipped toward Karina, and its roots shifted at their feet. Before Karina could say anything, before she could see too much, Lynx grabbed Karina's hand, pulling them both from that place and into the real world once again.

The silence of her room was stark. They were still standing close, but they were no longer touching.

'Lynx,' said Karina. 'What happened to your tree?'

Lynx thought of the yew tree that grew in Karina's grief place. That strong, powerful, vibrant tree with its scarlet berries and muscled limbs. So unlike her own tree, barren limbs reaching toward the sky like drowning people. What could she say?

Lynx sensed grief, a brassy taste. They both looked toward the door a moment before the knocking started, and pulled away from one another. While Karina turned to open the door, Lynx quickly let the dress fall away and pulled on trousers and a shirt.

Vela stood in the doorway. She still wore her short red dress and heels, and she was shivering.

'You weren't in your room,' Vela said.

'Can she come in?' Karina asked, looking over her shoulder at Lynx. Lynx nodded, and Karina stepped aside to let her in and shut the door behind her.

Vela spun the bracelet on her wrist and paced, not seeming to notice or care that Lynx was also there. Her whole body trembled, and Lynx noticed the sweat beading at her hairline, a glassy sheen in her eyes. 'I can't lose you. I simply can't. It's been running through my mind since dinner. Relentless. I can't—' Her face crumpled, and Lynx was astonished to see tears rolling down her cheeks. She reached forward with her mind. Vela's grief had grown. Instead of one mirror hung several, all tall and long and framed in gold.

'You'll find another nurse,' said Karina.

Lynx felt as if the world as she knew it was shaken like a snow globe and turned upside down. Where was Vela's coy smile? Her pretentious air? Her enthusiastic Brightness? And why did Karina act as if nothing were unusual at all?

Vela shook her head, the red tips of her hair splaying outward. 'No, I won't. Mensa found you for Sculptor.

He won't do the same for me.' She took a shaky breath and rubbed her arms. 'Crater was supposed to be your guardian. That's what Sculptor wanted. I didn't – I didn't think there would really be an investigation. Someone must have hated Sculptor more than they liked my money.' She tried to unclasp her bracelet, but her fingers slipped. She clawed at it, looking as if she were prepared to snap it in two, when Karina took her hands.

Vela froze. Lynx thought she would pull away. Rub her hands raw the way Solina had done when she'd accidentally touched Lynx's skin. But Vela did not. Instead she looked up at Karina and her body relaxed. Her breath was still ragged, her nostrils flaring, but the tremors that ran through her stilled.

Karina gently curled her fingers over Vela's token. 'You'll find a way,' she said. Karina looked at Lynx. 'Do you want some?'

'Of her grief?'

Karina gave her a small smile. 'Yes, her grief.'

Lynx chewed her tongue. Vela looked at her, her expression vulnerable and open. Lynx shook her head.

Karina nodded once then closed her eyes. One hand fell to her side, the forefinger rubbing in circles atop the thumb. She was taking Vela's grief.

They stood together this way long enough for Lynx to imagine Karina holding Andromeda's hands instead of Vela's. She could see their fingers intertwined and Karina drinking and drinking of that sea.

Lynx swallowed, feeling raw. Then Karina lifted her hand away from Vela's and opened her eyes.

Vela exhaled a long, shaky breath. She swiped her thumb beneath each eye. She still didn't look like the woman who had worn a wedding dress to a death party, but she was rosier, clear-eyed. 'You're a star,' she said, sounding like her usual self. 'I know what I have to do. You're not going anywhere.' She glanced at Lynx. 'I'll see you at the party,' she said before walking through the door.

When the door closed, Karina sighed.

'I don't understand,' said Lynx, her voice feeling loud in the small room. 'Why did she let you touch her?'

'It's complicated,' said Karina, and for the first time she looked uncomfortable, as if she were struggling to find the words, or struggling to speak them aloud. 'The short answer is that she's desperate. Her grief is much like Sculptor's was. It grows too quickly.' She hesitated. 'I don't know why Sculptor's grief was the way it was. Maybe he was born that way, I wouldn't be surprised. Vela's grief wasn't always so abundant'

Lynx sat on her bed, and Karina sat beside her. Their knees brushed. It was strange, not having to worry about touching someone. 'Something happened to her?'

'Someone. Vela's childhood grief nurse. He kept her token, took her grief whenever he liked. He took it so often, for so many years, she grew accustomed to the constant grief-taking, and her grief grew in response. Grief is adaptable like that, I suppose.'

'I didn't think a grief nurse could do something like that.'

Karina shrugged. 'It makes sense. We have more power than anyone would like to admit. It's tempting to abuse it.'

Lynx's heart leapt. She knew what she wanted to ask, but she knew that she wouldn't. 'Why doesn't she have a grief nurse?' she asked instead. 'Surely she can afford one.'

'There is a reason Miss Deleporte needs the Asters' good name.' Karina glanced at the door. She spoke without looking at Lynx. 'She is whitelisted. When she was fifteen, her nurse was found dead. He'd apparently mistaken poison for sugar in his tea.' She looked back at Lynx. 'She'd poisoned him. It was obvious, but his death wasn't ruled a murder. Only negligence. The consequence for a guardian who neglects to care for a grief nurse is whitelisting. She won't be granted a nurse in her own name, not through official channels.'

Lynx was silent for a moment, imagining a young Vela Deleporte, slipping poison into her grief nurse's tea. She felt anger on the grief nurse's behalf, that his death was never deemed a murder. But anger also for Vela, that someone had taken advantage of a child in ways that had profoundly shaped the rest of her life.

Alongside the anger was surprise, almost delight, at the possibilities of what a grief nurse was capable of. Her mind's fingers could do more than take grief. They could shape it, change it. Lynx wasn't accustomed to feeling powerful; her instinct was to shrink away from the feeling, as if were gifted to her by accident. 'How do you think she means to get you back?'

Karina sighed. 'I think we will shortly find out.'

CHAPTER 13

Karina wrapped her fingers around the teacup and blew gently across its surface. White wisps of steam danced in Lynx's direction before fading into nothing.

'What do you like to do when the Asters aren't hosting death parties?' Karina asked her.

Lynx leaned her hip against the table. They were in the servants' hall with the expanse of the table that stretched through the length of the room all to themselves. She held the cup near her face so she could feel the warmth of the steam against her cheek. She had her own cutlery and crockery, stored separately from the others in its own lonesome cabinet. But when Karina had asked for tea, Lynx had taken cups from the general cupboard instead. She'd felt a spark of joy, watching as the dark liquid flowed into each cup. She never would have thought to do such a thing if Karina weren't here. She liked the feeling. 'I like to be out on the hills. Even when the weather is unfavourable. I think, especially when it is.'

Karina sipped her tea. 'You like being on an island then?'

Lynx nodded. 'Yes, but I'd like to see the mainland. To visit the city. I'd like to see it again—'

The doorway darkened. She looked up to see Orion standing there, his gaze trained on Karina. He was frowning and looked as if he were searching for something, hoping to find it among her features.

'Good evening,' he said, when Karina turned and saw him. His gaze shifted to Lynx. 'Master Crater is here. He requested to see you both.'

'I didn't expect you to be awake at this hour,' said Lynx, and the slight twitch in Orion's lip suggested that neither had he.

'My princess of pain,' said Crater, his voice echoing down the hall, surely waking someone up. He had changed his attire. His suitcoat had been replaced by a green velvet jacket embroidered with flowers, bursts of pink, yellow and blue among green leaves. His cravat was silk, just as colourful, and should have clashed but somehow managed to complement. 'I wanted to be the one to escort you to this evening's diversion.' He shot a look at Orion, who maintained an expression of disinterest.

As Karina rose, and Lynx moved toward the door, Orion entered the servants' hall. Karina picked up her cup and moved as if to place it on the draining board, but Orion caught her, taking the cup into his palm. 'I'll take care of these,' he said.

Karina looked surprised, but she let him take it. 'Thank you.'

Distantly, the grandfather clock upstairs chimed. It rung three times.

'The witching hour,' said Crater. 'Are you ready?'

'Lead the way, Mr. Aster,' said Karina, giving Lynx a small smile. The crow on Crater's shoulder appraised them. Dread. He was frightened of the games, perhaps as much as Lynx was. Karina looked fondly at it, as if she wanted to take it into her arms. 'Is my Dread showing?'

he asked, looking uncomfortable.

'Should we take it?' Karina asked in reply.

'No, no.' Crater's throat worked as he swallowed hard. He adjusted his cravat. 'No need. Just come with me.' Without saying another word, he led them down the hall.

The house was even more subdued upstairs, where faintly the ticking of the clock could be heard. Their footsteps felt like an intrusion.

'This one,' said Crater, reaching for the doorknob of a room in the summer wing. The wood of the door was carved, the intricate dips and groves revealing themselves on closer inspection to depict a scene. A summer's day with a hare hidden among the stalks of goldenrod flowers, a tree reaching to the sky, and a sun whose rays filled every available space. It reminded Lynx of a room with animals painted on the walls – she bit her tongue before a memory rose up.

Crater didn't knock. Instead, he turned the knob gently and opened the door just a sliver. A yellow line of light cut into the hall, and Lynx could now hear voices from within.

'Well it must have been the Sorrow,' Mensa was saying. 'It's not uncommon, that someone should be driven mad from grief.'

'I don't know,' Eridanus said, but Vela interrupted before he could finish.

'Walking barefoot into the snow in the middle of the night? It's the very definition of madness,' she said. 'Awful timing. She could have waited a day until everyone had gone. Saved us the trouble of enduring Dread for an hour. Your mother was furious,' she added, with a smile in her voice.

Crater huffed. 'Boring,' he whispered. 'I thought perhaps I'd catch something of interest.' He straightened and rapped on the door as he pushed it open. 'Hello, hello,' he said as he let himself into the room. Mensa and Eridanus were occupying the two armchairs beside the fireplace, while Vela sat in the centre of her bed, her dress splayed around her in a scarlet circle. 'I come bearing grief nurses,' he declared.

'Finally,' said Vela.

'Help yourself to a drink,' said Mensa, nodding to a crystal carafe on a table beside the window. Crater was already halfway to it.

Lynx took up her usual position against the wall, and Karina stood beside her. Her presence soothed the anxiety that seemed to be twisting Lynx's stomach into knots.

'I hope I didn't interrupt an interesting conversation,' said Crater.

Mensa shrugged. 'We were making guesses at why the maid chose to fall asleep in a snowstorm.' Mensa's legs were crossed, the toe of his shoe barely brushing against Eridanus's ankle. Why had he acquired a nurse for Sculptor? Why hadn't he kept her for himself?

'It's annoying how the most delicious grief lives inside the most troublesome people,' whispered Karina, noticing Lynx's lingering look.

'Would you really call it a snowstorm?' said Eridanus, looking out the window. 'I didn't think it was that cold.' It was clear to Lynx he hadn't had his Dread removed. His thumb constantly tapped against his glass, and even across the room, Lynx felt the heat radiating from his heart. No one else seemed to notice or care.

'Perhaps she was sleepwalking,' said Crater, after taking a sip of his drink. He leaned against the windowsill.

'I'm not quite sure what's more frightening. Dying of grief or literally sleeping to death,' said Vela.

The door opened, and everyone turned.

'Here she is,' said Crater. 'The girl of the hour.'

'Please tell me you aren't talking about death,' said Andromeda, stepping into the room. 'I'm only here because Miss Deleporte promised a distraction.'

'You'll be distracted,' said Vela, looking eager to see her. 'And you'll have to start calling me Vela.'

'Why? You're not family anymore,' said Mensa, taking as sip of his drink, and watching Vela over the rim of his glasses. 'Do you think you'll ever be invited to Mount Sorcha after tonight?'

'I thought we were being civil tonight, Laurient. Can't we agree on a truce or something?' said Vela.

Andromeda closed the door sharply, nearly cutting off Vela's words. For a brief moment she looked at Lynx as if she were drinking her in, as if she, too, felt the current of desire in the room.

'Is it true you've already had proposals?' said Mensa to Andromeda. 'Have you made a choice?'

'Why so many questions? I've only just arrived.' Andromeda gripped the bedpost and kicked off her heels, which she deftly swept under the bed.

'Andromeda, would you be so kind as to get that little golden box on the vanity table?' asked Vela, pointing across the room to a low table with a trifold mirror atop it. Scattered across the table's surface were tubes and jars of makeup, lying amongst necklace chains and jewelled bracelets. Andromeda took the box as Vela instructed

136

and opened it. 'Just tip it out on the table.' After she'd done so, she handed the now empty box to Vela, who was unclasping her bracelet. Vela held the box up and dropped her token into it.

'This first game,' Vela said, shaking the box slightly so her token rattled. 'Is called mixing. I think you know of it, but I'll explain the rules. First, you must put your token in this box. Once we've all done so, a grief nurse, either one.' She looked to where Lynx and Karina stood. 'Will select two tokens. The two fortunate winners will have their grief mixed.'

'But what exactly happens?' said Crater, looking as if the question had slipped from his mouth without his permission.

'You feel the other person's grief,' said Mensa. He ran his fingers along his tie. 'How would you describe it? As if you suddenly knew them, even if you've never met them before.'

'You'll have to see for yourself,' said Vela. She held out the box to Andromeda, who dropped her pin inside. Vela hopped off the bed and went to the two men in armchairs. Both Mensa and Eridanus placed their tokens in without a word. She turned to Crater, who twisted the diamond earring before removing it and setting it into the box. He looked as if he was about to be sick, but he tried to hide it by taking a large gulp of his drink.

'Who will choose?' Vela held the box out toward Karina and Lynx. The box was charged with energy, all those tokens nestled together, a treasure chest of potential. Lynx had never seen such a thing before, such an offering. If they knew how much power they were handing to a nurse when they handed over their token, would they still do it?

Karina must have noticed Lynx's hesitation because she pressed Lynx's arm as she said, 'I will.' As Karina reached inside the box, Lynx felt the lingering sensation of her hand on her arm, the ease of that gesture.

Crater moved beside Vela, and Andromeda craned her neck to watch whose token Karina pulled from the box. She held the first one up. A brass thimble. Mensa looked pleased. She reached in again, this time Eridanus's gold chain trailing between her fingers as she grasped his locket.

'Well,' said Crater with a sigh. 'Now what happens?'

'We watch,' said Vela.

Mensa laughed. 'I'm not so uncouth as to mix among company.' He looked at Eridanus and stood. 'Shall we go into the other room?'

'That's such a boldface lie, Laurient,' said Vela. 'But I accept the request, given that the venue is far more proper than your usual haunts. I appreciate that you have to keep up appearances.'

'Thank you for your understanding, dear,' said Mensa, as he walked past her, Eridanus not far behind him.

Vela waved at him dismissively.

'I thought you had no interest in mixing, Dani,' said Crater.

'I've changed my mind,' said Eridanus. 'Perhaps I'll find something worthwhile in it.'

Karina and Lynx followed, as Eridanus and Mensa stepped through to the room's attached bathroom. The floors and walls were tiled, most of them a bold indigo with the occasional tile painted with bursts of gold and bronze. It was all very modern, being attached to one of the better guest rooms, with a generous lion-clawed tub, a fireplace, and a painted glass window that in the morning would let in a soft rainbow light.

'I wouldn't be surprised if they already have their ears pressed against the door,' he said. He perched on the rim of the tub, while Eridanus stood staring into the fire, his hands in his pockets. 'You've never mixed before, Mr. Deimos?'

'Somehow, I've missed the trend,' said Eridanus, not looking up.

'No offence, but I don't find you to be particularly modish.'

Eridanus chuckled. 'I'll take that as a complement.'

'You should,' said Mensa. 'It's refreshing.' He considered Eridanus. 'Why have you not had your grief removed all evening?'

Eridanus raised his head. 'You've noticed?' He paused, and Mensa waited. 'I'd like to see if there is anything good in grief. That's why I accepted Miss Deleporte's offer to come tonight. I want to see what is so enthralling about grief manipulation. Maybe I've been missing something by refusing to partake.'

'You have a very scientific approach to something that is very unscientific.'

'Is it, though? Or do we just think it's unknowable because we don't take the time to get to know it?'

'You cannot accuse me of not knowing grief,' said Mensa with a smile. He looked to Karina. 'Would you please? I'd like to show this gentleman the fickle nature of grief. It will hurt you one moment, fill you with joy the next. It's best to reserve your judgement.'

'Joy?' Eridanus asked, but Karina was already pulling

his token from her pocket. She held Mensa's thimble in one hand, Eridanus's locket in the other. Both men watched her intently.

Lynx closed her eyes to more easily observe Karina reach toward each man's grief. She drew away a thread of flame from Eridanus's heart, coaxing it forward into Mensa's orchard. She let is loose across the ground, where it smouldered, black smoke rising into the sky. Karina's white fingers shepherded the flame toward the nearest tree, dappled with oranges. The fire engulfed a low-hanging fruit, and Lynx drew a long breath. The joined griefs were impossible to resist. She couldn't take them without the men's tokens, but she could taste them. Her fingers joined with Karina's, dancing among the flames, curling around the branches of the orange tree.

Time stopped. She felt everything all at once. The power vibrating through Karina's fingers. The smoke and fire and the soft breeze that blew through the orchard. She even sensed her own tree, and for the first time in a long time, she let its song whisper through her.

There were memories in grief. Karina was drawing them forward, waiting for one to ignite. Suddenly, one did.

Lynx was no longer in Mensa's orchard. She was no longer herself. The way her body moved, the thoughts that flowed through her mind, they weren't hers. She was Laurient Mensa, the son of tailors, now a shadow minister in parliament who had a penchant for grief-taking and good wine.

Mensa was watching the young MP command the attention of a gaggle of rich fools, who he was greasing up for donations. He was oafishly ambitious, thinking that a golden tongue could get him a seat on the front benches.

Mensa sipped his wine, savouring its fruity notes. What the young man didn't know was that a golden tongue was useful, yes, but a willingness to barter beneath the table would get him far further if it was the attention of aristocrats he was after.

Mensa was an outsider. He grew up in the back of his parents' tailor shop, the clack-clack-clack of a sewing machine echoing in his ears, the scent of shoe polish sinking into the fabric of his clothing. He'd seen more of the world than any of these wealthy dolts ever had – and he knew that what they wanted more than anything was what they couldn't have. A taste of the real world. A bit of a pain. A dance with grief.

The young MP's name was Kuiper, and he'd recently acquired a grief nurse, who he was sorely underusing. The nurse stood beside the doorway. Mensa felt his gaze on the back of his neck. He knew the nurse was probably exploring his grief, getting a good taste of it, as much as he could without a token. Mensa turned. The nurse's gaze didn't break. He was young, early twenties most likely, with white hair worn perfectly straight down his back. He wore a silver disc in each ear, two flashing full moons.

Mensa sipped his wine, weighing up the risks. He looked again at Kuiper. His hair must have been naturally blond because his entire mop was dyed blue. Cobalt strands fell roguishly into his eyes, and he was constantly swinging his head to move them aside. Now that Kuiper had a grief nurse, he was someone to contend with, but he was such the epitome of all that Mensa despised in a politician – arrogant, naïve, and rolling in money – he found himself unable to care. And the grief nurse was still watching him. Kuiper might as well have been handing

Mensa an invitation.

After setting his wine glass on the windowsill behind him, Mensa went to the door. Without looking at the nurse, he said, 'I'll be in the dining room,' before heading out into the hall. He had just enough time to clean his glasses before Kuiper's grief nurse appeared in the dining room doorway.

'Let's make it quick,' said Mensa, reaching inside the breast pocket of his jacket for the thimble kept tucked away beneath a handkerchief.

It was quick but intense. The nurse was as hungry as Mensa had hoped. He felt the shock of invasion, the growing sharply-sweet anticipation as the nurse explored his grief, and the eventual bliss as he drew it from Mensa's body. He felt weightless, untethered. Always in the moment after a grief nurse took his grief, he felt the most free.

The nurse's lips were soft, clearly unused, unaccustomed to the touch of another.

'What is this?'

Kuiper's voice made Mensa pull away. He was too relaxed to move quickly, but the nurse knocked into a chair, nearly causing it to tumble over.

'You aren't allowed to use my nurse,' said Kuiper, who was standing in the doorway.

Mensa took off his glasses and cleaned them. 'Ah, Mr. Kuiper, my apologies. I'd assumed he was free for the taking.'

'You assumed wrong,' said Kuiper. He motioned at his nurse, who hurried from the room. Kuiper's simple brain was struggling to keep up, but it was clear he was working himself up to some sort of plan. Mensa cursed himself for letting temptation get the best of him again. Kuiper had just made it too damn easy.

'Well, this certainly is not the water closet,' said a man who'd walked into the room and quickly came up short. He was dressed well, albeit he wore no tie or ascot, and there was a heavy gold watch on his wrist.

Kuiper pointed a finger at Mensa. He looked like a little boy, on the verge of a tantrum. 'This man is a Fader. He was touching my nurse. He was kissing him.'

The man glanced at Mensa, then again at Kuiper. 'Where's your bloody water closet, Kuiper? I'm about to burst.'

'Did you hear what I just said?' Kuiper scowled. His hair fell into his eyes and he shook it away with an angry whip of his head.

'Yes, you're accusing the shadow minister of kissing your grief nurse. Where's your proof? I can't trust the judgement of a man who builds a fucking labyrinth and calls it a house. Perhaps I'll just take a piss here.' He reached for his belt.

'Aster, you've seen them together. You'll vouch for me.'

'No.' The man considered a potted plant nearby. 'Here maybe?'

'You have to,' said Kuiper. 'I know your family is running out of money. You want to get off the back benches? Vouch for me. Let's take him down.'

'No,' the man said again.

'Looks like it's just my word against yours,' said Mensa. 'I've been in politics for a long time, Mr. Kuiper. You've only just arrived. I wouldn't recommend slinging mud just yet.'

'You dirty fucking Fader,' Kuiper said, a moment

before the wad of spittle landed on Mensa's cheek. Kuiper rushed at him, ready to grab him by the lapels, but he was yanked suddenly backwards. The other man had grabbed Kuiper's arm, and just as Kuiper was swung around to face him, the man slammed his fist against Kuiper's jaw. Kuiper cried out, swinging wildly, missing with one fist before making contact with the other man's eye.

'Lucky hit,' said the man, dancing back. He pressed his fingertips against his eye, shrugged when he saw the smear of blood. He grinned. 'See you around, Kuiper.' Kuiper stood panting and fuming as the man left the room.

In no particular rush, Mensa unfolded the handkerchief from his pocket and wiped his face. It wasn't the first time he'd been called a dirty Fader. In fact, he'd been called far worse.

'What is his name?' Mensa asked.

'What?' Kuiper snarled.

'The gentleman who slugged you in the jaw. What's his name?'

Kuiper shook his head, his blue hair becoming even more dishevelled. 'Sculptor Aster.'

Mensa nodded once. He returned the handkerchief to his pocket. 'Pardon me,' he said, stepping past Kuiper. He stopped at the threshold of the room, not even bothering to turn around. 'You ought to feed your nurse more regularly. He was desperate for it.'

He found Sculptor Aster in the game room. He was leaning against the edge of a billiards table and staring at the floor. He looked ferociously glum, not even attempting to Brighten his features when Mensa entered the room.

144

'Mr. Aster,' said Mensa, leaning against the table beside him. 'I have to ask. Why would you endanger your political prospects for the sake of a dirty Fader?'

Sculptor didn't look up. He nodded, as if remembering. His lashes were long and dark, his eyes the colour of caramel. Mensa had a vague recollection of another Aster, a man with a seat in parliament years ago. 'I don't like being told what to do.' He paused. 'I know someone who is a Fader. If anyone tried to out her, I'd do far worse than knock them in the teeth.' Sculptor took one of the billiard balls and tossed it toward a pocket. He missed, the ball glancing off the table, leaving a hearty dent in the wood. He chuckled. 'Anyway, don't worry about my political prospects. Kuiper was right. I'm out of money. My mother is draining my inheritance on a house she can't afford.' He glanced sideways. 'Also, I pissed in one of the billiard pockets.'

Mensa laughed. He slid a card from his pocket, flipped it once and held it toward Sculptor. 'I'll let you in on a secret, Mr. Aster. It's not money that gets you power. It helps, but every fool in parliament has money. Grief nurses give you power. Not having one, but procuring them. In that respect, I am at your disposal.'

Sculptor took the card. 'Worth the black eye then, wasn't it?' Sculptor said, shaking Mensa's hand.

When the memory faded, Lynx blinked open her eyes. Karina still stood with each men's token clutched in her hands. She sensed Karina about to take their grief, and she reached out, grasping Karina's arm. 'Not Eridanus's,' she said. Karina gave her a puzzled looked, but she nodded.

Mensa and Eridanus were no longer looking at Karina.

Instead, they were watching each other.

'What did you make of that, Mr. Deimos?' said Mensa with a small smile.

Eridanus returned the smile. 'I never understood why my brother liked you, but now I have a sense that—I feel as if I know something about you that I didn't only moments before, but I cannot recall quite what I've learned.'

'It's more of a feeling than anything particular. Let it settle. It'll ripen nicely.' He held out his hand, and Karina placed his thimble into his palm. 'Shall we?' He motioned to the door. 'The others will be desperate to have a go.'

Lynx was the last to leave. She could still smell the mingling scents of smoke and citrus.

CHAPTER 14

Eridanus twisted his token in his fingers instead of placing it around his neck. 'I'm pleasantly surprised at how enjoyable that was,' he said to Mensa, as they entered the room, where the others were waiting for them. Andromeda had moved to Eridanus's chair, and Crater looked as if he had downed several drinks in the short time they were away.

'The pleasure was mine, Mr. Deimos,' said Mensa.

'How do you feel? Tell us everything,' said Vela.

'I stole your chair.' Andromeda started to rise.

'That's alright,' said Eridanus. 'I'll stand.' He looked to Mensa. 'A drink, Laurient?'

'Absolutely.' Mensa sank into the armchair and crossed his legs. 'Who's next?'

'That's it? You two are as giddy as children. What happened?' Crater asked. For the first time Lynx could remember, Eridanus was Brighter than Crater, who was struggling to keep his smile convincingly wide.

'Just as Laurient said.' Eridanus handed Mensa a drink. Although he looked refreshed, younger, with a new shine in his eyes, this Bright Eridanus was only temporary. His Sorrow was still there, though tamed for now. 'It's a particular kind of Brightness, that's all. The same sort of feeling you get when you go out and unexpectedly have a brilliant night.' He stayed beside Mensa's chair, and

147

placed his hand on the chair's back.

'Exactly,' said Mensa.

'I think we should play a different game,' cut in Vela. 'Since we're in the unique position of having two grief nurses. Let's have them take someone's grief at the same time.'

'I'm keen,' said Mensa. 'For once Miss Deleporte talks sense. She won't likely find herself in such a position again.'

'But whoever they choose has to stay here. There's no running away to another room,' said Vela.

'Agreed,' said Mensa.

Vela directed a finger at him. 'No, you two don't get to put your tokens back inside that box. Let one of us have a shot.'

'If Mr. Mensa's so keen, let him try his luck,' said Crater.

Vela ignored him. 'Alright, Karina, take your pick.'

Karina took the box into her hands again and reached inside. After she set the box onto the table, she held out her hand and uncurled her fingers.

A sand star hair pin rested in her palm.

Lynx felt as if a wave had crashed over her, knocking the breath from her chest. Could she refuse to play? But what excuse could she use that wouldn't implicate Andromeda? Her stomach churned with anxiety. A hundred 'what ifs' buzzed in her mind. What if she lost control? What if she couldn't resist Andromeda's grief, and she took and took... Cool fingers brushed against her arm. She glanced up at Karina, who gave her a short nod. Her worry was still there, but it was a great relief to know she wasn't alone. Maybe Karina's presence would be enough to keep her in control.

'Oh,' said Vela, sounding disappointed.

Crater cleared his throat. 'Lucky you,' he said to Andromeda.

'You could always decline,' said Mensa, surprising Lynx with a genuine look of concern in Andromeda's direction.

'Why would she do that?' Vela asked.

Even though Andromeda appeared confident and certain, Lynx felt the flaring of her Dread. 'No, I'll do it,' she said with defiance.

Lynx wished Andromeda would for once in her life think before taking up a challenge. Why did she have to be this way? Stubborn and reckless, unwilling to weigh up the consequences. Unable to admit that she couldn't be as free as she wanted.

Crater moved to the bed beside Vela to watch. Karina and Lynx stood in front of Andromeda. Karina held out her hand, palm upward, with the token resting atop. Lynx placed her hand beneath Karina's, so Karina's hand rested in her own. Karina's hand was cool, steady. None of it felt real, this moment, another person's skin against hers, the impending thrill of Fader grief, and the fear that she wouldn't be able to resist it. That she'd lose herself and do something she'd regret.

Lynx ran her thumb along the token, feeling the dip and rise of the diamonds. She closed her eyes, shutting out the room, mind eagerly stretching forward. She bit her tongue. Don't linger, she told herself. She sensed Karina, fingers unfurling alongside her own. Together, they dove into Andromeda's grief.

Her heartbeat soared, her breath becoming short and shallow. She felt herself suspended in the grief-water, the gasping thrill as waves crashed over her, salt stinging her eyes. She was lifted up then dragged under. Her whole body was beneath the surface, and the water was clear. She could see to the very bottom, through the ebbs and whirls of currents, to the seabed.

'Go on,' she heard Andromeda say.

As she drank, her fingers twisted and curled around Karina's. She felt Karina's desire, and it fed her own. The water was ice-cold, kicking her heart into a painful tattoo. Still, she drank, revelling in the taste of brine, the bracing chill, the stinging scent. She drank until she was no longer herself, until she was a restless young woman with a secret that could destroy her. Who ran away but always returned, tethered as she was to the place she both hated and loved. Who tried every day to trick herself into believing a lie – that she could have the life she was promised with the freedom to be herself.

Lynx lost herself, unsure of where Andromeda's thoughts began and hers ended. She imagined Andromeda coming toward her, slim fingers brushing her neck, the nick of her nails as she clawed through her hair, pressing her lips to hers—

'Lynx,' she heard someone say. She was torn suddenly from the sea. Her eyes shot open. Andromeda's lips were against hers, her fingers in her hair. Lynx pulled away immediately. She no longer held Karina's hand. Her connection with the token had been severed, ripping her from Andromeda's grief. Karina pressed Lynx's shoulder, forcing her a step away from Andromeda. Andromeda gasped, and her eyes fluttered open.

'It was good then,' said Vela, who had taken oven the armchair. Her legs were crossed, revealing much of her thigh.

Andromeda sat back. There was a tremor in her hands. She looked up at Lynx, and Lynx couldn't bear it. She looked away.

The silence made it obvious that everyone had seen. Eridanus and Mensa exchanged a glance. Andromeda stretched out her hand to Karina. 'My token.'

Karina placed the pin in Andromeda's hand.

'I couldn't understand why you seemed so disappointed to be inheriting Karina,' said Vela. 'Now I think I know why.' She looked at Lynx. 'You already have a grief nurse, and she obviously suits you well.'

Andromeda cut a look at Vela, whose hand rested on Crater's knee. 'I don't want Karina because I don't want to be Mother's puppet. Does that answer satisfy you, Miss Deleporte or is there something else you'd like me to say?'

'Meda,' said Crater, frowning. 'Why would you do that?'

'It was an accident.' Andromeda did not look at him.

'That was an accident?' Crater's face twisted in a look of disgust. Lynx wanted to stride across the room and grab him by the cravat. She was tired of him. Tired of his fear and his frivolity. 'You kissed her. Are you mad?'

Andromeda set her glass gently on the table. She straightened and looked down at her brother with such intense calm, Lynx feared what was coming next. 'Am I what?' she asked, her voice perfectly steady.

'Do you know what it's like to have your grief removed by multiple nurses at once?' asked Mensa.

'No,' said Crater, not looking at him.

'Then withhold your judgement.'

Crater shook his head. 'You don't tell me what to do. What I can't say to my own sister. None of this should have happened.' He waved his hand at the room. 'The Asters are a respectable family. We don't play grief games. We don't kiss our nurses. If you insist on being a rebel, Meda, be like Eridanus. Marry low. Don't do daft things like kiss your grief nurse. If anyone—' His voice caught. 'We already have one Aster in the madhouse. We don't need two.'

'We all know about you, Crater,' said Andromeda. She walked toward the bed, where she bent and retrieved her shoes. They dangled in one hand. 'We know you're afraid of grief-taking, of grief nurses. That's why you make a big show of making Lynx trail after you like a dog. You're a hypocrite, and I'm glad Mother chose me instead of you. You don't need Karina. You'd use her to start a career in politics, and once you'd tired of that, you'd use her for something else, always for yourself."

Crater rose. He pressed his drink into Vela's hands. 'Everything I do is for the sake of the family.'

Andromeda snorted. 'Everything you do is to please Mother. Don't pretend it's anything else.' She didn't let him respond. She slammed shut the door as she left.

Crater took a step toward her, but Vela grabbed his wrist, holding him back. 'Let her go.' She looked at him and smiled. 'Let's go for a walk. I have a proposition for you.'

CHAPTER 15

The morning room was made up for breakfast even though it was nearly midday. Ms. Aster was sitting with a newspaper spread out on the table before her, her husband beside her, and Eridanus was just settling into a chair. Plates of sausage, eggs, and potato scones were huddled together in the table's middle, where Ms. Aster had pushed them away to make room for the paper. There was a dazzling pitcher of orange juice and a steaming carafe of coffee.

Lynx sat in a chair against the wall. It'd been strange to be awoken by a gentle rapping on her bedroom door, the timid face of the kitchen maid appearing instead of Solina's. She had donned her usual uniform, since the dress was impossible to put on by herself. She'd awoken hoping the events of the previous day had been merely a dream. But she remembered the feeling of Andromeda's lips against hers, the taste of her, and she knew it was all real.

Sitting in the morning room, she felt sticky with guilt. Everything her mind observed – the way the light filtered in from the large windows to shine across the blue and gold tiled floor, or the blue velvet of the chairs, embroidered with gold filigree, or the comfortable scent of coffee – was tainted by an ugly sensation at the base of her neck. A constant reminder of what she'd done. She'd kissed Andromeda. She'd exposed her in front of a room full of people. She only hoped that everyone present at the grief games would keep the revelation to themselves.

She was relieved neither Andromeda nor Karina was present. She dreaded their arrival.

'Good morning, Eridanus,' said Ms. Aster, not looking up from her paper.

'Haven't you missed Cook's scones?' said Mr. Aster, brandishing one with his fork.

'I'm not quite sure how I've managed without them,' said Eridanus.

'I'm not quite sure how you've managed without a grief nurse,' said Ms. Aster.

Eridanus poured himself a cup of coffee, waving away Orion who tried to pour it for him. 'Most people don't have grief nurses, Mother.'

'We aren't most people.'

'You're looking Bright this morning though.' Mr. Aster refilled his wife's glass with orange juice before doing the same for himself. 'Did you try Andromeda's nurse, or did you go to Lynx?'

'Neither,' said Eridanus. 'I haven't used a grief nurse for three years.'

His mother's head snapped up.

'Good morning, everyone,' trilled Vela as she came into the room. She wore another elaborate yet emphatically modern dress. An off-the-shoulder gown, beaded in gold at the bust, with flowing sheer fabric. Her slip was visible beneath, a darker shade of blue. Her hair was pinned back with a multitude of golden pins, each in the shape of a many-rayed sun.

Orion pulled out a seat for Vela, who smoothed her

dress and sat.

'What would you like, Miss Deleporte?' Orion held a plate in his open palm, the other hand was in a fist behind his back.

'Just a soft-boiled egg,' said Vela. She searched Ms. Aster's newspaper. 'That's yesterday's paper. Haven't you received today's?'

'We always receive the papers a day late,' said Mr. Aster. 'The one downside to living on an island.'

'The only one?' said Vela with a smile, but Mr. Aster was too good-natured to notice the sarcasm in her tone. Orion placed a plate with a single soft-boiled egg in a shiny ceramic cup before her. Vela took up the tiny gold spoon and looked askance at Eridanus. 'Good morning, Mr. Deimos. Did you sleep well after last night's excitement?'

'What exactly happened last night? After the guests went home.' Ms. Aster was as Bright as the sun, but her voice was like ice.

Vela pressed her lips together, smoothing away a smile, and looked down at her egg. Eridanus glared at her.

'Grief games,' he said. 'Miss Deleporte's idea.'

'And you attended? You just told me you hadn't used a grief nurse in three years.'

'Used a grief nurse. Last night I had my grief mixed with Mr. Mensa's. It was never removed.'

Ms. Aster grimaced, looking like Crater. 'I don't care about this mixing, grief games. I don't want to hear about it, but do you mean to tell me you've been grieving all evening? That you have grief now, stinking up this beautiful morning room, while we're eating our breakfast? I may as well have Lynx touch everything in sight.'

Eridanus gripped his fork, its prongs pressing into the tablecloth. 'Mother, grief does not work like that. It's not a disease. You cannot catch it.'

'Is that so? Then what has happened to you? Your mind has been infected if you think this is proper, keeping your grief. Unless you're doing this to spite me. You must be. Why else endure it? I hadn't realized how much you hated me.'

Eridanus rose, his chair sliding back. 'I don't hate you.' He lowered his voice. 'I have every right to, but I don't. I asked Lynx not to take my grief. I am determined to keep it, long enough to disapprove my husband of the notion that there is something good in it. But maybe Syril is right. When my grief was mixed with Laurient's I felt something new. A revelation. A feeling of suddenly seeing clearly. A sense that I knew him, and all the prejudice I had carried within me until that moment was challenged. That moment reshaped me. Is that what grief can do?'

No one spoke for a long time. Vela dipped the very tip of her spoon into the egg. A drop of yolk clung to the spoon's tip and she brought it to her tongue.

'I'm done,' said Ms. Aster, pointedly returning to her paper. 'We remove our grief when it arises. There is no good in it, and to think otherwise is absurd. Cepheus, you will no longer send him money. I will not bankroll someone who insists on shaming this family.'

'I'm not someone. I'm your son,' said Eridanus, but Ms. Aster did not look up. He sank back into his chair and sat motionless, his hands in his lap. Lynx swallowed, tasting soot. She bit her tongue, pressing hard with her teeth. For a moment, the room was filled with smoke. It rose up to

156

the ceiling, obscuring the noonday light, filling the room like an oven.

Then she was in the drawing room, years before Sculptor's engagement, before Eridanus's marriage, drawn there by his grief.

'Come, Sculptor. I'll bet my horse in this round,' Crater said. He was three whiskies deep. The first three buttons of his shirt were undone, revealing the creeping dark curls of his chest hair. He had brandished a deck of cards from his back pocket.

'You know I hate riding.' Sculptor stood beside the fireplace, his arms across his chest. He hadn't been drinking. Lynx watched him fill his glass with water, pretending it was gin on the rocks.

Eridanus was sitting beside the fire, a glass of wine at his elbow, one hand marking his place in a book. Sculptor had called away the servants, and Eridanus had taken the opportunity to slip off his shoes.

'I'll play,' said Andromeda. She strode up to Crater and adjusted his collar. She wore a fuchsia gown with long, dreamy sleeves that bared her arm to the elbow as she reached up.

'I'm not looking to lose,' said Crater, winking at her.

'Your games are boring,' said Sculptor.

'Card games too old fashioned for you?' Crater asked.

'Not old fashioned.' Sculptor pulled the piano's bench out with a jerk and slumped into the seat. He always moved like he was on the verge of crumbling to pieces. 'Just fucking dull.' He pushed up his sleeves and hovered his fingers over the piano keys.

'Want a top up?' Andromeda slid the glass out from between Crater's fingers. She turned toward the bar tray in the room's corner. She looked over at Lynx, as she filled her own glass and Crater's. 'Lynx?' She raised her glass, cocking her head at the question.

Lynx smiled and shook her head. She was content to be here, sitting in a chair beside the windows, watching the rain bleed down the glass. She was glad to be away from the chill of the servants' quarters and was wondering already if Andromeda would find an excuse to come and see her that evening.

Sculptor pressed a piano key and then another, holding them long so they lingered. He kept his gaze firmly on his fingers. He was frowning, but that wasn't unusual.

Crater groaned. 'Please spare us.'

'You know what's worse than Sculptor's playing is your complaining about it,' said Eridanus. Sculptor chuckled at that. Eridanus looked down into his book, as if he didn't care what his brothers thought of him.

'Let's talk about something interesting then,' said Crater. 'How about that young man I saw you with at our cousin's wedding?'

'What about him?' asked Eridanus.

'To Eridanus, who is finally falling in love.' Andromeda raised her glass.

'Not falling in love,' said Eridanus, raising his glass of wine for a moment before taking a sip. Andromeda beamed at him.

Sculptor played a quick, dark tune on the piano in way of a reply.

'He's quite low, Eridanus,' said Crater. 'You better not tell Mother.'

'There's nothing to tell,' Eridanus replied.

'You mean Syril Deimos, don't you?' said Andromeda,

looking at Crater. 'He was kind enough to tell me I had a thread dangling off the back of my gown. He was very sweet.' She laughed. 'I was very much impressed by his beard.' She looked toward Eridanus. 'Do you think you'll marry him?'

Eridanus nearly choked on his wine. Sculptor started pounding out a song, and everyone's attention was pulled away from Eridanus, to his obvious relief.

'That really is awful, Sculptor,' called Andromeda over the music.

He continued to watch his hands and shake his head as he played.

'Speaking of love,' said Andromeda. 'What about yourself, Crater? Didn't I see you with an eligible young lady? Whatever happened to her?'

Crater waved his hand. 'I'm not interested.' He shot a look at Eridanus, who was still pretending his book interested him more than the conversation. 'In compromise.'

'I thought compromise was a tenant of marriage,' said Andromeda.

Sculptor made a terrible racket at the piano. 'That's what they want you to think, Meda,' he yelled over his own music. 'So that you'll make a lousy, politically advantageous match and pretend for the rest of your life it was your idea. For once I agree with Crater. Let the fucker do what he wants.'

'Thank you.' Crater raised his glass toward Sculptor.

'And why shouldn't Eridanus marry this Deimos fellow?' Sculptor continued. 'Mother deserves a good shock.'

'It's not like that,' said Eridanus.

Sculptor shrugged.

'She's looking out for our best interests,' said Crater. 'Do you really want to marry someone who doesn't have his own grief nurse?'

'How do you know that?' Andromeda asked.

Crater scoffed. 'It's obvious. His suit wasn't even tailored properly.'

'I don't care about his suit,' said Eridanus.

'Well you should. You don't want to marry someone who makes you look poor.'

'You're exaggerating.'

'I'm being practical.'

'You're being irritating,' said Sculptor.

Crater's eyes narrowed. 'Well, if you're not going to play, then I'm off.' He set his drink onto a table with an angry clink and left the room. The mood had soured, the room less full without Crater there.

Sculptor played a few more lingering notes on the piano before abruptly shutting the lid. All that could be heard was the ticking of the clock. Eridanus started to read again, but when Sculptor began walking towards him, he looked up.

Sculptor clapped him on the shoulder. 'I was serious about what I said about Deimos. If it's what you want, you need to take it. You shouldn't be trapped. Leave that to me.'

Andromeda looked toward Lynx. Inexplicably, Lynx felt as if she were missing something, as if she had let something slip through her fingers.

'I'm not sure it is,' said Eridanus.

Sculptor shrugged. 'That's up to you.' He smiled.

Lynx didn't get the chance to hear what Sculptor had

said next, what had followed one of his rare, genuine smiles. The memory spit her out into the real world, where Eridanus's grief was still flaring, where Ms. Aster was still standing at the breakfast table, the newspaper spread out before her while Vela took delicate bites of her egg.

Crater walked into the room, making everyone look toward the door.

'Good morning,' he said, dropping into the chair beside Vela. He nodded at Orion to serve him. 'Looks like Andromeda is having a lie in.'

'Laurient,' said Ms. Aster in relief, looking beyond her youngest son. 'You're the very person I was hoping would walk through that door.'

Mensa looked around at those already seated. 'What a delightfully warm welcome, Cassiopeia. I take it you had a good night despite the unfortunate disruption?' He lowered himself into a seat.

Ms. Aster opened her mouth to speak, but Crater said loudly, 'Now that everyone is here, Miss Deleporte and I would like to share some marvellous news.'

'There's no need to call off the wedding.' Vela smiled.

Ms. Aster's brow crumpled for only a moment before she caught herself and smiled. 'Pardon?'

'Miss Deleporte and I are engaged to be married.' Crater placed his hand atop Vela's. She pulled back almost imperceptibly before relaxing.

'When?' Eridanus stared at his brother. 'You said nothing of this last night.'

'There was nothing to say last night,' said Crater. 'Miss Deleporte and I took a turn around the house this morning. She wanted to see the gallery, and as I was narrating our family's history, I realized an engagement would be the perfect way to end Sculptor's death party. I asked her if she would marry me. She graciously said yes.'

'I thought it was such a shame, all this beauty falling prey to decay, everything this family worked for crumbling to dust. I wanted to save it.'

Mr. Aster set his hand atop his wife's. She looked speechless.

'Crumbling to dust?' said Eridanus flatly.

'I suppose it has nothing to do with you wanting his grief nurse,' said Mensa.

'Do you mean Lynx?' Crater asked. 'She isn't mine. Mother is her guardian, and she stays here in Mount Sorcha.' He looked at his mother. 'I've fixed everything. You no longer have to worry.'

'Crater...' Ms. Aster looked as if she were working out a puzzle, trying to determine if she was walking into some sort of trap. The trap of course being Vela Deleporte.

'Well, then,' said Mensa. He held up a hand to Orion, who was about to set a full plate before him. Lynx sensed his grief, flowers blooming, leaves unfurling. 'I see what's happening here.' He rose. 'I must beg your apology, Cassiopeia, but I'll be leaving on the next ferry.'

'Laurient—'

'Sculptor cared for you,' Mensa said, spinning toward Vela. 'He confided in you. The least you could do is respect a dead man's wishes.'

Vela twirled her spoon in her fingers. 'I think he'd rather have liked me marrying his brother. It would have saved him the trouble of marrying me.'

Mensa glared down at her. 'That's not what I mean.' He looked meaningfully at Crater. 'Think before you do something that will make you hate yourself for the rest of your life. How much is a grief nurse really worth?' He turned to Orion. 'Get my bags.'

Then, he was gone, and the room hung with quiet in his absence. Eventually, breakfast was eaten, the paper passed around, pointless conversations started up and drifted away. Another servant appeared to serve in Orion's place.

Lynx was on tenterhooks, waiting for Andromeda and Karina to arrive. They never did. As the breakfast carried on she found her guilt transforming, as it so often did, to anger. Andromeda never should have agreed to let her grief be taken. She should have known that she'd lose control – Lynx had told her as much. But she had to play the rebel. She had to prove herself, despite everything that was at stake. She never seemed to realize that all the rebellious things she did – running away, carrying on as if she had no secret to hide – not only hurt herself. They hurt Lynx, too.

Suddenly, just as Crater and Vela were making their way toward the door, Lynx tasted oranges. Mensa marched into the room, pushing passed Crater who was near the threshold. His face was puckered in anger. 'The ferry has stopped running.' He took his hat off and handed it to a servant. 'It seems we're trapped.'

CHAPTER 16

The bells in the signal box above the door were still and silent. Lynx counted them, repeating in her mind the word scrolled above each one: Lady Aster, Sir Aster, Master Sculptor, Master Eridanus, Master Crater, Miss Andromeda.

She imagined Orion carrying a ladder into her room, propping it against the wall and asking her to keep it steady as he climbed to the height of the signal box. He'd paint away 'Master Sculptor.' Replace it with 'Lady Vela' in scrawling gold paint.

What would Sculptor think?

Good riddance.

Or would he rally against his family's forgetfulness? She wondered if Eridanus was right. Did removing your grief make you truly forget? There were memories in grief – she knew that, she felt it often enough – but how powerful was grief, really?

She spun the white shard of sea glass in her fingers. The entire collection sat in the hollow made by her crossed legs. If Crater was right, and his engagement to Vela fixed everything, why did she feel a looming presence, the sensation that something horrid was coming their way? She thought of Mensa's reaction to the news, the way his Sorrow had bloomed, the anger that it had sparked. That's not what I mean. But what did he mean?

Lynx was turning the white shard of glass around in her fingers again and again, when a distant flare of Dread made her drop the glass into her lap. She slipped on her shoes and opened the door, peering out into the hall. Karina was not far away, standing in the corridor, her head cocked, focusing on the same Dread that had sent Lynx from her room.

'Something isn't right,' said Karina slowly.

'Upstairs,' said Lynx, and they were both running, propelled by that awful Dread. It grew as they thundered up the stairs, and soon they could hear a wailing to accompany it.

When Lynx opened the door to the upper corridor, the scent of oranges made her step back. Karina held a hand against her nose, and Lynx swallowed hard. Not just oranges, but the stink of rotting fruit.

'What is that?' Lynx asked.

'That's the smell of death.'

Lynx swallowed and stepped forward into the hall. The housemaid, a girl with a nick of a scar on her lip, was gasping with sobs. She was stumbling from Mensa's guest room when Lynx and Karina arrived in the summer wing. Eridanus was already there. He took her by the arms, and she wriggled in his grasp, wailing an indecipherable stream of words like a moan.

'Petra,' he said, surprising Lynx by remembering the girl's name. 'Petra.' At the sound of her name, the maid abruptly threw her arms around him, pressing her wet face into his chest. He looked up at Lynx and Karina, his expression taut. 'I'm afraid to know what she's discovered,' he said, as he gently unwound Petra's arms. He rose without saying more.

The door to Mensa's room gaped open. The room was dark, the curtains apparently closed. Eridanus approached it, hesitating for only a beat, before entering. As he disappeared inside, Petra began sobbing again, low and lilting. The only word Lynx could make out was dead.

A moment passed before a flare of Dread made Lynx's heart jump. She didn't think. She rushed into the room, coming up short as she crossed over the threshold, the stink of rot making her almost stumble. Her feet were silent on the carpeted floor. Everything seemed hushed and pensive. As her eyes adjusted, making sense of the looming shapes, she braced herself for what she would find.

Eridanus stood before the open wardrobe, his Dread flaring wildly. The heat was almost unbearable, but Lynx came up beside him. For a long moment, her mind couldn't understand what she was seeing. Then, just as the green stroke of silk in the snow had within the span of a breath revealed itself to be Solina's frost-covered body, she understood.

Mensa hung by a necktie from the bar in the wardrobe. He was naked, his bare toes brushing the wooden floor. In his mouth was an orange. Lynx stepped past Eridanus. As if in a dream, she reached up. She brushed her fingertips over the dimpled hide of the orange. It was hard, unyielding. She had expected it to be soft with rot.

It was the orange that stayed with her, long after the others had arrived, the body taken down, the door to the guest room firmly shut. She saw it, encircled by Mensa's blue lips, the man's blood-shot eyes wide as if in surprise. An orange, as vivid as the oranges of his grief.

166

CHAPTER 17

Moonlight streamed in through the wide windows of the drawing room. Outside, the lawn glittered in white as the snow continued to fall. It was dinner time, but no dinner was served. Instead, Ms. Aster had instructed the servants to bring meals to everyone's rooms. Lynx presumed that those meals had gone largely untouched, as not long afterwards, the guests and family members migrated to the drawing room, either unable to eat or unable to resist the temptation of gossip.

The Dread hung thick in the room, close and heavy like the air of a thunderstorm. Lynx couldn't stop seeing the orange, couldn't stop worrying about what it might mean.

She stood beside the window, letting the chill seeping through the glass transport her. She wanted to feel the wind on her face as she stood on a craggy hillside, the thrill that one wrong step could send her tumbling to her death. She craved that reminder of how glad she was to be alive. She buried her hands in her pockets. She had scrubbed her fingers raw, thinking that the scent of oranges still lingered on her skin, but she couldn't scrub the fingers of her mind.

'Stay beside me tonight,' said Crater, handing her a drink. He wore the same jacket he'd worn to breakfast, a burgundy affair with traceries of umber and orange and flared sleeves. His cravat was gold, complementing the burnished gold pin of an oakleaf on his lapel. Although he was impeccably attired, there was something changed about him. His Dread was palpable, and it was growing. The crow perched in the chandelier above him and rustled its wings.

The scarlet cocktail in her hand smelled of berries. She peered into it, seeing a hazy reflection of her face. Crater didn't notice as she slipped it onto the windowsill behind his back. He looked out at the room as he spoke, 'Two deaths in two days are making people jittery. This is my opportunity to prove how Bright I can be despite it all.'

'Prove to who?' she asked, surprising herself by actually speaking the question aloud.

He looked at her, obviously just as surprised as she. 'I—' He huffed, nostrils flaring, and turned just as Eridanus walked past. He reached out and grabbed his brother by the elbow. 'Dani, I heard you saw the body.'

'Yes,' said Eridanus, frowning as he looked his brother over. Eridanus glanced at her. 'Hello, Lynx.' He noticed the full glass behind her on the windowsill.

Crater raised his eyebrows. 'I'm sorry to say, but you look terrible.'

Eridanus glowered at him. 'Thanks.'

'You haven't spoken to anyone, nor done anything but cling onto your drink and look pensive. It's not a good look. You'll make Mother anxious.' Their mother wasn't yet in the room. Most likely she was still managing the logistics of having two dead bodies in the house.

'I don't care what Mother thinks'

'You saw the body. You should go to Lynx.'

'Did Mother send you over here? Are you her little

messenger?' asked Eridanus.

Crater scoffed. 'If you want to destroy your reputation, that's your business, but since you're here, have a little respect for mine. You're making all of us look bad.' He sighed and watched the room for a moment, but Crater was never good at letting silences linger. He looked eagerly at Eridanus. 'Is it true about the orange? Did you see it?'

Lynx could see it now, still feel its rind beneath her fingers. She hadn't been able to shake it from her mind since she'd first seen it crammed in Mensa's mouth. The object of his grief made sexual and deadly. Eridanus looked as if he remembered it vividly, too.

'Don't be so morbid,' said Eridanus.

'He was going to get me a grief nurse. Now all my hard work is to waste.' A shadow passed over Crater's features, but it was short-lived. He was soon smiling again. 'There's nothing for it but to wring out the juicy details.'

'Have some respect,' said Eridanus.

Crater groaned. 'Why are you being so boring, Dani?'

'I'm always boring. Or did you forget?'

'No one liked the man,' said Crater. 'The least we can do is have a little fun since we're trapped here.' He shot a pointed look at Eridanus's empty glass. 'Back on the sauce?'

Eridanus turned away. 'I'm fine.'

'You're right. You're boring. Why do I even bother?' Crater shook his head.

'Lynx, what do you suppose happened?' Eridanus asked.

'Why are you asking her?' Crater gestured with the hand that held his drink. Some of it splashed over the rim, drops raining toward Eridanus who took a step back.

'She found the body.'

'But you're acting like it isn't obvious.'

'It's not,' said Eridanus. 'He was hanged.'

'He hung himself.' Crater slapped his brother's arm with the back of his hand. 'Do I have to give you the talk?' He grinned. 'You know, sometimes, when a man is alone in his room, he—'

Eridanus sighed. 'Crater—'

Crater's eyes were glittering, almost feverishly. 'He was clearly enjoying himself when he died. I do hope that he actually reached the end before reaching the end, do you know what I mean?'

Had it really been an accidental suicide? It seemed that way, yet Mensa was a powerful and controversial man. Lynx could think of any number of people who would prefer him dead. Then there was Solina's death…

Lynx thought of ice and oranges and bit down on her tongue, hard. She had to remain composed. Stay in control like she was taught – a grief nurse must be detached from the flurry of emotions around her. She must stay poised and unaffected in the face of great feeling. With all that had happened since Sculptor's death, she was finding it increasingly difficult to keep her feelings knotted up within herself. There were so many unanswered questions.

Eridanus shook his head and stared at the flakes of snow dancing in the wind outside. He took a long drink. His Sorrow had grown. Of course it had. He had Sorrow for Sculptor and Solina and now Mensa burning within him. Lynx was amazed he hadn't given up yet, but he had gone three years already without a nurse. He was stronger than she realized.

Even as she thought this about him, his gaze shifted just enough so that he was no longer looking out the window but looking at her. He'd never looked at her with desire before, with longing, but as he looked at her now, she felt his want. He wanted her to take his grief. He wanted all of it gone. She would have happily taken it save for the question nibbling at the back of her mind. Why was Laurient Mensa dead?

'What a shame,' Crater said, swirling his drink. 'Years spent in parliament, on course to be prime minister if the tides turned, and he's strangled himself to death with a fucking necktie and a piece of fruit.' Crater laughed, joyless and hollow. 'He should have just called Lynx. Much safer to fuck a grief nurse than try to manage it on your own.' Crater glanced at Lynx. 'I don't think she's strong enough.' He looked across the room at Karina. 'But that other nurse could have handled him properly. She's probably got strong hands.' He flexed his fingers, grinning.

At the mention of Karina, Lynx almost lashed out, but before she could, Eridanus grabbed his brother by the cravat. 'What's the matter with you?'

'Just saying aloud what everyone is thinking,' said Crater, trying unsuccessfully to pry Eridanus's hands away. 'Mensa was a pervert. He slept with any grief nurse he set eyes on. That's probably why he got into politics in the first place. Where there's power, there's grief nurses.'

Eridanus released him, shaking him so that his drink spilled all over his shoes. Crater exclaimed and danced back, kicking his feet so that drops flew at Lynx's ankles.

'Honestly, you've gone mad,' Crater said. He looked past Eridanus, toward Orion, who was near the door, speaking with Andromeda. 'Orion.' Crater pointed to his shoes. 'Come here, please.'

Orion said something more to Andromeda, who nodded absently. Andromeda saw her staring, but Lynx couldn't look away. She looked like her usual self. She wore a blue dress, so dark it was nearly black, embroidered with constellations. Her hair was loose, held back only by her sand star hairpin. What had Lynx expected? Did she think Andromeda would look different now that someone else knew her secret?

Her grief was more potent than it'd ever been, and for a long moment, Lynx really felt as if the sea churned around her, covering the entire floor of the drawing room. Then, Orion approached them, distracting her enough to pull herself away from Andromeda's ocean.

'How may I be of assistance?' he asked Crater.

'I need a handkerchief. My brother has attempted to destroy my shoes.'

'Don't you have your own?' Eridanus asked.

'Yes, but I don't want to dirty it.' Crater looked annoyed.

Orion took a cloth from his pocket and handed it to Crater. 'Here you are, sir.'

Crater didn't take it. Instead, he looked down pointedly.

Orion's mouth twitched and he cleared his throat. 'A handkerchief.'

For a moment, Crater looked as if he would really do it, as if he'd ask Orion to get down on his knees – but he didn't have the courage, not under Orion's hard stare. 'Get me another drink,' he said, taking the handkerchief. He swung his foot up onto the windowsill and cleaned off his shoe with a flourish. Once he'd done the same for the other one and a new drink was in his hand, he said in a voice just a bit lower than his usual register, 'What are we going to do about Andromeda?'

Eridanus's eyebrows drew together. 'Nothing.'

'We can't do nothing.' He glanced at Andromeda, who was talking to the woman Ms. Aster had attempted to pair her with just the night before. It seemed like a lifetime ago. 'She's a liability. The wrong person finds out, and it could destroy my career.'

'What career?'

Crater ignored him. 'Or do you think it was just a mistake?' He took a long sip from his drink and stared at Andromeda, as if he could tell she was a Fader just by looking hard enough. Eridanus made a point not to follow his brother's gaze. 'Maybe she'll get over it,' continued Crater. 'Or perhaps she's just being ludicrous on purpose. It's something she'd do – like all those times she's 'run away'. It's just a big show to get a rise out of us. Once she marries, she'll calm down. She'll forget about all of this.' Crater waved vaguely in Lynx's direction.

'Or maybe,' said Eridanus in a low voice. 'She just likes Lynx.'

Crater seemed caught off guard. Eridanus broke the silence before his brother did. 'Lynx,' said Eridanus. 'There is something I've been meaning to ask you. You know my grief. What is it?'

Crater shifted, clearly uncomfortable. Obviously, it was exactly the reaction Eridanus wanted.

'You mean is it Sorrow or—' she started.

'You said Crater's grief was a crow, and our father's a rose. What is mine like?'

She hesitated, wondering why he was asking. 'It's a fire.'

Eridanus frowned. 'It's true, isn't it, that the mad die like their grief?'

'What does that even mean?' Crater asked, but Eridanus's question wasn't absurd. She wished he hadn't asked it.

'Yes, that's right,' she said, thinking again of the orange, of the frost that mottled Solina's skin.

'If I were to go mad, then, I would find myself up in flames,' said Eridanus. 'Would you be able to know, just by looking at my grief, that I was succumbing to madness?'

'Listen to yourself,' said Crater. 'You're being improper.'

'Says the man who wanted me to describe the way a dead man looks when he's hanging by his neck in his closet.'

'Are you so out of touch, Dani? You do know he was a Fader, don't you?'

'I don't see how that's relevant.' But he did, of course, they all did. Faders were considered sexual deviants, perverts who got pleasure from grief-taking. And the way Mensa had died...

'It was his own fault, that's all I'm saying.'

'I can't wait to get off this island.'

'I'm taking his death as an opportunity,' said Crater. 'The press will be swarming here as soon as the ferry is running again.' He smoothed down his lapels. 'It'll be a chance to position myself. Anyone who has ever associated themselves with him will be scrambling to make excuses about how they didn't know he was a Fader. Opportunities will arise, and I'll be there to take them.'

'Who was a Fader, darling?' Ms. Aster had slipped into the room without notice. She hadn't even been in the room long enough to acquire a drink. Her grief was gone, but when she said the word Fader, her voice was cold.

'Mother, you look perfectly Bright.' Crater turned, his smile faltering.

'Who was a Fader, darling?' she repeated.

'Ah.' Crater glanced at Eridanus, whose expression made it clear he would not be throwing his brother a lifeline. 'Mr. Mensa,' he said, and after seeing his mother's widening smile, quickly added. 'It was an open secret.'

'A secret I wasn't aware of?' said Ms. Aster. Her smile had grown enough to make it clear she was displeased. 'I hope you are not slandering a good man's name for the sake of "opportunities".'

'Mother, everyone knew, they just kept their mouths shut because Mensa was good at getting what people wanted,' blurted Crater, his words tumbling over one another.

'He's not wrong,' said Eridanus, sounding reluctant.

Ms. Aster was silent. Lynx sensed the brothers' flaring Dread. She was afraid, too.

'Lynx, was he a Fader?' Ms. Aster asked. Her tone was light, as if she were asking about the weather, but there was a current of tension running beneath it.

Lynx's throat tightened. 'He was, but—'

The snake was coiled around Ms. Aster's neck. Its thick, muscled body was layered upon itself loosely. Lynx could not find its head, not until Ms. Aster turned to her sons, and the snake's eyes gleamed beside her ear.

'It seems I have been made a fool of,' said Ms. Aster. 'I invited a Fader into my house. Let him eat at my table. Let him use my grief nurse.' Her nostrils flared as she pressed her lips together. 'You should have told me. Both of you.'

'It's different on the mainland,' said Crater. 'Everyone knew.'

'I don't care what's fashionable on the mainland, if everyone is gallivanting with Faders these days. This is my house, and you know where I stand.'

'Grandmother is still alive, isn't she?' Eridanus said. His fire was burning. 'Don't lie and tell me she isn't because I found her. You sent her to the House of the Sickle Moon. Syril was doing work there. He found her name in the record book.'

'I sent her nowhere,' said Ms. Aster. 'My father made the choice to protect his only daughter, to protect me and my future. My mother deceived us for years. She would have ruined our family if your grandfather hadn't sent her away.' The snake flicked its tongue, as if whispering secrets into Ms. Aster's ear. 'Faders belong in madhouses, all of them. It's sick, what they do. It's not natural. Let them have their grief nurse children. That is all they are good for.'

From across the room, Andromeda watched her mother, her gaze unwavering even as the woman beside her continued to speak. Lynx knew she was hearing every word.

Crater and Eridanus did not look at their little sister. Their gazes did not wander, but they were afraid. They were afraid, but they said nothing.

The roots within her shifted. She blinked, and her vision was spidered with black tendrils. She felt the anger twisting inside her. She tried to hold it down, but the roots shifted, sliding over one another, stretching. That inescapable urge rushed through her. She wanted to scream until her throat was raw. She wanted to reach out and raze this house to the ground. She wanted to destroy everything, the way she had destroyed her tree, stripping its leaves, tearing its roots from the earth.

She peeled away from the conversation until the Asters' voices were distant nonsense in her ears. Her legs urged her to run, but she kept herself steady as she came up beside Orion.

'Where is the body?' Lynx asked.

Orion frowned. 'The game larder. To keep it cool until the ferry is running. Lynx, why do you want to know?'

'I just want to see.'

She didn't tell him what she was really thinking – that she needed to see the body. That she needed to know the truth.

CHAPTER 18

The larder was cool and dry, the floor slate, the slim windows covered only with a fine wire mesh. The walls were tiled, floor to ceiling, painted with vibrant scenes of game: a vixen slinking from her den, a grouse with a ruby crown, a stag and hind in the rut. It was gaudy and romanticized, a lewd backdrop to the rabbits on hooks around the walls, the small birds suspended from the ceiling.

None of it rivalled the bodies stretched out on a table, feet near the upturned pheasants, heads by the marble chopping block. The bodies of Solina and Mensa.

Solina's body was covered in a blue cloth, only the smallest finger of one hand escaping from beneath the cloth's edge. Lynx took a long breath and moved toward Mensa's body.

She thought she could still smell the oranges on him, but she must have been imagining it. The larder smelled only of blood and peat. Mensa's body was uncovered, and he was dressed as he was the night she first saw him in the great hall in his cranberry suit. His eyes were closed, his hands clasped together. The collar of his shirt hid most of his neck.

Lynx moved closer. She felt like an intruder and her instincts told her to get out, but her gaze caught on the breast pocket of his jacket. The handkerchief he usually wore there was gone.

She pressed her nails into her palms. She felt no fondness towards this man. She wouldn't ever forget his fingers on her skin, his conviction that he could take from her what he wanted because of who she was. He was a hypocrite. A Fader who struck deals with anti-Fader lobbyists. He was a trafficker of nurses, a wheel in the machine that kept Lynx in her place.

She did not care that Laurient Mensa was dead, but she hated how they treated him now that he was silenced. He could not speak when they called him a dirty Fader, a pervert who deserved his death.

As she leaned over the body, her hair fell around her face. Faders were called perverts, unnatural, but what was done to grief nurses was worse. Taken from their families, trained to work for people who saw them only as tools. They could not go where they pleased. They could not run away. What happened to a grief nurse who was disloyal? Who made too many mistakes? Faders were sent to madhouses, but what happened to grief nurses was far worse.

Their trees were ripped from them. As a child, she had heard the screams of nurses who had transgressed, who had been brought back to the school after failing their guardians. She did not know what happened to a grief nurse without a tree – the children were never told – but she had felt their fear. Though she had often imagined plucking her own tree, she could never bring herself to. Always, an instinct stopped her, a warning woven into her bones. To have her tree taken would be a violation so great, the thought make her sick.

For her own sake, she needed to know what had

happened to Mensa. She needed to know what had happened to his grief.

Gently, she touched Mensa's fingers, ran her fingertips across his knuckles. She felt nothing inside him and her heart sank. Just the day before, she was sinking her teeth into the fruit of his grief, raking her fingers through the vines of it. Now all that bounty was gone. But she was certain – a hint of orange. She could smell it. She hesitated, her fingers hovering above Mensa's heart. A body was temporal; flesh rotted so quickly, even bones eventually crumbled, but an object, a token – Lynx slipped her fingers inside the breast pocket of Mensa's jacket and grasped the thimble.

She was back in the orchard, the scent of it shocking her senses, and she gasped. It was not the same as it was when Mensa was alive. She could see it rotting, skin puckering, leaves drying to brittle flakes, but some fruit still clung on. Bright bulging oranges, shiny plums, grapes turned red but still plump and whole.

As Lynx took a step farther into Mensa's orchard, dry leaves cracked beneath her feet. She let her mind's fingers tumble out and spread across the ground. She felt the papery sensation of leaves, the downy skin of a shrivelled peach. She wanted it. She wanted all of it.

Lynx ignored the temptation. Instead she focused on the way the grief felt beneath her fingers, the taste of it, the scent. She was searching for something. A feeling or a realization. Something that would give her proof. She was seeking evidence of madness. Had Mensa gone mad with grief or had he been killed another way?

Lynx, like the rest of the world, knew very little about madness. She did not know what she was looking for. She had hoped that upon entering the orchard it would come to her easily, like an instinct. As her fingers roamed the orchard's trees and shrubs, her frustration grew. She had tasted madness before. She had felt it with her mind. She should know—

The grief began to fade.

Trees at the far end of the orchard began to shrivel, their branches curling in on themselves like dead spiders, and the ground receded, giving way to whiteness.

If there was evidence here, she needed to find it fast.

Panic rose within her, desperation that made her unable to think. She could not focus. She felt everything at once, and memories were hurtling toward her, images that did not belong to her. The gunshot sound of a sewing machine. A needle pricking her thumb. The rough green fabric of a seat in parliament.

She shoved them away, but more rushed in to take their place, and as her panic grew, a memory sunk its teeth into her mind and would not let her go. It did not belong to Mensa. It was hers.

A bell rang, tinkling and persistent, a sound Lynx was used to hearing bouncing from the walls of the tiny, painted room.

'That'll be the shortbread,' her mother said, and she was already climbing down the ladder. She left her paint brush on the cloth spread across the floor. A tiny pool of silver formed around its tip. If it were any other colour, Lynx would have taken it and brushed it through her hair. She just wanted to see what it would be like to have hair that wasn't white. She considered the other colours in their jars – blue, green, purple, red. Which did she like the best?

Before she could pick, her mother returned, carrying a block of shortbread wrapped in paper.

'I'm going downstairs to bring this to Ms. Io,' she said. She broke off a piece and handed it to Lynx. It was still warm, and Lynx imagined that this was what it would be like to hold a little bird in her palm, its warm breast against her skin. 'Don't leave the flat. Don't open the curtains. Lynx, are you listening?'

Lynx looked up. She nodded.

'Good.' Her mother smiled and bent to give her a kiss on the nose. 'Think about what animal I should paint next. A sand star maybe?'

Lynx popped a piece of shortbread into her mouth. 'No, I hate those,' she said. Her mother only smiled and shook her head as she closed the door behind her.

Lynx heard the click of the lock, but she placed the shortbread on the ground and ran to the door anyway. She tried the handle. It didn't budge, even when she shook it as hard as she could. Defeated, she returned to her place on the floor, drawing her knees up to her chest.

For a while, she was content, enjoying the buttery sweetness of the shortbread. But eventually, it began to taste like dust in her mouth. She threw the remaining crumbs as far as she could, annoyed that none of them landed as far as the paint jars.

The window was open, making the curtains shiver. Spots of sun speckled the floor. She looked to the unfinished painting of the ocean and tried to love it, but the more she stared at that silver moon, the more she wanted it gone. She didn't want the room full of paintings. She wanted the real world, the one everyone else got to see.

She went to the window and gripped a fistful of the dark fabric. It would be bad to open the curtains. It would be a naughty thing to do. She stood for a moment, straining to hear any movement in the stairwell outside. When she was certain no one was coming, she peeled the curtain away.

A swatch of sunlight filtered into the room, settling on her skin, gilding the hairs on her arms. She held out her hand and cupped her palm, feeling as if she could scoop up the warm sun with her fingers. She laughed and stood on her tiptoes to press her face against the glass.

She could see straight into the flat across the street, but there was nothing really to see. Just a pair of old curtains, an empty pink vase on the windowsill. The street was empty, only a few scraps of rubbish littered the gutters. Then a face appeared in the window opposite. A man with emerald hair who wore round, gold-rimmed glasses. He looked right at her, and she ducked beneath the sill.

Lynx's heart beat so hard she had to bite her tongue to keep herself in the present. She had a little tree inside herself she liked to visit .at night. She'd go there sometimes when she was upset or frightened, but she didn't go there now.

Slowly, she lifted herself up and peered through the window again. There was no one at the window across the street. But as she reached for the curtain, the man appeared again, this time accompanied by a woman. Lynx froze. The man said something to his friend, and he pointed in Lynx's direction. The man and the woman exchanged glances. They looked pleased.

Lynx dropped to a crouch, sliding the curtain closed as she did so. She wanted to go inside herself, but she was too afraid to remember how. Her heart was so loud in her ears.

Just then, the door opened and her mother stepped through.

'Lynx,' she said, a puzzled look crossing her features. She seemed to realize something, her gaze flickering to the curtains, which were still moving from when Lynx had shut them so quickly. 'Lynx,' her mother said again, and this time, something strong and delicious and horrible rushed toward Lynx, enveloping her, suffocating her—

Lynx was on the hillside again. It was night-time now. The full moon hung above her. The wind was wild, and it tore at her hair and made her eyes water. This time, she did not feel happy. She felt hopelessly and terribly afraid—

With all her will, Lynx forced the memory away. She had no more energy left to resist the grief. She let her mind take over, let it do as it pleased. For once, she took without limit, without caring for the consequences.

When she had enough, she let her desire give way to anger. She no longer wanted to take. She wanted to destroy, to dismantle, to see this grief crumble. Her mind's fingers whipped through the orchard, tearing at branches, ripping fruit off their stems. She was tired. Tired of obeying, of hiding, of standing against the wall and watching as the Asters lived their lives. She never let herself feel anger. Anger was dangerous, as dangerous as the hunger that vibrated through her. Anger and desire made her lose control, and she would not hurt someone again – but Mensa was dead. She could not hurt him.

His grief place was already fading. She felt it slipping away. She let herself strip the trees of their leaves and tear their roots from the earth until the ground was slick with crushed fruit, the air filled with their sweet scents.

She tore and broke and crushed until the vines and branches withered beneath her fingers. She tried to hold on to the dying grief. Everything was fading fast, leaves browning and curling and crumbling to dust. She was thrown out of Mensa's orchard and into the real world. The dark larder, the hulking shape of Mensa's body. Her heart was thunderous, and blood beat so hard in her head, she felt battered by it.

Shaking, Lynx grasped Mensa's token, reached her mind forward, probing for his orchard. It was destroyed, leaves shredded, fruit scattered across the ground, their skin burst. She touched a leaf and it crumbled and was gone. A moment later, there was nothing left, only a white emptiness and the lingering scent of orange.

She turned at the sensation of someone watching her.

Karina stood at the threshold, her pale eyes vivid in the shadows. She had seen everything.

CHAPTER 19

Mensa's grief was destroyed, and what remained of it had withered away. The token in her fist was empty, silent. It was nothing more than a thimble belonging to a dead man.

The body was unchanged despite the violence she'd inflicted.

Lynx placed the thimble back into Mensa's suitcoat, her fingers shaking. The vicious energy that had coursed through her only moments before was dissipating now, leaving behind an ache in her bones, a heaviness in her limbs. She had never done such a thing before. She hadn't known she was capable of such violence.

She was acutely aware of the intensity of Karina's gaze.

Karina had seen everything. What would she think of Lynx now?

'I lost control,' said Lynx, not yet turning around, not yet ready to face the look of revulsion she would surely find in Karina's eyes.

'You destroyed his grief,' said Karina. 'I've never seen a grief nurse tear someone's grief apart like that.'

'I didn't mean to—' Lynx started, her voice raw.

'It was incredible.' Karina's footsteps were loud in the small space. She came to stand beside Lynx, her fingertips resting on the table where Mensa lay. Reluctantly, Lynx looked up into Karina's eyes. 'When I first saw you, I thought there was more to you than appeared,' she said.

'This isn't me.' Lynx shook her head. She wanted to undo it all, go back and fix everything she had broken. She'd been taught so little about what grief nurses could do. There was grief-taking and grief play like mixing. She'd learned, through Vela's story, how nurses could change grief, too. She never knew a grief nurse could tear a person's grief apart. What would have happened if Mensa were alive? What could she have done? She stepped away from the table, but Karina caught her hand.

'Wait. Go inside. Visit your tree. Take me with you if you want.'

To see her tree was the last thing Lynx wanted to do, but she felt compelled. She felt drawn to it, as if something there would help her understand what she had just done. And Karina would be with her. She squeezed Karina's hand and reached out with her mind. Her mind's fingers found Karina's and she clasped them and took them inside herself. Soon, they were both standing beneath Lynx's tree.

She couldn't understand what she was seeing.

'Lynx,' Karina breathed.

Where her slim and broken oak once stood, burst a great black tree. Its biggest branches were thicker than the oak's trunk had been. Some reached into the sky, while others dipped down to nearly brush the ground. Its roots spread far, erupting from the earth in places. At her feet, rolled a cluster of smooth, ebony acorns. In the tallest branches of the trees, black leaves shivered in the faint wind.

It was her tree, she realized. It was the very tree she had torn and bent the day before. It was almost unrecognizable. For the first time in years, she listened for its singing. The sound vibrated through her body, a hum that felt like a heartbeat.

She opened her eyes and returned to the larder with Karina's hand still in hers.

'What happened?' Karina asked.

Lynx bit her tongue. She didn't know. Not only was her tree black, it had grown, was growing still. How had it grown so quickly? Why was it sprouting leaves again? Lynx closed her eyes and stretched forward with her mind. Her mind's fingers curled outward, but quickly they changed, white tendrils transforming to black. She pulled them back inside herself, heart hammering in panic. 'Something is wrong with me.'

'It's beautiful,' said Karina, shaking her head, and Lynx looked at her in surprise.

Beautiful? Karina's tree was beautiful, not hers. Karina's yew was strong, vibrant, with pine needles and berries. It was the perfect complement to Karina herself, confident and certain. With her many white braids and skin dusted with freckles across her nose. Her hands that weren't slim and dainty but strong. Her body that took up space and commanded it.

'Mensa said something to me. You're not beautiful. None of you are. I believed him. I've believed it all my life,' Lynx said. 'Until I met you.' Her cheeks were hot. Before Karina could say anything, before Lynx could stop herself, she continued, 'I can't stay at Mount Sorcha. Something is wrong with my tree. It's dangerous. Who's to say I won't hurt someone's grief again? If I do this to someone who is alive, what will happen to them? What will happen to me?' She shook her head, her throat tight.

'They'll take my tree.' I need to leave the island.' She took a shaky breath. 'Will you come with me?'

She wanted to turn away, to avoid seeing Karina's reaction, but Karina's lips tugged into a smile. 'You're right,' she said. 'You can't stay here.' Lynx held her breath. 'But the ferry isn't running.'

'I couldn't take the ferry anyway. There's an old boat not far from the dock. I could take that.'

'In this weather?' Karina dropped her gaze to meet Lynx's.

'I can't wait. I have to try.'

'No.' Karina shook her head, and her braids softly rustled. 'You'll get yourself killed. Wait. Wait for the weather to improve, until it's safe. Wait, and I'll come with you. We'll run away together.' Karina's white tendrils flickered around her, darting across her skin, and Lynx wondered how she'd ever let herself believe that this wasn't beauty.

Lynx grabbed Karina's hand, and she pulled her toward her and she kissed her.

CHAPTER 20

Lynx sat on her bed, fingertips still buzzing at the memory of Karina's touch. She packed all her possessions into a bag, which lay now on the floor, forlornly leaning against the wall. She swept the sea glass that usually sat in a row atop the dresser into a now-empty drawer. Though she closed the drawer with conviction, a moment later she couldn't help herself. She took one of the shards and dropped it in her bag with the rest of her belongings. She pushed away the spark of misgiving the glass ignited. Was this the right choice?

Even as that question rose in her mind, she knew that there was no choice, not truly. She had to leave or risk the lives of everyone on the island, including her own. What she wanted hardly mattered and wasn't worth thinking of.

Tentatively, she unfurled her mind's fingers, bracing for what she'd find. They were still black, and they were stronger now; she could feel the power vibrating through them. A bell rang, and she yanked the tendrils back inside herself.

A bell in the signal box above the door was shivering, Crater's name inscribed in gold above it. She took a deep breath and let the bell's chime fade away before walking out into the hall.

When she reached the autumn wing, Crater was

standing in the doorway of his room. He was wringing his hands through the ties of his robe. 'What took you so long? I was almost ready to come down and look for you myself.' He turned into his room as soon as he saw her, and she followed after him. He tore the diamond from his ear and placed it with a clink onto the bedside table. 'Are you trying to make me suffer?'

'It's quite a distance from the servants' quarters,' said Lynx, looking down at the token, but not touching it, not yet. She glanced at the window. Snow was still falling.

Crater's throat worked as he clenched his teeth. 'You have one job, Lynx.'

She had always thought of Crater as a harmless gossip. The loud one, who despite being occasionally obnoxious was generally bearable. Looking at him now, knowing that she would be leaving soon, she saw his flaws for what they were: he was selfish and self-centred and, above all, obsessed with his mother's admiration.

The crow on his shoulder cocked its head at her, as if it knew what she was thinking.

'What are you waiting for?' Crater snapped. 'Take it.'

She knew his anger was a shield for his fear. She picked up the earring, resting it in her palm.

Crater watched her, and when she did nothing more, he turned away. He strode about the room as he spoke. 'Mother's arranged a deer stalk tomorrow. I couldn't stop thinking of blood—you know the look of blood on fur?' Crater snorted, as if offended at the mere mention of it. 'Suddenly I was thinking of Mensa. Although there was no blood.' He shook his head. 'And Sculptor. I keep wondering how he did it.'

She felt the Dread as a rustling of feathers, a musky

scent, the taste of earth and crisp air.

'I'm not going to do anything until I'm certain,' Crater said as he continued to pace. 'I'll feel better without all this Dread sticking to me—' His flicked his hands, as if he could fling the Dread off his fingertips like mud.

She couldn't delay any longer. She let her mind's fingers stretch forward like an offering. The crow shivered as she touched it, fluffing up its feathers, revealing dusty brown plumage beneath the glossy black.

The crow hopped away, avoiding her. Before she could stop them, her dark fingers shot forward, grasping for the crow, who shot into the air, wings fluttering like the pages of an upturned book.

Lynx turned her hand over and the token fell to the ground. The black tendrils relaxed, and Lynx pulled them back into herself.

Crater's back was to her, and he was still speaking, oblivious. 'I need that nurse,' he said. 'With Mensa dead, I'll never get off the waitlist. I need her.'

Lynx bent and picked up the token, biting her lip as she did so, fighting the urge to reach forward with her mind again.

She could not take his grief. She couldn't trust herself, not with her mind changing as it was.

She picked up the token again, careful this time to keep her fingers coiled tight within her. She closed her eyes and waited, counting each breath as the grief called to her. Her mind's fingers itched, but she held them back, and when she couldn't resist any longer, she opened her eyes.

'That's it?' Crater looked relieved and sceptical as he watched her place the earring back onto the table.

'There wasn't much,' she said, not looking at him.

Crater's brow was furrowed, and he didn't seem to believe her, but he put the diamond back into his ear. He moved to the window. 'Well, it appears we'll be hunting in the snow tomorrow.' He drew his finger through the frost creeping along the edges of the glass. Lynx took a step back toward the door, and he noticed. He turned around, stopping her mid-step. 'What was wrong with Sculptor?'

The question was so unexpected, she froze. 'You mean—'

'I mean, what was wrong with his grief?'

'It grew too fast.'

Crater let out a long breath and nodded. 'I see.' His face was drawn, an unusual expression of vulnerability in the downward curve of his mouth. He turned suddenly. 'I have to find something to wear tomorrow that I don't despise.' He looked at his reflection in the mirror and tightened the knot of his robe. 'I was right about Sculptor. He was even more fucked up than me. I wish he was here, just so I could tell him so.'

As Lynx left the room, she glanced over her shoulder. Two crows sat on the windowsill. As she snapped shut the door behind her, she could still hear their screeching.

CHAPTER 21

Lynx watched Crater press his palm against his horse's velvet mouth. With his other hand, he tugged a knot out of the horse's mane. He was dressed in unusually dull colours – in green and gold-striped trousers, with a light brown shirt under a tweed vest. He looked vulnerable without a cravat. Even from a distance, she could smell the alcohol on him.

His Dread was even stronger now than when she'd left him in the dark hours of the morning. What was he afraid of?

The air was biting, the sunrise little more than a glow in the sky. The chilly quiet made the memory of what she'd done to Mensa feel stark and raw. She imagined what could have happened if she had done the same to Crater's grief, if she'd been unable to rein in her corrupted fingers. She rubbed her hands together and blew into them for warmth. She'd slept terribly, rocking in and out of her dreams, forgetting if she was herself or Mensa, his memories still haunting her.

'Good morning,' called Vela, who was trotting across the lawn, two rifles slung across her back. She wore a brimmed hat, her hair twisted into one perfect curl beside her left cheek. A scarlet scarf was wrapped around her neck. She pecked Crater on the cheek, and he seemed surprised. She patted his lapel, and Lynx noticed a new diamond ring glinting on her finger. 'You look empty. Have this.' Vela tugged off her scarf and wrapped it around Crater's neck. She spent a moment tucking and adjusting it before stepping back, pleased with herself. 'Lovely. It suits you.' Already, flakes of snow dusted the scarlet wool.

'You're very Bright this morning,' said Crater with an edge of suspicion.

'I have every reason to be,' Vela replied. 'I'm so looking forward to this evening.'

Crater's crows had returned. They sat on his shoulders, glassy eyes alert. Crater touched Vela's arm and turned her halfway around. 'Why two guns?'

'One's for you.'

'I don't shoot.' He patted his horse's withers.

'But you can, and today you should. You might miss the perfect opportunity.'

'I'm not fond of dead things,' he said.

'Though a dead brother suits you well.'

He said nothing to that, as he took the gun from her and slung it across his back.

Grooms arrived with more horses and the band of ponies that would carry the dead hinds back to the larder. Eridanus and Mr. Aster were not far behind them. At a distance, the similarities between them were clearer. They both bent their heads as they spoke and held their shoulders in the same way.

'Crater, you're shooting?' Mr. Aster said, as they approached. 'Good morning, ladies,' he said to Vela and Lynx.

'Miss Deleporte believes it will be an auspicious stalk,' said Crater.

'Well, I trust Miss Deleporte's intuition,' Mr. Aster said. 'I'm afraid your mother won't be joining us. She's taken ill, but she insisted she'll be well by this evening.' There was a hint of sadness in his smile. 'Our final dinner before you all run off again.'

'Even Mother's illnesses do as she says,' said Eridanus.

'Where's the stalker?' said Crater, cutting in.

They all turned to watch as Orion emerged from the house. He, too, was dressed in muted colours and carried two rifles. He was almost unrecognizable without his crisp suit. His arrow token was pinned onto the small pocket of his coat.

'I think you have your answer,' said Eridanus.

'Good morning,' said Orion, nodding once. 'Our usual gillie doesn't stay on the island. She was to come yesterday, but with the weather, she couldn't make it. I will be your stalker this morning.'

'I prefer you anyway,' said Crater.

'Is Andromeda joining?' Mr. Aster asked. The others exchanged glances.

'Oh, there she is,' said Vela, pointing across the lawn. Andromeda, flawlessly dressed in a tweed suit, brown leather shoes and gloves, and a green and gold tartan scarf, strode through the snow. She was striking in a suit. It suited her better than a dress.

Lynx felt a heartbeat of desire, but her attention was immediately drawn away from Andromeda to Karina walking beside her. Like Lynx, she was dressed in white, but while Lynx's hunting attire was made of wool and waxed leather, Karina was draped in white furs and velvet. Her gloves were cuffed with fur, and her boots were studded with silver moons. More moons were embroidered around the edge of the cloak around her shoulders.

Lynx was familiar with the crags and glens of the island, the ashen rock rupturing the sides of hills, the wind-blown grasses and the burns that cut tumbling white fissures through it all. She knew Karina's attire wasn't suited for a deer stalk, but Karina looked so much like a queen, like she ruled this island, that Lynx believed she could do anything. She was tempted to take Karina's hand and run, leave right now though the snow was still falling.

Crater crossed his arms, looking uncomfortable in his hunting gear. 'We make all this effort to blend in, and you dress your grief nurse like that?'

'I assume this is a Miss Deleporte creation,' whispered Lynx, running her gloved fingers over the fur on Karina's shoulders.

Karina's pale eyes shone. 'I suppose I needed a turn at being overdressed.'

The wind rose, bringing with it the scent of the sea. Lynx turned to see Andromeda watching her. Her fingers fell away from Karina's shoulder.

'This was the only suitable outfit she had,' said Andromeda, turning to her brother.

'Suitable?' Crater raised an eyebrow. 'The deer will be spooked.'

'I'm sure they aren't frightened of grief,' said Eridanus.

Crater rolled his eyes at him. 'What I mean is, the nurses are too conspicuous.' He looked down at himself. 'Why are we dressed like dirt, when we're toting around veritable white beacons?'

'I still intend to get my hind,' said Vela.

'Do you suppose our party is too large?' Eridanus asked Orion. 'Perhaps we should send the nurses back.'

'I will tend to Cassiopeia,' said Mr. Aster before Orion could reply. 'And leave you all to fetch us dinner.' He gave Eridanus a meaningful look before a smile lit up his face and he turned away.

Vela was already pulling herself into her horse's saddle. 'Are we going to waste the whole morning?' she said cheerfully.

With that everyone busied themselves with mounting, while the grooms began rounding up the ponies, who had scattered across the lawn, happily chomping the short grass and kicking up snow and black earth.

They left the lawn and surrounding forest behind and were now cutting across fields that in the summer would be ablaze with heather. Lynx knew it would be the kind of day that never seemed to start. A heavy blanket of clouds obscured the sun, making it impossible to know if it was morning or afternoon.

Lynx curled her fingers through her horse's mane. Snow fell onto her cheeks, and she felt as if it were mocking her. She needed to leave. She kept her mind to herself, but she was terrified of letting her guard down. Already, she was exhausted from the concentration it took to not explore the grief around her.

'Was Father conspiring with you to send you money behind Mother's back?' said Crater, who rode his horse beside Eridanus's. Lynx watched him sneak a sip from a bronze flask he kept in his jacket pocket.

'You know he's unwaveringly loyal to her,' said Eridanus. 'Why don't you fill your pockets before you leave tonight?' Crater smirked. 'We've got hoards of useless junk that I'm sure would fetch a fortune on the mainland.'

'If anything in that house truly fetched a fortune, Mother would have sold it already. Nobody on the mainland has use for anything here. Mount Sorcha was out of fashion before it was built.'

'I suppose, you could get a divorce. That would get the money flowing again.'

'Or, perhaps, I could get a job,' said Eridanus.

Crater laughed. 'Really?' He grimaced. 'You're serious? What would you do?'

'I don't know yet,' said Eridanus.

'Divorce seems far easier. I really don't see why you're bothering.'

'You really don't know much about love.' Eridanus urged his horse forward, and Crater fell behind.

Lynx let her horse pull back until she was the last in the group, only the pony boys trotting the ponies a good distance behind her. As they rode, hump-backed hills, dappled in shades of grey and green and white, rose onto the horizon. Without the distraction of the others' conversation, she found herself remembering a hillside much like this one, the scent of gorse and heather arriving on the wind, the way the sun would tip itself above the highest peak in the distance, golden rays gilding the distant hills.

She encouraged her horse forward, letting its quickened pace knock the memory from her mind. Orion, at the head of the hunting party, raised his hand. Those up front stopped their horses, the ones behind dancing back to keep from colliding with the others. The wind was stronger now, buffeting the snow.

The party had reached the foot of the hills, and everyone was dismounting. The pony boys caught up with them just as Lynx had stepped down from her horse. One stayed with the ponies, while the others led the horses away.

Orion lifted his chin, and Lynx knew he was feeling the wind on his face. 'This way,' he said, and they began climb.

'Poor Mr. Mensa,' said Vela, trailing her hand along a rock. 'I think he would have liked a hunt.'

'Luckily, he's indisposed. We're already too large a group as it is,' said Crater, cracking a smile that no one returned.

'What do you suppose will happen now?' Andromeda asked. 'Once everyone hears what happened?'

'Mother isn't ill,' said Eridanus. 'She's working out a way to smooth all this over.'

'I think Mother should burn the house down and start over,' said Crater. 'It's obviously bad luck.'

'She'd never do that. She loves that house more than us,' said Andromeda.

'Get down,' came Orion's voice.

In the distance, a group of deer skirted the ridge. There were five of them, the one at the head of the group staring with upright ears at the hunting party.

They all dropped to the ground, Vela pulling the rifle from her back, Orion handing his to Andromeda. Andromeda balanced her rifle on a grassy knoll. 'It's your shot, Miss Andromeda,' said Orion. He looked up at Crater, who was still standing. 'Master Crater.' The ears of the leading deer twitched, and Crater dropped into a crouch.

'Not yet,' came Orion's whisper on the wind, as Andromeda cocked her rifle. 'Wait. They're out of range. Let them come closer.'

As everyone's attention was focused on the deer, Vela pulled away from the group. She came up beside Lynx, who felt a twinge of her brassy grief.

'Take it,' Vela whispered. Her token was already in her hand, and she dropped it in the snow beside Lynx.

'I'm not your grief nurse, Miss Deleporte,' said Lynx. Take it. Take it. Take it. A voice in her mind echoed. She balled her hands into fists.

'I'm part of this family.'

'Ms. Aster doesn't think so,'

'Well, aren't you loyal?' Vela sighed and took up her rifle. She set it on a rock, but instead of turning it toward the deer, she swung it around to face the hunting party. The barrel was directed straight toward Andromeda. Vela squinted one eye as she looked down the barrel's length. 'I'm a very good shot. Of course, at this distance, if I missed her, I would surely hit someone else.'

'Don't—'

'They say the second time is easier than the first.'

'Miss Deleporte—'

The gun's safety clicked off.

'Take it,' Vela said again, not taking her hands from the gun, not breaking her gaze toward Andromeda.

Lynx tore off her gloves and scrambled for the token. As soon as it touched her skin, her mind's dark fingers unfurled, lifting around her, jubilant to be let free.

The mirror hung, suspended in empty air. Lynx's fingers were reflected in its surface, like curls of dirty smoke. They brushed the glass, and it rippled. It was pliable, and she found herself able to manipulate its shape, stretching it, moulding it into a circle. Beads of molten glass dripped off the gold frame like tears.

Take it. Take it. Take it.

Stop, she wanted to scream, but she had already tasted the grief and it was impossible to break away. As the grief shifted beneath her fingers, memories rose up. At first she ignored them, focused instead on trying to resist, but then she realized – perhaps they could help her.

She plucked one at random. A memory that vibrated in the bones above her heart. She surrendered to it and tried to stay calm as she was pulled out of herself and into the mind of Vela Deleporte.

CHAPTER 22

That night, Vela was high from a party, and everything seemed so perfect. She had taken off her heels ages ago and they dangled in her hand. Her toes sank into the fabric of the staircase. As she climbed, she trailed her hand along the wall. Her fingernails were painted maroon but they looked black in the shadows. Her dress looked nearly black, too, even though it was a vibrant tangerine.

Just before she reached her room, she crashed into someone, and she cried out, feeling someone's hand on her, catching the scent of mint mingled with tobacco.

'Watch where you're going,' said Sculptor.

'What are you doing here?' she asked, pushing him away from her. He immediately recovered and slid his hands into his pockets. 'I thought you were visiting your family on their little island.'

'I decided not to go.' Sculptor pushed the strap of her dress back onto her shoulders. His touch left her tingling. 'Where have you been?'

'That's none of your business.' She pressed her toes into the carpet. 'Why are you still up?'

'I'm an insomniac,' he said. The shadows of the hall exaggerated the dark circles beneath his eyes, but he was still handsome with perfect lips, thick eyelashes, dark stubble on his chin. She pressed her hand against his chest, but he took her fingers.

'Are you sober?' he asked, gripping harder and leaning close.

'Obviously not.' She rose onto her tiptoes and kissed him. His lips always tasted of cigarettes and the mint he tried to hide it with.

He tore away from her. 'You were with someone.'

She huffed. He always did this. Ruin a perfect moment. Like tearing out the cornerstone of a perfectly-built house.

'Such is the nature of the games I play,' she said, and she could sense the potential for a fight churning beneath her words. She hoped there would be a fight. She preferred Sculptor's anger to whatever this was. This dull listlessness, when he didn't seem to care about anything.

His velvet eyebrows knit together. 'I know.'

She pressed herself against him and kissed him again. For a moment, he conceded. His mouth opened against hers, his fingers pushed the strap of her dress down, the one he'd just righted. She was pleased with herself. Everything would be fine. Sculptor Aster hadn't been a mistake. He was moody sometimes, that's all. And he'd gotten her a grief nurse. She'd love him forever for that.

Then, suddenly, he stopped. He drew away from her, taking her hands again and forcing them away from him.

'We can get Karina,' said Vela.

'No, no I don't want her,' he said, and she noticed the watch on his wrist was missing.

'Well, what do you want?' she asked, angry now. She snatched her hands away from him.

'I'm going for a walk,' he said, brushing past her.

She stood in the hall alone. The high she'd felt had dissipated. She felt powerless and empty. She clenched her teeth at the urge to see Karina. Instead, she went to bed.

That night, Vela lay atop her bed, shivering in the darkness. She felt herself in pieces, spread out on the bed like a dissected corpse. She pressed her fingertips into her eyes, feeling their perfect curves. She tried to let herself drift off, but with every heartbeat, she thought she felt a twinge of grief.

She threw herself out of bed. The dressing table was a hulking shape in the darkness. She'd thrown a blanket over it, to hide the trifold mirror. Her fingers itched to pull the cover down. Instead, she strode to the window and threw open the curtains. Silver-blue light soaked her skin. The sun was clawing its way over the tree line, and the snow took that scant light and lit up the world. She saw it all through her murky reflection.

She pressed a hand to her heart. Was grief there? Her heartbeat was steady, but she thought she felt its pace quickening, and then she was certain of it. Heartache. She felt the dragging, wretched sensation of Dread, too, not in her heart but in her head, like a knife held to the nape of her neck. The grief weighed her down. Her whole body now felt it, as if her bones were made of stone.

She needed it gone.

She fumbled for her wrist, but it was bare, and a quick glance at the nightstand confirmed her bracelet wasn't there either. Panic coursed through her. Without her token, she'd never be able to feel like herself again. She clutched her arms, fingers pressing deeply into her flesh. Had she given Karina her token? She didn't remember. All she could recall was Sculptor's kiss and then him pulling abruptly away. She didn't remember going to

205

Karina, but perhaps she had.

Her dress was discarded on the floor. She knelt and rummaged through the fabric then picked it up and shook it out. The bracelet wasn't there. She looked beside the washbasin, under the bed, she tore off the bedsheets and shook out all the pillows. Eventually, she turned to the vanity mirror, hidden beneath its cover. It had to be there, mingled with all her other jewels. It had to be.

Vela yanked down the cover. The mirror's glass shone in the meagre light. She saw herself reflected, face naked and drawn. She noticed she was shaking.

She wanted nothing more than to see the mirror's surface shattered. She could do it—with her bare fist even. She wanted to break every mirror in this house. Instead, it seemed to catch her first, holding her there, willing her to lean toward the mirror until she was so close her nose nearly brushed the glass. She looked into the depth of her irises, at the flecks of green and brown.

She didn't know how long she stared, but when she pulled away, she was no longer in her room. She was in a room with no walls and nothing but darkness above. A room hung with mirrors, mirrors rising from the floor like stalagmites, her reflection flickering back. A red scarf was tied around her neck like a wound. She tugged at the scarf, clawing her fingers beneath the silk, but it would not loosen. The knot was firmly tied, and her fingers were weak.

She pressed her hand against the closest mirror, half-expecting she could walk through it. It was cold and unyielding at her touch.

'Let me go,' she said, but who was there to hear her? She pounded her fist against a mirror. 'Let me go.' The room was deathly silent. Here, her voice had no echo.

She began to walk. Every time she saw a flash of herself in the mirrors, she was reminded of what she'd done, how even then she hadn't saved herself. She was broken. A failure. Soon she was running, trying to outpace the hopelessness and the fear. She ran, stumbling over the mirrors that burst from the floor. She fell, hands outstretched, and cut her hand on a mirror's edge. The glass was speckled with her blood, but she pulled herself up and began to run again.

Vela knew that there was no way out. She knew it and still she ran. She fell again and again, and her hands were bloody. Her night dress was streaked with red. She was no longer running now, but crawling, oblivious to the shards of glass that cut her. She didn't look up, only down at her hands, even though the mirrors seemed to sing to her, calling her to look.

She was a failure. She needed Karina. She could not beat this on her own.

She pressed her fingertips to her eyes. She would crush those perfect orbs if it meant being free of grief. She pressed harder, thinking of Percy, her first grief nurse. Thinking of an overturned cup of tea, his pale eyes still opened. Of the red scarf she'd worn that day, tied around her neck, and how her fingers had worried over the silk as she waited for Percy to die.

She pressed and pressed until she saw no more darkness, only colour. When she peeled her fingers away, she was looking at her own reflection in the trifold mirror of her bedroom. Her eyes were rimmed in red. She wore only her nightgown, no scarf, and her hands were clean.

She would go to Karina and everything would be fine.

The air was colder in the hall. Across the way, the door to Sculptor's room was ajar. It swung softly and a cold breeze snaked around her ankles as she approached. Had he gone for a walk and not yet returned? She walked inside, immediately seeing the source of the breeze – all the windows were thrown open, their curtains billowing. She crossed her arms against the cold.

The bed was empty, the blankets crumpled and one pillow lying on the floor. The door to the adjacent bathroom was open, too. She took a step back. She could slip away to Karina, go to bed with a light heart, and deal with all this in the morning. Surely, Sculptor was fine. But as soon as she had that thought, she was afraid.

She took a blanket thrown over an armchair and wrapped it around her shoulders. It smelled like him.

'Sculptor,' she said, as she pushed aside the bathroom door.

There was no answer.

The one window in the bathroom was open, too, but the curtain was stilled. The wind wasn't blowing this direction. The bathtub was full, and as she thought how strange, she saw him.

His head, leaning against the tub's rim, was tilted toward the ceiling. His eyes were open just enough for her to see the whites gleam.

She approached the tub, her fingertips brushing the surface of the water. 'Sculptor,' she whispered, but she knew he was dead.

She thrust her hand into the water.

At the very bottom of the bathtub, she found the knife. Beside it rested the wristwatch, the gold looking like silver in the gloaming. She held each object in her hands. It was too dark to truly see colour, but she knew her skin was slicked scarlet. Her nightgown was flecked with comets of water – of blood.

She had never known grief before, not like this, not the kind of grief so thick she could chew it. Her knees buckled. The knife and the watch clattered to the floor.

One hand, fingers splayed, braced itself against the bathtub's side as she pressed her forehead to the cool floor. As soon as the Sorrow seemed unbearable, like it would tear her apart from the inside out, it was gone.

She lifted her head. Karina stood in the doorway, Vela's token in her fingers.

CHAPTER 23

A gunshot reverberated around the hills. Vela's token tumbled into the snow. The black tendrils slithered away from the mirror, and Lynx gathered them up inside herself once again. Her mouth was dry, her throat sore as if she'd been screaming. The taste of blood coated her tongue.

Sculptor had taken a knife to his wrists.

What she'd always suspected proved to be true. He'd gone mad with grief.

'I still feel it,' Vela said, kneeling beside her. The others were rising now. Apparently Andromeda had missed her shot. Vela snatched up her token and slipped it into her pocket. 'It's still there isn't it?' she said, as she reached for her gun. Instead of preparing to fire it, she slung it across her back.

Lynx said nothing. The party began to move again, and Vela went with them. Her absence was a relief.

They picked their way over the rocks and around the low shrubs of the hillside. They were higher now, and the wind was stronger.

Lynx needed to speak with Karina. She needed to tell her that they couldn't wait any longer. Lynx was too dangerous, her mind too unpredictable, and she couldn't control it. The only reason she hadn't taken Vela's grief was because the gunshot had wrenched her from the memory. And there was the truth of Sculptor's death. That madness had killed him...

She quickened her pace to catch up with the others, but when she did, she was hit with a wave of grief, all of them mixing together. Water and fire. The earthy scent of the crows, the coolness of Vela's mirror. She stopped suddenly, her mind's fingers dancing before her, reaching forward when she refused to move.

But she had to move. She had to follow. She pressed forward despite the heady sensation of grief all around her. Karina walked beside Andromeda, and when Lynx neared them, she was slammed with a wave of Andromeda's grief. It took her breath, made her stumble and nearly slip. She scrambled to steady herself, fingernails catching in mud and turf, snow sending a jolt of cold through her fingers.

She stood there, letting the others pull ahead. The hill was steep, the path they took narrow. If she had fallen, she would have tumbled down the rocky face, most likely to her death. She looked out across the expanse of hills, remembering the other hillside that until two days ago, she had forgotten. She had buried the memory so deep and yet here it was, as fresh as if it had happened yesterday. If she left the island, she could leave the memory behind, too.

When Lynx had steadied herself and caught up with the others, the party had stopped again. They had found the deer. The five hinds were still together. One of them was clearly older than the others. Her body was bony compared to the muscled youth of her companions. Orion signalled for the hunting party to drop where they stood.

'Master Crater,' he said, turning his head so his words were snatched in the wind away from the hinds. 'You have the best shot.'

Crater gritted his teeth as he set his rifle against the rock, hunkering down to take the shot. He watched the deer with intense focus. He would aim for the old one. She was at the head of the group. The deer cocked her head, nose in the wind.

'Now,' said Orion. 'Master Crater, now.'

Crater fumbled at the trigger. His crows fluttered, anxious wings rustling. One let out an unhappy caw. The deer's ears twitched and then she bounded forward, just as Crater took the shot.

She leapt up, hind feet kicking high into the air. The deer behind her scattered, dashing off across the hills. The old hind fell onto her forelegs, but she was still half-way up, still living.

'Again, now,' said Orion his voice sharp.

Crater's breath was heavy. His crows had lifted into the air and were wheeling above him. His fingers trembled. He fired again, the gunshot bursting through the silence. The hind reared her head, eyes wild. She was dying, and the second shot had missed.

Orion took his own gun into his hands and rose. He held a hand up, the simple gesture as potent as a command, and Crater took his hands from the gun. Orion scrambled down the side of the hill, boots slipping on loose rocks, but he remained steady. He was making his way toward the dying hind, looking for the closet place to get a clean shot and end her suffering.

Suddenly, Lynx was dragged below the sea's surface, the sounds of the physical world becoming muted and distant. Andromeda had come up beside her.

'Lynx,' she heard Andromeda say. Everyone was standing now, moving toward Crater to watch Orion kill the hind.

Andromeda took her hand. As Lynx was rocked in and out of her grief, desperately trying to keep her head above the waves, Andromeda pulled her away, up and over a lichen-shrouded boulder, out of sight from the others. Lynx had wanted to take Andromeda's hand for so long that this moment felt impossible, like a dream.

A gunshot cracked, and Andromeda startled. Lynx pulled her hand away. Her fingers tingled.

Andromeda's lips parted, revealing the gap in her front teeth. 'I needed to tell you.' A pause, and Lynx was pulled under again. Her body felt so heavy. It would be easy to let herself go, drop to the very bottom of the seafloor, and let everything, all the events of the past three days, float away with the currents.

She thought of Karina. Of her black tree. Of the orange in Mensa's mouth. No, she couldn't stay here. She had to leave. She kicked her way to the surface, gasping for breath as she broke through. 'I meant it. The kiss,' Andromeda said. Her gold eyes shone.

All the desire and longing and hope that Lynx had bottled up for years suddenly was free.

She couldn't stop herself. She plunged into Andromeda's grief, making her gasp. She flickered in and out of it, one moment surrounded by water, the next pressing Andromeda against the rock, kissing her both under the waves and on the hillside.

'Lynx,' Andromeda said, their lips apart for only a moment before she closed the space between them.

213

'Lynx, I'm leaving.'

Andromeda brushed aside a lock of hair that had blown in front of Lynx's eyes as they pulled apart.

'My brothers know I'm a Fader,' Andromeda said. 'They wouldn't tell anyone, but Vela knows, too, and she has no reason to keep quiet. Mother will send me to a madhouse. I know she would.' She wrapped her arms around Lynx's shoulders, her fingers playing at the nape of Lynx's neck. 'Lynx, I want you to come with me.'

Lynx was dizzy from the taste of Andromeda's lips and of her grief. She couldn't believe what she'd just heard. Andromeda wanted to run away with her. All these years, and all she'd wanted was to hear these words.

She could do it. She was leaving anyway. And she had been in and out of Andromeda's grief just now and nothing had happened—

As Andromeda leaned toward her again, ready to kiss her, a dark thread crept over her shoulder. It wound around her neck, down her shoulder, her arm. Take it. Lynx stepped back, pushing Andromeda away from her. 'No,' she said.

She hadn't known she was doing anything. She hadn't felt—

'Andromeda.'

They both froze.

'So it's true,' said Crater. He stood behind them, red scarf wound round his neck.

Lynx shut her eyes.

CHAPTER 24

Crater stood with his arms crossed, red scarf fluttering in the wind, the crows perched on his shoulders. Andromeda's sea was throwing itself against rocks, foam and spray hurling into the sky, and the air was thick with the scent of brine – of seaweed and fish and salt water.

'The hind is dead, I suppose,' said Andromeda, as she pulled on her gloves.

'You should commit yourself. Save Mother the Heartache of doing it for you,' said Crater. He wasn't even trying to look Bright.

'I'm not going to a madhouse,' said Andromeda.

'It's where you belong,' said Crater, and even Lynx felt his words like daggers. The white spray of Andromeda's waves clawed at the rocks as they smashed against them, as if they wanted to drag the entire sea onto the shore, defy the tides, the moon. 'At the grief games, I thought it was just a mistake, or you did it on purpose to get a rise out of us.' His lips twisted. He pointed at Lynx. 'That wasn't a mistake.'

'No, it wasn't,' said Andromeda with only a slight tremor in her voice. 'I'm a Fader.'

Crater winced at the word. 'You don't belong at Mount Sorcha.'

'I'm a Fader, but I'm still your little sister,' said Andromeda, and even though her voice was steady, and she looked up at him with an unwavering gaze, tears rolled down her cheeks.

'I'll have to tell Mother,' said Crater. 'She deserves to know.'

'You don't have to,' said Andromeda, not wiping away her tears, but Lynx felt her disappointment shift into anger. 'You don't have to do anything. You could walk away and never tell anyone about me. But then you'd miss an opportunity, and Crater Aster never misses an opportunity, does he?' Andromeda pushed the hair from her face. 'I think you've been waiting for this your entire life. Finally, you can prove to Mother that you are the best, the most perfect of her children. You have never managed to succeed at anything, but at least you aren't a Fader, at least you didn't kill yourself or marry low. Well, there you have it, Crater.' She lifted her arms out to the sides. 'You've won. Mother will give you Karina once she finds out what I am. You'll finally have your grief nurse.'

Crater was caught in the silence, and for once he didn't try to fill it. He let it drag on, until eventually he said, 'I'll wait until after dinner tonight. We'll act as if nothing has changed. Then I will tell her. It's Mother decision what she will do with you.' His gaze shifted to Lynx and Andromeda stepped forward, as if her body was protection against her brother's betrayal.

'Tell her I'm a Fader, but don't mention Lynx,' Andromeda said. 'She has nothing to do with this.'

'It didn't seem that way,' said Crater. He stared at Lynx with a hardness she'd never seen before. 'I'll see how I feel.'

Andromeda's jaw tensed. She looked at Lynx, but Lynx looked away. She sensed Andromeda waiting for her, to say something or to take her hand.

She did neither. She'd chosen to let her go, and now she was certain in that choice. She had to get off this island before Crater told Ms. Aster the truth, before Ms. Aster invariably decided to send her away. She couldn't take Andromeda with her, not with her black tendrils hungering for grief. Already she'd done enough.

Crater stayed where he was, staring out at the hillside.

When Lynx returned to the others, they were busy loading the deer's body onto a pony's back, lashing the hind so her head lay against her back, her hindlegs dangling. The fur on her chest was matted with blood, and her eyes stared, unseeing.

CHAPTER 25

Lynx paced her empty room until the sun set. Then she slung the bag onto her back and crept out into the hall. After she had just turned and shut the door, a door at the end of the corridor rattled. She froze, pressed her back against the wall so her bag was hidden, and held her breath. The door opened and a footman, now casually dressed, stepped out. When he saw her, his gaze immediately dropped to his feet. He hurried away, shoulders stooped.

The corridor was quiet once again, and Lynx released her breath. She looked about her, expecting to see the black tendrils snaking around her, looking for grief. Briefly, she dipped inside herself. Her tree stood strong and dark. Wind rustled its leaves. It was unsettling to see its black crown stretching far above her, but she began to see the beauty in it. Worry burned her throat at the thought of what might become of it if Ms. Aster sent her away.

Already, the servants were preparing for dinner. She didn't have much time. Still, there was one person she needed to see.

Lynx realised she was holding her breath as she approached Karina's door. Was it right to ask Karina to come with her, knowing that doing so might put Karina in danger? If she left with Lynx, she'd be implicated alongside her. Karina, she reminded herself, was capable of making her own decisions. She didn't want to leave without giving her a choice.

Lynx pressed her palm against the door and grasped the knob with her other hand. She was about to turn it when she heard a voice from within. A man's voice. Crater.

'You're certain there is nothing left? You've taken all of it?'

'Yes,' came Karina's reply.

'But I can feel it,' Crater growled, his voice rising. 'I am not like Sculptor. There is nothing wrong with me. It is this house. It's making our grief grow. That's how the others died. They went mad—they went mad with grief—'

Lynx stepped away, far enough that Crater's voice became muffled. With a shock, she saw her dark tendrils creeping at the door's edges, trying to work their way inside. Fear shuddered through her as she pulled them back. She could not wait for Karina, and she felt like a fool for ever thinking Karina would come with her. How could Lynx have been so selfish to ask Karina to leave her life behind? And for what? A broken girl like Lynx. A single kiss. A fruitless hope.

She left through the servants' door and was immediately hit with a wall of cold. As she ran across the lawn, the snow was above her ankles. It was a wet, heavy kind of snow, the kind that melted easily against her skin but chilled her to the core. It was mixed with an icy rain that did nothing to lessen the snow that had already accumulated on the ground.

The path Lynx wove across the grounds was a familiar

one. The moon was lost behind the clouds but she didn't need its light. The shapes of trees, bare and clawing toward the sky guided her. She knew each one. The towering oak, over two hundred years old, the oldest tree on the grounds. The slender lime trees lining the forest path. The rhododendron that marked the curve that would lead her toward the sea.

The chill seeped into her boots. She couldn't think beyond each footstep, else she'd be consumed by her own Dread. She didn't know how she would survive without the Asters or even where she would go. She didn't dare think beyond the island.

She slipped her hands into her pockets to warm them and found the edge of something. Andromeda's shard of sea glass was in her pocket It was still sharp, not completely worn by the sea. She felt it cut her, but she held it tighter. The snow whipped around her, almost blinding her. Soon, she heard the roaring of the sea. She scrambled down a small deer path until the mud of the forest became sand.

The sight of the sea made her come up short. She had forgotten the power of a winter storm. Dark and rolling waves threw themselves at the beach. For as far as she could see, the sea was wild. It was a long way across the bay to the mainland.

The fishing boat was exactly as she had remembered it. It was overturned, its bow in the undergrowth covered in dark sodden leaves. Its stern lay in the sand where the tide threatened to overtake it. It was a one-person rowboat, an old fishing dory that she'd discovered while exploring the island when she was young. She had never told Andromeda about it, and she realized now why she'd kept it a secret. She hadn't wanted Andromeda to run away without her. Now, she was doing what she'd always thought was impossible. She was leaving the island alone.

Lynx placed the sea glass carefully into her pack. She hooked her fingers beneath the edge of the small boat and heaved upward. Some of the wood gave way in her hands, but she managed to flip the boat upright. Parts of the rail had rotted away from where it lay in the mud, but when she checked the other planks, they seemed sound. The oars were still tucked neatly beneath the thwarts.

She pushed the boat out into sea, gasping as icy water seeped into her boots. When the boat was far enough into the water, she pulled herself inside and took up the oars. She had just set the oars in place when a wave crashed over the boat, lifting the bow and sending freezing water down her back. She gripped the oars tighter and rowed. Her muscles ached, but she wasn't tired. She would make it if she could get far enough away from the shore, where the waves were strongest.

Despite it all – the snow, the icy water, the waves that rocked the boat – she couldn't help but feel a small spark of Brightness. If she left this island she would be free. It was not the sort of freedom she had always dreamed of, but it was enough to give her hope. This was her chance to truly start over, to leave her past and its regrets behind.

In the very next moment, this small spark was extinguished. She felt the wave before she saw it. The sudden change of the water's pace made her glance behind her. She had only enough time to look away and brace herself before the wave tumbled over her, pummelling the boat and sending it on its side. She tried to throw her weight against it, to force the boat to right itself, but she was weak compared to the strength of the sea.

She was thrown into darkness. The cold knocked the breath from her lungs, and she gasped, water coursing down her throat. She did not know which way was up, and she panicked. Pain pulsed through her body with every heartbeat.

She felt her mind's fingers unfurling, and it seemed as if she could see them, inky tentacles in the almost-black sea. She closed her eyes, letting herself feel instead of think, and as she surrendered herself to the sea, to the guidance of her instincts, she remembered.

Her mother rushed to the window. She knelt and grasped Lynx by the shoulders.

'Did someone see you?' she asked. 'Did anyone see you at the window?'

Lynx shook her head. She felt ill, her stomach turning in knots.

'Lynx, don't lie to me, please. Did someone see you?' Her eyes were pleading, and Lynx felt that delicious sensation that made her want to close her eyes and lose herself in that other place, that hillside.

Lynx nodded. 'There was a man at the window. And a woman.'

Her mother rose and peeled away the edge of the curtain. She peered out and then knelt again before Lynx. She kissed her once on the nose. 'We have to go.'

'Go where?' Lynx asked. Her mother was already moving about the room. She pulled a case from under the bed and was throwing things inside.

'Somewhere else. We can't stay here anymore.'

'Because of my hair,' Lynx said.

'No,' the woman said, and she slammed shut the suitcase, snapping closed the locks. 'Because the world is broken.'

'We'll fix it then,' said Lynx, and for some reason this made her mother cry. Tears rolled down her cheeks, but she swiped them away.

'You have to do as I say,' she said. She placed a hat on Lynx's head and tucked her hair inside and then she scooped Lynx up into her arms. There were voices in the stairwell that made her gasp. 'You have to be very good, and everything will be fine.'

'I'll be good,' Lynx said, and she buried her face in her mother's neck.

And as her cheeks pressed against her mother's warm skin, everything changed. She was among the hills again, the moon above her, the wind blowing her hair around her face. And this time, there were white tendrils, too. They curled around her. Take it. Take it. Take it, they told her.

They were her, and they were hungry.

CHAPTER 26

The house was like a crown, studded with jewels. It was dark save for its shining windows. Lynx was stiff and sore and so cold she could hardly feel, but somehow, after the sea had spit her out, she dragged herself back across the island to Mount Sorcha. She didn't know how long she was gone, but it must have been late evening, perhaps already past midnight. It was early enough for two servants to still be up, hanging outside the servants' entrance. Their occasional laughter punctured the night and made her feel more alone than she had ever been. She tried to wait for them to leave, but when she saw the orange glows of their newly lit cigarettes, she gave up. She was too cold and too wet to stay outside much longer.

She approached the house from the front, and as she climbed the steps to the great double doors, all she could think about was the fireplace that would greet her and how much she wished flames were still burning in its grate at this late hour.

For all their grandeur, the doors yielded easily. She stumbled up the steps, her wet boots slipping on the marble floor, and nearly collapsed at the hearth. The fire was small but strong, and the tiles around it were warm.

Her pack had been lost to the sea. She had nothing else to wear but the sodden clothes that stuck to her skin. She would sit by the fire for a while, until she was warm enough to feel again and then she'd sneak downstairs to her empty room.

Lynx brought her knees to her chest and rested her forehead between them. She let the warmth of the fireplace wrap around her. Why, after all these years, was she thinking of her mother again? Wearily, she pushed the thought away.

She slipped in and out of sleep and wakefulness, occasionally drifting into a dream – of those black fingers, of her growing tree, of the bodies in the larder.

A brassy taste and the coarse rustle of feathers against her skin woke her from her dream and she raised her head. She heard footsteps echoing around the great hall. Her heart was in her throat. Anyone standing in the great hall would see her. She was far from inconspicuous. There were many rooms extending off the hall's great expanse, and she could slip into one of those, wait until the night owls who were roaming the house wandered away.

She darted into the nearest room, a reception room where guests could be entertained if the great hall wasn't being used or if they wanted a break from the hall's festivities. The fireplace was empty, but colourful rugs covered the floor and tapestries hung along the walls, giving the room a warmth the marble hall lacked.

She nearly sank into one of the velvet settees, but then the doorknob rattled. She dropped behind the settee instead, feeling foolish and fearful all at once.

She heard Vela's laugh and Crater's less enthusiastic chuckle. For a moment, Lynx's senses in the physical world were overpowered by the taste of brass and feathers. When she managed to pull her mind away and keep it there as best she could, she peered around the edge of the settee.

Vela had her back against the wall. She was working her fingers through the silk knot at Crater's throat. 'Gloominess is a terrible look on you.'

'No one has seen her all evening,' Crater said, and Lynx wondered with a jolt if he was talking about her. Crater had changed from his hunting attire into a bronze silk jacket with peacock feathers embroidered across the shoulders. Normally, he would have worn it with panache, but he looked uncomfortable and awkward, as if he'd borrowed the jacket from a man off the street just to stay warm. Even from a distance, Lynx could smell the scent of alcohol hanging in the air. 'Something isn't right.'

'Maybe she went for a dip.'

'At midnight? In a snowstorm?' Crater asked.

Andromeda. They were talking of Andromeda.

'Well, maybe she ran away or maybe—' Vela shrugged. 'What difference does it make? She was going to a madhouse anyway. Were you really planning on visiting?' Vela smiled triumphantly as she undid the cravat's knot and pulled it off his neck with a flourish.

'She's my little sister.'

Vela began undoing the buttons of Crater's jacket, while he looked distractedly away.

'She knew I was going to tell Mother,' Crater said. He reached for his throat, but the cravat lay at his feet. 'I told her.'

Vela sighed, rolling her eyes. 'I never said we should tell her.'

'We planned this together.'

'It was your idea to wait until tonight. You insisted we find more proof. We had enough proof from the grief games!' She held the lapels of his jacket, drawing him closer. 'She kissed your fucking grief nurse,' she said, her lips not far from his. 'What other proof were you looking for?'

'A kiss could have been an accident.'

Vela raised her eyebrows. 'Have you ever kissed your grief nurse by accident?'

'It's done. We don't have to ruminate over it.' Crater pulled away from her and shucked off his jacket, which he tossed behind him.

'You're acting like Sculptor, and it's annoying.' Vela picked at the buttons of his waistcoat. 'I pulled you in here to celebrate.' She looked up at him, a genuine smile on her face. 'We have a grief nurse now.'

'I have a grief nurse,' he said, as though trying the words out in his mouth. 'Finally.' He looked at her, gaze flickering over her body, lingering on her long, bare neck. He took her hands, pulled them away from his waistcoat, and kissed her. He ran his hands along her arms, down her waist, one hand fumbling with the hem of her dress.

She leaned her head back as he hitched up her skirt. She rocked her hips, encouraging him further, and when he wrapped the fingers of his free hand around her neck, she gasped. He held her this way for a while, her hands down at her sides, pressed against the wall, her lips parted, a moan sometimes escaping between them.

Crater took his hand from her neck and began undoing his belt with one hand.

'You can pretend it was an accident,' said Vela, her voice breathless. 'Try to save yourself a scandal. Assuming, of course, none of your disloyal servants calls for an investigation. That's obviously what happened to me.'

'No, it isn't,' said Crater. He couldn't manage the belt with one hand and pulled away from her to unclasp it. Vela's skirt fell around her knees, but she kept her back against the wall. 'Your servants didn't call for an investigation. I did.'

Crater succeeded in undoing his belt, and he pressed toward her again, hands roaming along her waist, lips on her neck. Just as he lifted her skirts again, Vela snorted with laughter.

She pressed her hands against her mouth, holding in more giggles. 'Really? Are you serious?'

'What? What's so funny?' Crater's crows launched from his shoulders and spun circles around the tiny room, occasionally letting out strangled cries of indignation.

Vela shook her head. Her mouth worked, but she was breathless. Crater grabbed her by the shoulders and slammed her back against the wall. 'Tell me,' Crater said.

Vela's eyes grew wide. She took a breath, nostrils flaring, but she was clearly shaken. 'I'm laughing because if you hadn't called for an investigation into Sculptor's death, his will would have been valid. You would have inherited Karina anyway.' She waved her hand. 'Without all this nonsense.'

'You read it?'

'Of course I read it.'

'What do you mean I would have inherited Karina anyway?'

'You act like Sculptor hated you. Obviously, he didn't.'

'Vela, just answer my fucking question.'

Vela shrugged. 'He bequeathed her guardianship to you,' she said, saying the second word long and emphatically, leaning toward him as she did, so their noses nearly touched. 'He wanted you to have Karina.'

Crater pulled back. 'He gave me his grief nurse?' he said in a low voice.

Vela started to laugh again, and she immediately slapped a hand over her mouth to stifle it. 'You didn't need to marry me to get her.'

'I still don't.'

Vela's features transformed. From mocking mirth to a look of fear. 'That's not true. I can get you more than a grief nurse. You need my money to save this house.'

'Now that I have a grief nurse, I can get money myself. I can save this house on my own.'

'No, you can't. A grief nurse is useless if you don't know how to use them.'

'If Laurient Mensa can do it, so can I.'

'Mensa was vile, but he was clever,' said Vela.

'And I'm not?' Crater slid his hands into his pocket, apprising her. He looked more like Sculptor than he ever had, a wild edge to his smile that made Lynx uneasy. 'You're the one who isn't clever, Miss Deleporte. I know everyone's secrets, and you are no exception. You're whitelisted. Without me, you won't ever get yourself a grief nurse.' He looked at her wrist and the bracelet she was clutching. A mirror appeared behind Vela's head, Crater's grin reflected in the glass. It loomed over her. 'You need one, don't you?' said Crater, coming toward her, his voice lowering. 'You'll do anything to get one. You should be on your knees begging me to marry you.'

'I will. I'm sorry.' Vela scrambled to her knees, her hair falling around her face as she knelt at his feet. She held her hand to her chest, the token on her wrist pressing against her heart. 'Marry me, please. I need you.'

He grabbed her hair, pulled her head back so she was looking up at him. 'Unfortunately for you, I don't need you.'

The crows settled onto his shoulders. They cocked their heads and looked toward Lynx. Crater's eyes darted in the same direction. Lynx drew back, heart pounding. A cawing above her caught her attention. A third crow roosted in the chandelier above.

'Did you hear that?' she heard Crater say. A pause and then she heard rustling and beyond that the sound of distant footsteps on marble. 'Someone's coming through the front door.'

The crow above swooped down, and when she looked out from behind the settee, she saw Crater striding toward the door and yanking it open. His crows fluttered around him, screeching with anticipation. 'It must be Andromeda,' he said as he stepped out into the hall.

Vela stood. She paused, looking down at herself, a look of disgust on her face as if she hated what she saw. Soon, she followed Crater out of the room, and Lynx moved to the door's threshold.

'Master Crater,' said Orion, his voice the sudden crack of a whip. He was climbing the steps of the lower vestibule. Over his arm was a fuchsia coat, lined with fur dyed pink. Lynx's heart beat a jack-rabbit rhythm.

'Why aren't you using the servants' entrance?' Crater asked.

'We found this,' said Orion, holding out the coat. It was stiff with ice. 'I believe it belongs to Miss Andromeda.'

'Where did you find it?' Crater asked.

'On the shore, not far from the dock.'

No, no, no. The word spun around in her mind like

raindrops caught in a gale.

'But where is she?' Crater asked. 'Have you checked the hunting lodge? The gardeners' sheds? The glasshouses?'

'We've looked everywhere,' said Orion. 'I'm sorry.'

Lynx blinked and she was standing beneath her corrupted oak. The black roots beneath her feet shifted, lifted from the earth and twisted into the sky. The tree was even taller now, and its trunk had grown in girth. More leaves rustled in its crown. It seemed impossible that all this power belonged to her.

This was who she really was, who she'd always been.

She looked at her tree, and she finally admitted the truth she'd been running from the moment she saw Solina's body in the snow: she was a monster.

Andromeda was dead, and Lynx had killed her.

CHAPTER 27

There was grief in the air. She felt the thumping of Orion's hare in her temples. She didn't know how long she'd been waiting for him. Nothing existed beyond the present moment. The familiarity of Orion's realm – the brick and iron plate safe looming behind her, the napkin press squatting in the corner, the sharp scent of wine mingled with a copper tang – it all seemed absurd.

As if she were made of nothing herself, just a vast emptiness, she felt hollow. No anger, no sadness, no fear. She looked down at her hands, and half-expected them to act on their own accord. Her body belonged to someone else. It certainly didn't seem to belong to her.

Eventually, the door to the butler's pantry opened.

'I'm so sorry, Lynx,' he said when he saw her. The hare was at his feet. Its long ears twitched.

'Have they found a body?' she asked.

'Not yet.'

Lynx nodded. 'I know how she died. How all of them died.'

Orion's forehead furrowed. He shut the door. 'It was their grief,' he said carefully, as if he thought his words would break her.

'No, it was their grief nurse.'

'It's not unusual to go mad with grief.'

'You know that isn't true.' Lynx stood. She brushed her

fingertips over the back of the wooden chair she'd been sitting on. It was familiar, but it seemed altered, as if it had changed from walnut to maple. Everything in the room seemed this way. Familiar but changed. 'I drove them mad. Not on purpose. Something is wrong with— something is wrong with me, with how I take grief. I can't control myself.'

'Perhaps they didn't die of madness,' he said.

'They did. I know because to die of madness is to die like your grief. Solina's grief was ice. Mensa's an orchard filled with orange trees.' She paused. 'Andromeda's was the sea.'

He considered her for a moment. Orion never spoke unnecessarily. 'I understand,' he said after a while. He turned and opened the door. 'Come with me.'

She guessed he was leading her toward her room. She knew he had a key and could lock her inside. What would happen next? He would tell the Asters what she'd done. Her tree would be taken. She didn't know what would happen then – if that would kill her. She found she didn't care. It was the taking she was afraid of most.

When they reached the middle of the corridor with its indigo tiles curving above them, he did not turn left. Instead, he walked straight, toward the door that would lead them outside. She hesitated before following after him.

The freshness of the air made her gasp. She realized she hadn't taken a full breath in ages, so she took one now, sucking the chill into her lungs. Orion stood gazing out at the lawn, which was dark and colourless, a void stretching before them. Somewhere out there, the sea threw itself against the rocks of the shore.

From his pocket, Orion took a cigarette and a lighter, which he flicked to life. He didn't take a drag of the cigarette. Instead, he held it out to her, and without even thinking, she took it. 'I'll go pack you a case,' he said.

He turned. As he walked past her, she stood in his way. 'What do you mean?'

'I'm letting you go.'

'You can't do that.'

'I can,' said Orion simply. He nodded to the cigarette, the tip now grey with ash. 'Enjoy that, before it goes out.'

'You can't do that. Something is wrong with me. I could hurt someone else.'

'I won't ever know what it's like to be a grief nurse, but it seems an unfair life.' His green eyes were the only spot of colour in the night. 'There's much you don't tell me that I wish you would. I know that you're a kind person. I know you want to be happy, as much as they do. I know you deserve better than the lot you've drawn. It's nonsense, what you're saying.'

'I lose control. I'm broken.'

'Losing control doesn't make you broken, it makes you human. The Asters are broken. It's their inheritance.' Orion looked behind him at Mount Sorcha. 'Geminus poured his money into this house, trying to secure his legacy, trying to atone for what he'd done, but building a beautiful house doesn't absolve you of your selfishness. There is no gift he could give his daughter that would make up for sending her mother away.'

'I can't leave. The ferry isn't running.'

'We won't take the ferry. I know another way. Meet me in the smallest glasshouse. I'll be there as soon as I'm able. I'll bring you a case with new clothes, and I'll help you leave.'

'Orion—' She watched the hare lift itself up, its forelegs just barely brushing the ground. 'I could hurt you, too.'

He held her by the shoulders, a fierce look in his eyes. She thought of the first time she'd met him, and the handshake that had made her feel less alone. 'You won't. I've had my grief for many years. I will not be giving it up. You couldn't take it if you tried. I wouldn't let you.' He smiled, and she almost believed him. 'You're not leaving this place alone.'

She felt the flaring of his grief, the thudding of a hare's feet against the earth. Then he turned away and the door shut behind him.

CHAPTER 28

Lynx stood outside the servants' quarters, breathing in the sea air. She knew she ought to be making her way to the glasshouse now, but she found herself tethered to this place. She found it hard to move from Mount Sorcha's shadow.

She realized the snow had stopped falling.

As she tucked her hair into a hat, she was reminded of her mother's fingers doing the same the day they had tried to run away. The emptiness that had opened inside her the moment she saw Andromeda's frozen coat began to shrink. Something was moving in around the edges, not something she wanted to become acquainted with. She tugged the stolen coat Orion had brought her tighter around her shoulders, looked once behind her and began to walk.

Lynx tried to think forward, of a future off this island, but her mind conjured only a blankness. She knew what the harbour looked like, was familiar with the sounds and smells of the city, but she couldn't imagine herself there. She could only think of Mount Sorcha, monstrous and empty with Andromeda gone, and a flurry of memories she'd do well to bury inside herself and let be forgotten: The gap between Andromeda's teeth when she smiled, her hands in Lynx's hair, the diamonds of her hairpin and the feel of them against her fingers, the turning of a card against the cold floor of her bedroom, a silhouette of a girl sitting in a lightning-struck tree. She bit her tongue while she walked and tried to think of the present instead, of the cool air prickling her eyes and the squelch of the snow and mud beneath her boots.

Lynx stopped, breath billowing in a white cloud around her. The emptiness was gone. It was grief – her own – that had come rushing to fill it. From it, she felt a rising despair. Nothing would ever be the same again.

What did a grief nurse do with her own grief? Her mind's fingers shivered, but there was no object to sink them into, no sea to dive beneath. She felt bereft, unable to understand what she was feeling. This mix of emotions felt elusive, unformed. This was her own grief, but she couldn't grasp it. She seemed to hear the soft rustle of leaves and felt an urge to slip inside herself, but she ignored it.

She was ready to push it all away and continue on, when she sensed that she was not alone. She looked over her shoulder. Though the night was dark, the moon shown with just enough light that Lynx could see a figure striding across the lawn. Tall, thin, shoulders bent. His pace was quick. He was coming for her.

She looked away and hurried forward, hoping that somehow he hadn't seen her. It could only have been Eridanus. When she tasted the bitterness of soot, she was certain it was him.

The heat of his grief reached her first, fire sweeping across the ground, flames licking at the snow, black smoke spiralling into the sky. Then there was a hand on her shoulder, spinning her around, and she was looking into the hopeful eyes of Eridanus. The hope was gone like a spark, and his hand fell away. He took a step back.

'Lynx,' he said. 'What are you doing here?'

The coat and hat she wore weren't white, and he had mistaken her for someone else. Her throat tightened at the realization of who.

He had a coat slung over his arm. One of Andromeda's.

'I'm running away,' she said, and even though it was true, it came out easily like a joke.

He laughed, a low huff. 'You'll get in trouble, wearing that.'

'I didn't expect anyone to see me.' She was amazed at how natural it was to have a conversation, despite the heaviness inside her. She knew Eridanus felt it too, this act they were putting on. She wanted to stay in this place of pretending. 'I was going to the shore. To see—' She let her voice catch, and she glanced at the coat in Eridanus's arms.

'She's alive,' he said quickly, and the fire roared to life around them. Her mind's fingers stretched forward, but she snapped them back. 'She'll be missing a coat.'

Lynx thought of the black tendrils wrapping themselves around Andromeda's neck. She wished she had hope like Eridanus.

She nodded, thinking that would be the end of it and he'd continue on ahead of her, but he stayed beside her. Something was on his mind. She knew because the fire grew hotter, the blaze an uncomfortable warmth in contrast to the cold air. She willed him to go. Her jaw ached from holding in her hunger for the grief that raged around her.

'I've lost at my own game.' Eridanus took the wedding band from his finger. 'I can't stand the Sorrow.' Lynx noticed that his token was missing. His neck was bare. 'I was foolish to try. Mother has given Karina to Crater, and

I have no way of saving Syril. There is a space between us that I can never close.'

She understood that. There had always been a space between her and Andromeda.

'I should throw it in the waves.' He clenched the ring into his fist. 'Better to save myself the grief. Better to move on, get a grief nurse, be Bright like Mother always wanted.'

'You've given up.' She couldn't help it – she was disappointed. She'd admired Eridanus for being different than the others, a quiet rebel against Ms. Aster. Even he'd been bested by grief.

'I tried,' Eridanus said, his grief flaring, tongues of white flame bursting forth across the ground. 'I tried to live with the Sorrow, and I thought I'd found something in it. It gave me memories I didn't know I had. It reminded me of who he was and why I loved him.'

'Isn't that good? Isn't that what your husband said you would find?'

'What good is there in loving someone who is gone?'

Through the flames, she saw Eridanus reach for the necklace that was no longer around his neck. He lifted his head, his shoulders dropping, as he looked beyond her toward Mount Sorcha.

She followed Eridanus's gaze, and something caught her eye.

A dark shape against a gabled tower. Someone stood on the thin railing that wound round the spire. A flock of birds flew above the figure's head. In the light of the moon, she saw Crater, poised to jump.

Eridanus slid the ring back on his finger, dropped the coat into the snow, and began to run.

CHAPTER 29

Standing alone on the lawn, she had a choice. She could let Eridanus try to save his brother on his own, make her way to the glasshouse as she'd promised Orion. She could leave the island without ever having to think of the Asters again.

Or she could try to save Crater. He was mad, she was certain of it, and it could only have been her fault. Maybe she could find a way to undo what she'd done. But if she went back into that house, she would be throwing away her only chance at freedom.

What kind of freedom would it be, to live her whole life with guilt?

Her own grief seemed to shift within her. She felt the movement of her tree's branches.

No, she didn't have a choice, not really.

She felt the magnetic pull of the sea, of freedom, but still she turned and ran toward Mount Sorcha.

Lynx raced through the house. Like a twisted mockery of her childhood, she took the stairs she and Andromeda had taken countless times when they were children, challenging each other to sprints to the tower, daring to stand at the railing and look down without shaking.

She reached the final door. The wind whistled through the cracks around the hinges. Eridanus was there, trying the handle, but it was stuck. He reeled back and threw his shoulder against the door. Wind struck them, nearly pushing them back into the stairwell.

Crater stood on the railing, his toes over the edge, his arms outstretched. He was going to fly.

The wind made Lynx's eyes stream.

'Crater,' said Eridanus, his own grief flaring wildly around him. 'I'm here. It's Eridanus.'

Crater did not turn to look at him.

'Do something,' Eridanus said, turning to her.

Lynx took a breath and released her mind. Stay in control, she told herself. Her mind's fingers shot into the sky, racing towards the flock of crows that flew above Crater's head. Her mouth filled with the taste feathers, so strong she felt almost suffocated. She grasped at the crows, but they evaded her. Every time she willed her mind forward, the crows slipped away, flying higher.

Crater took a small step forward, and Lynx snapped her mind back. For some reason, she couldn't touch his grief.

'It's not working,' she said to Eridanus. 'Talk to him. You have to buy us more time.'

Eridanus took a soft step forward, reaching out. 'Crater, please don't jump.'

'Let me go, Dani,' came Crater's voice on the wind. Eridanus froze. 'You and Sculptor were right. I was afraid. I hated whenever Lynx touched my token. I hated to look into her pale eyes. I was scared out of my wits every time I felt that lightening of my heart. And when Sculptor died, I was afraid of going mad.' Crater laughed. He was still looking out at the lawn. From his height, he could probably see the sea. 'But I was wrong to be afraid.

241

It's so peaceful here.'

'Here?' Eridanus said, his voice no louder than a whisper.

Crater reached forward, hands extended. 'With the birds.'

Lynx tried again to touch his grief. She wanted to play with it, give him the same sort of high she'd given Sculptor countless times. If she could only touch his grief, she could calm him down, and Eridanus could convince him to step off the ledge.

But she could not touch it, and it was growing. More and more crows shrieked through the sky above them.

She felt the heat from Eridanus's fire getting stronger. She glanced at him. His grief was growing too, flames stretching above his head, smoke rising to mingle with the crows above.

'Fight it,' she shouted at him. 'He's the only brother you have left.'

Eridanus took a gulping breath of air. 'I asked Lynx not to take my Sorrow for Sculptor,' he said to Crater. 'Do you know what happened? It made me remember. I saw things I'd forgotten. There was one—there was one memory. I'd forgotten it completely, until the grief brought it back.' Still, Crater did not look at him. 'Sculptor and I were fighting. A real fistfight, out there on the lawn. Do you remember, Crater? He punched me right in the jaw, the scoundrel, and I thought I'd lost a tooth. I was furious because I was attending a party the next day, and there was a young man I had hoped to impress. I didn't want him to think I was a cur. I was about to round on Sculptor for destroying my chances, when suddenly you were there, between us, keeping us off each other.' Crater hadn't turned to look at his older brother, but he hadn't jumped, not yet. 'We were fighting over something absurd. I still can't remember what it was.'

'I remember,' said Crater, and his hands fell to his sides. 'He had taken your favourite cufflinks without asking, and he lost one.'

'Yes, that's right. I remember the look on your face when we told you. You broke out into the biggest grin. You were laughing at us, and we were both fuming. And you were laughing so hard, you were crying, and it was impossible to stay angry. In a moment you had us both laughing, too.' His words died away on the wind. Eridanus wet his lips. 'I love you, Crater. I won't let you go.'

Eridanus looked as if he were burning alive. Smoke whisked off his skin and tore off into the night. Crater hadn't moved, save to drop his arms to his sides, and she knew that it could go either way: either he would jump, or he wouldn't.

His token. If she had his token, she could take his grief. But the ear where his token usually flashed was bare.

'Where's his token?' she asked Eridanus.

He reached for his own token, which wasn't there. 'We gave them to Karina. Crater thought there was something wrong with the house, that the grief was growing somehow, and Karina said she could protect us if we gave her our tokens.'

A twinge of unease made her stomach flip.

'She has your tokens? All of you?'

'Yes,' Eridanus said, but she wasn't listening. Already she was reaching for Crater's grief. This time she didn't try to touch the crows. Instead, she watched them, and the more she observed them, the easier it was to see –

243

white tendrils twirled among them. White tendrils danced around Crater, too. She looked at Eridanus, and she couldn't believe how she'd missed it before. His flames were threaded with white.

Karina's white fingers.

She was driving them mad.

CHAPTER 30

Lynx found Karina in Sculptor's bedroom. She sat on the floor beneath the window, her eyes closed. The little pile of treasure she held in the scoop of her palms contained the lives of what remained of the Aster family – each of their tokens. A pocket watch. A signet ring. A locket. And a diamond earring. Lynx brushed her fingers over Karina's wrist. She reached with her mind, dark fingers flickering across Karina's skin. She closed her eyes, and the world shifted.

The room she knelt in was Sculptor's, but it was changed. The air was cold and carried with it the scent of pine. The muted silence of the house was replaced with the groaning of wood.

Lynx stepped into the corridor and swallowed her surprise at the yew tree whose canopy stretched toward the torn-away ceiling of the great hall. It was stronger even than when she'd seen it last, far stronger than her corrupted oak. She was uneasy looking at it, at its bulk, its animality. It was impossibly large, and it was growing.

She moved to the railing, but she couldn't see Karina through the layers of branches.

'Karina!' she shouted into the creaking quiet.

The branches of the tree shifted. They extended toward her, and she bit her lip to keep her composure. Needles brushed against her cheeks, ruffled her hair. Through the branches, Lynx caught a flash of white. She brushed a branch aside and looked down into the great hall.

Karina stood beside the trunk of her tree, her hair lifting lightly in the wind. She was beautiful. Confident and strong. Around her, all the grief she had ever taken glistened, and twisted, and fluttered. Why was she driving the Asters mad?

Lynx brushed aside branches as she made her way down the corridor. She reached the grand staircase, which was covered in a layer of roots. She half-fell down the stairs, but eventually made it into the great hall. The hum of the yew tree shook her bones. She felt it in her teeth, behind her eyes.

Karina was looking up, one hand at her side, finger constantly running across her thumbnail. Above her, crows wheeled and dipped. A snake wound around the tree's trunk, scales sliding against scales as it shifted Karina didn't see Lynx approach the tree, and she didn't notice when Lynx reached out her hand. The snake's head reared as if it would strike her, but instead it only flicked its tongue. Its touch sent a tremor through her fingertips.

As she expected, a memory rose to greet her—

Cassie was waiting. She was always waiting, but this past day had been the worst for it. At twelve years old, she had grown quite comfortable being her parents' only child. Months after learning she would shortly be usurped by a new baby, she was still in indignant shock. She'd never wanted to have a little sibling, and now she was so angry she could scream right into the expanse of the unfinished great hall.

She sat in the hall's centre with her knees pulled into her

chest and her head tilted up toward the scaffolding. The new house was almost finished. There was just the matter of the elaborate ceiling. Due to a shortage of a certain coloured glass, some of the skylights were still missing, and occasionally a flurry of raindrops snuck through the protective canvas to patter against the marble floor. One drop fell right on the top of her head, a cold shock. Outside, rain fell in torrents.

Not far away in the old house, the baby was killing her mother. Just because Cassie couldn't hear the screams or see the worried faces of the staff didn't mean her stomach wasn't squirming with Dread. Of course she'd seen the grief nurse not long ago, but she felt as if she hadn't been to him in months. She'd never been so afraid. She was nearly shaking. Tears stung her eyes, but she thought of what her father would think if he saw her crying. She swallowed and swiped the heel of her hand against her eyes.

I hate you, she wanted to shout. The only one to blame was the baby, who had decided to come far too early. Her father wasn't even here. He'd gone to the mainland four days ago and hadn't yet returned. News travelled slowly from the island, and he likely hadn't even heard what happened yet. What could happen.

She had a thought and spoke it before it flitted away. 'I hope it dies,' she shouted, her voice echoing through the hall. The words bouncing back at her felt harsher than she meant, but the guilt only made her angrier. If the baby couldn't be born... if her mother couldn't be rid of it... Cassie leapt to her feet.

Her footsteps were loud as she bolted through the great hall. She navigated through the many corridors and stairwells that led to the old house, a much smaller structure connected to the new house via a newly constructed wing. She hurried toward her mother's room. Someone stood outside it, baring her way. The midwife, all sharp nose and cheekbones with a constellation of freckles across her neck. The corridor was silent. Not a lovely silence like the morning room at dawn or the shore at dusk. A deathly silence. A hollow quiet. Cassie's heart pounded in her ears.

'Miss Cassiopeia,' the midwife said when Cassie reached for the doorhandle. The woman shifted her body, blocking Cassie's hand. 'I suggest you go to bed. It's late. You can see your mother in the morning. She needs her rest.'

Cassie almost laughed, the relief was so sudden. 'She's well.' She pressed her hands against her cheeks, feeling how warm they'd gotten. 'She didn't – the baby—Did it arrive? Was it born?'

The midwife flinched as if struck. 'Miss Cassiopeia...' She shook her head. 'Go to bed. Your mother needs to be alone.'

Cassie saw the lies written all over the woman's face. 'I want to see her.' She reached again for the doorhandle, but again the midwife blocked her.

'The baby passed. It did not survive,' the midwife told her, and Cassie drew back.

The baby was dead. Was its little body still there in the room? Was her mother holding it? She imagined its skin turned blue, its hands curled into fists that would never open. Cassie realised at once what she had done – her wish had come true, the baby's death was her fault surely. She wanted it dead only because it was killing her mother. The grief had made her do it. The grief had made her imagine a life without her mother, without her stories and her singing and the little notes of encouragement she snuck beneath Cassie's pillow sometimes when she was sad. She would be alone in this big house that was only getting bigger with a father who hardly looked at her and a houseful of a servants who thought her spoilt and plain.

She had only wanted her mother to live.

The midwife was blocking the door, but she had to go in. She had to see her mother and tell her what'd she'd done, how she hadn't meant the words she's shouted into the great hall, that she was sorry, that she was afraid to be alone.

'My father wants to see you,' she said, squeezing out a smile. 'He's returned from the mainland. He said to fetch you. You're to meet him in the drawing room. He didn't want to come here – in case—in case there was too much grief.'

The midwife nodded, looking stricken. More than that. She looked afraid.

'I'd call for the grief nurse on the way,' said Cassie. 'There's a bell pull in the vestibule before the staircase.' Cassie smiled wide. 'I'll go straight to bed.'

The midwife nodded again and strode off. Cassie let out a breath, took the knob in her hand, and stepped inside her mother's room.

The room was hot and sticky with the lingering scent of blood. Everything was perfectly tidy, as if nothing of importance had happened here. She saw the shape of her mother in the bed and the wooden cradle beside her. Cassie held her breath. She could hear her mother's steady breathing and—and a snuffling grunt, a strangled whine.

Cassie rushed to the bed. The blankets were pulled

up to her mother's chin, her dark hair splayed around her head atop the pillow. She was asleep, chest rising and falling. She looked thin and waxy, exhausted with a yellow tint around her eyes. Cassie heard the sound again, a kitten's cry, and with a bubbling sensation of hope ran to the cradle.

There was the baby, swaddled in blue cloth, a little cap atop its head. Its eyes were hardly opened, and its mouth was like a rosebud. It was ugly, with dark lashes and splotchy, wrinkled skin. Cassie stroked its cheek. It was warm.

'What a wretched woman,' Cassie said as she reached for the baby. 'What a horrible liar. You're perfectly alive.' Cassie investigated, unwrapping the baby expecting to find some disfigurement, some aliment to explain the midwife's deceit. She found what looked like a heathy baby girl. She held the baby in her arms, excitement thrumming through her. She had a sister. Everything was perfectly fine. 'Mother,' Cassie breathed. 'Mother, what is her name?'

But her mother didn't wake.

Cassie looked down at the baby and nuzzled her finger into the soft folds of her neck. 'What's your name?' The baby wriggled against Cassie's touch. Her cap slipped from her head, and Cassie nearly dropped her in surprise. She had hair, lots of it, and it was pure white.

The baby was a grief nurse.

Cassie looked at her mother asleep in the bed. If the baby was a grief nurse, that meant her mother was a Fader. And if her father found out...

Cassie bundled the baby against her chest. She didn't care when it started to cry. Now she understood why the midwife lied. She was protecting her mother. Cassie would do better. She didn't look back as she stepped into the hall. She shut the door carefully so as not to wake her mother, but as soon as it was shut, she walked away as quickly as she could. Her legs burned, but she resisted the urge to run. The baby was so small, so light, she was easy to carry, and she had stopped crying and only snuffled and grunted against Cassie's shoulder.

The anger was back. That grief. The baby had almost killed her mother, but it was not done. There was more havoc it could wreak yet. Such a small, stupid little thing could cause her family to fall apart.

As Cassie walked, she shuffled through her memories, all the memories of her mother. How had she never noticed? How hadn't she known that there was something different about her? Why hadn't she realised that for her whole life her mother had lied?

Cassie reached the corridor to the new house. She would go through the great hall, out the grand gold doors, and straight to the sea. She would destroy her mother's shame. She would save her family.

She was nearly there, halfway across the hall with the painted stars above her and the rain drumming against the roof, when a figure appeared at the foot of the staircase. Her father. Geminus. A slight, short man with the energy of a coiled spring. The baby began to cry, a wail that twisted like a wraith through the hall, and Cassie nearly smothered it, but it was too late. She was too late.

'Darling,' her father said, approaching with his arms outreached. He was smiling. He was always smiling, and the gold glinted in his teeth. 'Darling, what have we here?'

CHAPTER 31

Lynx returned to the cold and pine-scented wind of Karina's Mount Sorcha. She turned to find Karina's pale eyes watching her.

'Cassiopeia's snake,' Karina said calmly. Her finger still moved across her thumb, a small constant motion. Around her, the yew moved too, branches creaking, needles occasionally dropping from the canopy to be lost among the roots. 'What did it show you?'

'The baby,' said Lynx. 'The Asters had a grief nurse child.'

'Me,' said Karina. Her lips quirked into a smile.

'You're an Aster.' Lynx slotted the pieces into place to form a picture she hadn't imagined was possible. Karina was an Aster. She was born here, and her birth had exposed Andromeda's grandmother for who she was. A Fader.

'Not by name, but by blood,' said Karina.

'Ms. Aster is your sister.'

'Isn't she just brilliant at keeping secrets?' Karina motioned at the tree beside her, at all the grief among its branches. 'Aren't they all?' She shrugged. 'Perhaps that's the one trait we have in common.' She looked thoughtful, for a moment almost hurt. 'What a shame it ended up the way it did.' She looked at Lynx, a brightness flashing in her eyes that Lynx recognized as anger. 'I'm not special though, am I? None of our stories have happy beginnings. How can they? You either give up your grief nurse child or they take it from you. There are no other options.'

Karina was right. That was just the way things were. Geminus may have been cruel, but he wasn't exceptional in his cruelty, Lynx knew. 'But what happened? Afterwards?'

The light caught Karina's eyes as she considered Lynx. A moment passed before she spoke. 'My mother was sent to a madhouse and I was sent to a school for nurses. Geminus washed his hands of us both.' Karina's voice was even, but Lynx sensed the effort she made to keep it so. Like a pane of fractured glass, barely holding itself together. 'Like you, I was trained. I was assigned a guardian. As you might imagine, I wasn't very good at taking orders. Eventually, I left. Ran away. Ended up on the streets, and that's when I met Mensa, doing business as he usually was. He was looking to procure a grief nurse for a man named Sculptor Aster. You see how it all happened after that. It was an opportunity I couldn't turn down.'

Lynx understood Karina's hate. She understood what it was like to lose someone who loved you. The world was broken. She'd always thought it was foolish to try to fix it. Since Karina arrived at Mount Sorcha, Lynx had begun to see the world differently. She had always thought she had no power, that she was vulnerable without the Asters' protection. Now though her tree was growing stronger than it ever had, challenging all the lies she'd ever been told, all the stories spun to keep her in her place.

Yet... was this how she would choose to wield her power?

'You're driving them mad,' she said.

'The Asters need to suffer,' Karina said easily, as if it were a statement of fact. 'If I do nothing, every one of them will live their lives Bright and oblivious to what their family has done.'

Lynx thought of Geminus Aster, the man whose legacy was Mount Sorcha. He had forsaken his daughter, just as he had forsaken the wife he sent to the madhouse. This house was built on his guilt and grief.

'Geminus is dead,' said Lynx. 'The others don't know about you.'

'What Geminus cared about more than anything was his progeny.' Karina lifted her hand, and a root stretched to meet it. 'A perfect, pure line who would inherit his power and his wealth, who would have children who would continue the Aster legacy.' Her fingers met the root's wood, and she gripped it, veins standing out along her wrist. 'I want to end the Aster line because it is what he loved more than my mother's life, more than mine.' Karina's voice broke at that final word, and her expression was raw and unguarded. Her words left the air feeling thickened.

'Sometimes, I want to destroy them, too,' said Lynx. These were the words she'd always kept hidden inside her, that she'd never spoken aloud before because they frightened her. Because they were true. 'But to kill them, Karina?'

Karina sighed, and Lynx heard the disappointment in the sound. 'Madness is a peaceful death. That's more than they deserve.' Her voice began to rise. The roots around her shifted, as she looked up at the great hall around them. 'There is nothing the Asters love more than themselves.

There is no loyalty in the heart of a person who doesn't have to feel grief.' Karina smiled sadly, as if she knew what Lynx would ask next. 'Andromeda was no better than the others, Lynx. What made her special? Besides the taste of her grief, what made her different?'

Lynx thought of the space that had existed between her and Andromeda. It made her so angry to remember all those years she had hoped in vain that somehow it would just disappear. Even so, Andromeda had been her friend. They grew up together, and there had always been something between them, not just a gap, but a connection. 'I loved her,' she said.

'Don't be naïve,' Karina scoffed.

'You killed her,' said Lynx, and what she had moments ago thought of as confidence in Karina seemed to reveal itself to be a hunger for power. A desire not only to take but to destroy.

'I came here with a purpose, Lynx,' Karina said, voice low.

Lynx shook her head. 'She did nothing to you. She didn't even know Geminus.'

She imagined what it would have been like to sink her fingers into Andromeda's grief. Not to take it but turn it over on itself, encourage it to grow and grow until Andromeda no longer knew the difference between her grief and the real world. Until her grief consumed her so completely that all she wanted was to stay with it forever. Until her only desire was to let her grief take her. Until she slipped off her coat and stepped into the sea.

Lynx knew she was on the edge of losing control. She felt her fingers convulsing in her mind.

'What about Solina and Mensa? You killed them, too,' Lynx said.

'Solina suspected I was Geminus's daughter. She knew the rumours. And Mensa knew that I had wanted to work for the Asters. I had come to him, seeking employment with Sculptor.' Karina looked down. Icicles formed along the roots at her feet, and in the branches above her hung vibrant oranges. 'I needed the strength from their grief.'

Blood pounded in Lynx's head, and her cheeks were hot. 'What do you mean?'

Karina smiled. 'Look.' A root lifted from the floor of the great hall, slithered over the floor until it hovered before Lynx. 'Look what happens when we make them go mad.' Flames erupted along the length of the root, spitting orange sparks. Lynx stumbled back, but the root followed her, drawing closer. It was growing, expanding in girth as the flames engulfed it. It was devouring the flames, she realized. Taking its power.

The root that had reached for her, that had once been no wider than her wrist, had grown to be thicker than her waist. It dropped onto the floor of the great hall, cracking the marble as it fell. Flames still flickered along its length.

'Their grief gives us power,' said Karina.

'Power that kills.' Lynx looked up at the crows overhead.

'Yes, and so? In this world, we have nothing. We have no rights. They try to strip us of everything that makes us human, and yet—and yet, we can fight them with just a twist of our fingers.' Karina held up her hands. For her, it was as simple as that.

'I don't want to fight them.' Lynx's throat was tight, and she swallowed against the pain. 'I love them, even though I don't want to. Even though there is a chasm between us that can never be bridged, though they have done so much wrong.' She hesitated, trying to find the right words for a feeling she had never been able to express. 'I know I'm not one of them. I'll never be one of them, but they're all I have. And so I love them,' said Lynx, 'and I can't change that.'

Karina scowled. 'Well, they don't love you. You are an instrument and a symbol, existing only to make them look Bright.' She looked away, again tilting her head toward the tree's canopy. 'You will always be a grief nurse, Lynx. You've seen for yourself what happens when you try to destroy your own heart. If grief is power and that power is violence, then why should we deny it? Our very existence destroys people's lives. Right from birth, we bring destruction. How is what I've done any different?'

'You aren't finished,' Lynx realised. 'You're going to kill them all.'

'Yes.' Karina stepped toward her, stretched her hand out at if wanting Lynx to take it. 'Will you help me?'

She could, she knew that now – it was within her gift. She could destroy just as well as she had faithfully provided comfort and relief all these years. She could be the opposite of what she'd been told her entire life to be.

But even then, she would not be herself.

'I can't,' she said at last.

'You're lying to yourself. You don't need them.'

'It's not about that—'

'Do you know where I'm going once I'm done here?' Karina looked away, out toward the night, gesturing toward a place far from this island. 'There is a district in the city on the mainland called the Rue de Chagrin.'

Lynx had heard of the street of grief. A place where the poor went to have their grief taken by grief nurses without guardians. It was a dangerous place. Nurses were vulnerable there, where the law turned a blind eye.

'In the Chagrin, grief nurses are free, as free as they can be in a world like ours. They take their own clients. They keep what they make. They live alongside other nurses, and they wear their hair as they please.'

'It's a myth,' said Lynx.

Lines appeared around Karina's mouth as she frowned. 'No, Lynx, it's not. I've been there. It's very real.' She paused. 'It is not a beautiful place. It's not like this.' She looked around her at the imitation of the great hall. 'It's not what you're used to. Everyone there is breaking the law, one way or another, and you always have to watch your back, but you can be anonymous in the Chagrin. And you won't be alone. Help me, and I'll take you there.'

It sounded like a dream. Lynx swallowed hard.

Karina pressed her advantage. 'What do you want, Lynx? What do you really want?'

'I don't know. I've never thought—'

'Of course you haven't. We aren't meant to think for ourselves, have our own feelings, want things. They want us divided.' Karina's white tendrils unfurled toward Lynx, an offering. 'Let's fight them, together. We can change the world. Maybe that's what you want.'

Lynx didn't know what she wanted – she didn't know how to fix the world – but she knew she didn't want this. She reached forward with her mind, dark fingers brushing against Karina's pale ones, but she did not tangle them with her own. 'You have to let them go.'

'You cannot stop me,' said Karina harshly, her fingers drawing away.

The yew shivered as if a wind blew suddenly through it. A flock of crows rose up, wings fluttering, and more branches flexed forward.

'What good will killing them do?' Lynx said. The wind whipped up her hair, and for a moment, all she could see was white.

'I'm done trying to be good,' said Karina.

Lynx shook her head. 'There has to be another way.'

Karina laughed, and Lynx's heart sank at the sound. 'Why? Because you don't want them to get hurt?'

'Is it just about revenge?' said Lynx, feeling as if everything she loved about Karina was slipping away between her fingers.

'No.' Karina spoke the word with such conviction, Lynx felt its vibration in the tree that surrounded her. She lifted her arms at her sides. 'I'm doing this for you, too. For all of us. I'm becoming exactly what they don't want us to be. Strong. Stronger than them. With the power to destroy the world if we wanted.'

The air was filled with the sound of screeching crows. Lynx wondered if Crater had jumped.

'Their grief makes me stronger,' said Karina. 'This is how we're going to change the world, Lynx. We're going to become so strong, they cannot hurt us.'

It was an alluring lie.

'That's not true,' she said.

'Don't be a coward.' Karina's soft smile dropped away. 'Take what's yours.'

Lynx wanted to. She wanted a tree as strong and confident as Karina's. She wanted to radiate power and she wanted to make her own choices. She felt the anger within her, and she knew she was done hiding it. She could entangle her roots with Karina's and together they could take the Asters' grief until it killed them.

She wanted power, but more than that she wanted to be herself.

'No,' Lynx said. She called on her anger. She let herself feel it, let it course through her body, rise into her mind and she gave it permission to take over. She couldn't leave this island without trying. Karina had killed four people, and she was prepared to kill four more. She didn't deserve what had happened to her, what Geminus had done, but Solina didn't deserve to die alone in the snow. Mensa didn't deserve to be silenced, and Andromeda, who was destined for a madhouse, should have had the chance to run away.

Sculptor, for all his flaws, had deserved a choice.

'I can't let you kill them,' she said.

'If you won't help me, then stay out of my way.'

'Karina—'

Roots clawed their way across the ground toward her. Lynx stumbled back, kicking at a root that had snatched at her ankle. As her back pressed against the wall, she called on the fingers of her mind. They shot forward, and the dark tendrils entangled themselves with Karina's roots, keeping them at bay.

'You want them to love you.'

'Of course I do,' said Lynx. 'They were supposed to be my family.'

'But you know they never will be. So why choose them over me?'

'I'm not,' Lynx said. 'I'm choosing myself.'

'You're frightened,' said Karina, and the voice that could be at times so warm was cold with derision.

Lynx's fingers struggled. The roots were strong, and for all the anger that flowed through her fingers, she was not strong enough. Her strength broke, and the roots came tumbling forward, sliding over one another like snakes.

'You're a coward,' said Karina, and her voice was everywhere now, as if she spoke through the tree itself. 'You tried to tear away your own heart.'

The roots climbed her body, twisting around her legs, forcing them together, pinning her arms to her sides, wrapping around her throat—Lynx saw stars, blinking against blackness. Her lungs screamed to breathe, and panic seared through her brain.

Let them go, she wanted to say, but she hadn't the breath for words.

Just as the stars across her vision began to give way to darkness, as her breath struggled in her throat, as she felt as if her bones would snap beneath the power of those roots, the memory that had been piecing itself together the moment she had learned of Sculptor's madness reached out and took her once again.

CHAPTER 32

The sun was setting among the hills, and the sky was a vivid orange. The clouds were silhouettes, dark and curling along the horizon, and Lynx imagined they were horses galloping through the sea, rearing their heads as waves crashed around them.

Take it. Take it. Take it, the white tendrils whispered. They poured forth around her, spreading across the ground, lifting up into the air to taste the wind.

They were familiar, though she had never seen them before, and she sensed they belonged to her, or were her, but she didn't know what to do with them. Take it? She didn't know what it was, except that it must have been in everything here because she wanted to taste everything around her – the sky, the air, the heather blanketing the hills.

She took a step forward, and the fingers moved along with her. Take it, she thought and she opened her arms wide as if she could gather up this entire place. With a shock, she saw the white tendrils respond to her gesture. They shot forward, stretching out like her arms had done, and they began to pull it all inside of her.

It was the most delicious feeling she had ever known.

She laughed and twirled in a circle with her arms still wide. She wanted her mother to come here, the loveliest place in the world. If they had a place like this where they could be together, they'd never need to go outside.

She began to run. The fingers took and took as she ran. When she came to a stream, she splashed through it. She scampered up a boulder and stood at its top. This was her place, she decided. It all belonged to her.

Then something changed. The wind blew in a new direction. The white feathery clouds began to gather. Soon, the sky, which had turned blue once the sun had risen, was hidden behind them. It all still tasted sweet, but it was stronger now.

'Stop,' she told the white fingers, but they did not listen.

They took and took. Everything around her became too much. It was filling her up too fast, but she couldn't stop. She hugged herself, squeezing herself tight so the tendrils would do the same, but they did not change.

Rain began to fall, and the stream she had leapt through grew and grew until it was rushing through the hills. The purple heather shrivelled away, and yellow bushes of gorse pushed through in their place. Everything in this place was moving and changing.

Lynx hugged her knees to her chest and buried her face between them. Stop, stop, stop, she repeated in her mind, but the white fingers ignored her. They were hungry, so hungry, even though she felt sick with taking.

'I've never seen such a place,' she heard someone say. Her mother's voice. She looked up. Her mother stood not far away, looking out at the strange world around her.

'Mama!' Lynx leapt up. She rushed toward her mother and wrapped her arms around her. 'I can't make them stop.'

Her mother gently clawed her fingers through Lynx's hair. 'Let's stay here,' she said, but something was wrong with her voice. It was faraway, as if she were talking in another room but further than that.

'No,' Lynx said. 'I want to go.'

Even as she spoke, the fingers took and filled her up. She was dizzy, and she was seeing strange things, like memories but they weren't hers. She smelled bread baking. Heard the scraping of a poker against the floor of an oven so large it could have swallowed her whole. She saw rows and rows of sugared buns with cherries on the top of each one.

'Let's stay here, baby,' said her mother, and she pulled away.

Her mother began to climb the hill and Lynx tried to run after her, but every breath she took brought something new. A man's voice she had never heard before. The sound of a door slamming shut. Light streaming through the leaves of an apple tree. Her mother was climbing to the very top of the hill. Lynx couldn't reach her, so she stretched out her hand, and the white fingers stretched, too. They wrapped around her mother, and she looked so beautiful in that moment with the white tendrils like smoke flickering around her. And then Lynx was hit with another wave of memories. She felt as if someone were tearing her apart again and again, and then she was looking down at a tiny wrinkly baby with thin wisps of pale hair. The baby's eyes were screwed shut, and when she opened them, the irises were white.

Her mother laughed. She lifted her arms and took a step toward the edge—

The hills disappeared all at once. Lynx stood in the stairwell, the door of their flat open behind her. Her mother stood atop the railing, her body wavering as she balanced there. Her chin was lifted up and she was smiling. They were five flights up.

'Mama!' Lynx shouted, but her mother didn't hear her. She took one step and fell.

There was a crack, like a gunshot, that echoed around the stairwell.

Lynx gripped the bars of the railing. She did not dare look down. She shut her eyes and tried to go back to the hillside, to see if her mother was still there. But the hillside was gone.

CHAPTER 33

When Lynx surfaced in Karina's Mount Sorcha, with the roots of the yew still wrapped around her, she reached out with her mind and plunged her black tendrils into her heart.

The wailing of the wind suddenly cut away. The smells changed, from pine and winter air to gorse and peat. She no longer stood in the great hall. Instead, her shoes pressed into soft earth. She stood on a hillside, green all around her.

Her tree was still, its black branches like shadow puppets against the light sky. It had grown again, its trunk now almost as wide as the yew's, and leaves sprouted on all its branches. An acorn dropped from up high and fell at her feet.

She bent and picked it up. It sat like a gem of jet in her palm.

There was only the sound of her own ragged breathing and the low hum of the tree. She focused on the humming, willing it to call out to her. The song grew louder the more she listened. She could no longer hear her own breath, only the pulsing song. Her first instinct was to run. That sound contained the memories she'd been hiding from for years.

The memories. She squeezed the acorn in her fist.

Tall grass brushed against her knees as she walked

forward. She remembered the shame and anger that had caused her to rip the roots from the earth, bend the branches until they snapped. After her mother's death, after Lynx had been taken away, when the lights were out one evening in the place they called a school, she'd pulled herself inside herself and tried to destroy the tree. She bent its branches and tore its leaves. She'd never felt such anger in her life. She had almost uprooted it – she felt the creaking of its roots – but she'd been unable to truly destroy it. From that moment, it was broken. It never grew the same again.

That anger and shame weren't gone. She felt them in her body as aches, as a heaviness in her limbs, as something clawing at her back.

But now her tree was growing again, and she thought she knew why.

Roots shrank away from her feet as she moved, as if the tree were frightened of her.

'I'm sorry,' she said, as she pressed her palm against its trunk. 'Will you forgive me?'

A memory flared – a woman with blond hair pulled a tray of shortbread from an oven – and the tree shifted. A shiver ran through it, rustling its leaves. The branches stretched toward the sky.

The tree was her grief. Just as Mr. Aster's was a rose, Crater's a crow, Eridanus's a fire.

A grief tree sang in memories, and it wanted more than anything for someone to listen.

The memories gave it strength. Her grief was the source of her power.

CHAPTER 34

Lynx peeled her hand away from her oak tree. The bark had made indentations in the skin of her palm, and a tremor ran through her fingers. She knew what she had to do.

She pulled herself back into Karina's place.

Karina's Mount Sorcha howled with wind. Crows shrieked and the scent of smoke hung thick. The air was charged with grief. The great yew tree was growing, as roses burst along its branches. A murder of crows roosted in the tree's crown, the branches bending beneath their collective weight. Fire lapped at the roots, smoke rising in grey swirls. The snake still clung to the tree's trunk.

Lynx braced herself. She called on the fingers of her mind, urging them forward. They burst all around her, twisting like serpents, and still she pulled until the dark tendrils began to harden. Her mind's fingers became the roots of her tree. They wrapped around the roots that clung to her and tore them away. Then they launched toward Karina's tree, throwing themselves against the branches, sending needles erupting into the air.

The yew creaked, the sound like a scream. Lynx's breath was yanked from her throat, as the yew fought back. She stumbled forward, gasping. Lynx's roots were pressing toward the yew's trunk, but they were battered by the animal power of the yew's branches. Still, they pressed forward, and every time a root snapped, Lynx felt as if her heart were breaking. She thought bigger, of not just the roots but of her tree's branches, of its canopy stretching to meet the yew's.

She saw Karina then, standing beside the tree's trunk. Her hands were balled into fists, her hair lifting and rising around her face in the wind. She was looking at the highest branches of the tree, where the dark shapes of crows whirled and settled, whirled and settled. Lynx felt the surge of power, sensed her own roots falter, more breaking. The branches of her oak which had intertwined with the yew's were stripped of their leaves as Karina called on Crater's grief. Oak leaves floated around her. One landed on her shoulder before the wind took it.

Grief was power, but Lynx would not draw on another's grief to give her strength. She turned, and there beside her stretched her own oak tree. It was still firmly rooted in Lynx's grief place, on that hillside. She could hear the sound of birds twittering, smell the heaviness of the earth. Lynx found she could be there and here at once, and she pressed her palm against the tree.

An icy drop of water splashed against her cheek. She lifted her head up, and as the water rolled down to the ridge of her jaw, a memory flared up, burning away as quickly as it appeared— Her knees had been scraped raw from the climb up, but it was worth it. She'd smeared blood on her dress, and the sight of the scarlet mark made her happy. When she was alone, she didn't hate herself so much. She didn't mind being a Fader when there was no one to hide from. She'd never spoken the truth aloud before, not even to Lynx, who surely knew. The wind howled. The clouds were heavy over the sea. She stood on the cliffside and shouted into the impending storm, 'I am a Fader.'

Above Lynx, a black limb was slickly wet, and silver beads of rainwater shivered at the tip of every branch. Not rainwater. When she swiped the droplet from her jaw and brought it to her lips, it tasted of brine.

Her knees nearly buckled in despair. All that was left of Andromeda's untamed sea clung to the branches of her tree, nothing more than a few drops of water. Nothing more than a few quivering beads of memory. Without thinking, Lynx held out her cupped hands and caught the next drop, and the next. She tasted her own Sorrow, and it was sweet and bitter. She couldn't bear to see more, even as she craved to catch more drops into her waiting hands. She reached out again, letting the memories fill her.

Lynx gritted her teeth, even as each falling drop of grief seemed to hollow her out, the way rock can be moulded by raindrops given enough time. Soon there would be nothing left but a shell of herself, scraped out and sore.

Lynx drew in a long breath and loosened the ties that bound her heart. She had all her life refused to look directly at the squirming, needling truth: she had her own grief, just as much as anyone else. For the first time, she acknowledged it, as if it had been standing for years on a doorstep, shivering in the cold and wet, waiting to be let in. She welcomed it, even as it cut her, even as it sent painful memories flaring. Old, ugly thoughts snapped their teeth. This time, she listened. She heard it for what it was and let it go, let it settle inside her. She found that amidst the regret and self-loathing and worry, there was joy and bold, golden bursts of happiness, too. She realized that the tree was singing, and its song vibrated through her body. She was a grief nurse. She was grief. It felt like coming home.

Another drop fell from the tree, splashing against the nape of her neck, shocking her with its chill like a prick of a needle. The branch that had dripped with Andromeda's grief was dry, and when she felt a pang of Heartache at the loss, Lynx didn't fight it. She opened her heart to it, and it floated inside, a feather caught in the wind.

Lynx's shattered roots began to grow again, leaves burst from the tree's branches, and the oak surged forward. Its canopy was tangled with the yew tree, while roots snaked around its trunk. Lynx bit her lip, her fingers clawing into the bark of her tree, and made the Sorrow rise again.

She thought of her mother, who she had driven mad with grief. Who had tried so hard to keep her safe against all odds. Lynx had for her whole life hated herself for what she'd done. She'd ignored her grief and pushed the memory as deep inside her as she could. But the memory showed her what she had never noticed before. She had lost control in her mother's grief not because she was broken but because she was a child whose power the world feared and desired all at once. She hadn't known how to control herself. How could she have? Who was there to show her?

Her mother was dead, but her love lived on in Lynx's grief, in the bark and the branches and the roots of her tree.

The oak reared back, as Lynx called her fingers to herself. She would save the Asters. She would tear Karina's tree from the ground. She would drag it into her own grief place, freeing the Asters' grief. At first, the oak was strong enough so that the yew's roots began to lift from the ground, but Eridanus's fire flared into life, and the roots clung on.

Lynx was weak with grieving. She was kneeling now, pressing her cheek against the trunk of her oak tree. She could feel it shifting and groaning beneath her. Karina was too strong. She was tearing the oak out by its roots. Even Lynx's own grief wasn't enough.

Lynx lifted her head. The Asters' growing grief was pushing aside the other grief that lived among Karina's branches. An old grief, which had once grown close to Karina's trunk, had been pushed aside and was now flowering among the roots at the edge of the hall. A cluster of goldenrods. Lynx stretched out her hand and ran her fingertips through the flowers. She knew whose grief this was.

With one hand still braced against her tree, she wrapped her fingers around the goldenrods and she pulled.

The grief came away easily into her hand. She was hit with a flutter of memories, rushing at her all at once, and then it was gone. Her fist was empty.

Grief was pain, but it was also love. Lynx felt it in the bark that pressed against her palm, in the soft singing of the tree. Grief was love, and whoever said love didn't hurt? That it was always joy and happiness? Being Bright was a lie. It was an impossibility. Grief, love, it was a two-sided coin, a double-edged sword. One did not exist without the other. Lynx wrapped her arms around the tree, and silently she thanked it.

'No!' she heard Karina scream.

All at once, the crows fluttering in the crown of the yew tree lifted into the air. Their screeches echoed throughout the hall, and their wings fought the wind. They shot toward the night, away from the house. Black shapes blotted out the stars as they flew higher and higher until, eventually, their cries faded away. The yew shrank at the loss of the birds. Karina clenched her fists and stared after them, and Lynx watched, rapt, wondering if Karina would realize: all she needed to do was press her palm against the tree's trunk and call on her own grief.

If Karina knew, she did not do it. The oak lurched forward, and Lynx squeezed her eyes shut, preparing for the inevitable wrenching of its roots. But the vibrations shifted. The oak groaned, and the yew responded. They were locked together, two equal forces, their branches intertwined, their roots indistinguishable. Lynx called her fingers back, and the oak complied, dragging the reluctant yew forward. There was the sound of stone rending, as the yew lifted from the ground.

Lynx thought of the hillside where her tree grew, of the scent of summer, of the sound of the birds. When she opened her eyes, she was there, still clutching the oak. Her teeth vibrated at the sound of something crashing down around her. The yew. Its branches shook as it fell. Far away, Lynx heard a woman scream. Karina, trapped without her tree in the other Mount Sorcha.

Lynx was shaking, and her tree was shuddering, too. It heaved forward. It stood at an angle and its many roots were lifted from the ground. Its song filled her ears. All her grief and many others coursed through its trunk, through its branches and its leaves. The tree was the very heart of her. It made her a grief nurse. It made her human.

A knot rose like a fist in her throat, as she realized what would happen next. She threw herself away from her oak, just as it fell, crashing to the ground, still entangled with the yew.

As Lynx fell, she felt something inside her snap. All she could see was white. The sounds of the hillside were gone. Her cheek pressed against something soft. When she opened her eyes, and her vision returned, she was lying in a puddle of golden hair. She turned her head to see who it belonged to and realized that it was hers.

CHAPTER 35

Karina was gone. The Asters' tokens lay scattered across the floor, putting Lynx in mind of Ms. Aster's overturned jewellery box. She knelt beside them, letting the blood rush back into her limbs, but she didn't touch them. She felt—an absence. The golden hair fell around her face. She reached up and tugged a fistful. Her hair.

Lynx pulled herself up. There was a mirror hanging on the wall across the room, and she walked toward it, her body heavy and her movements slow. She wasn't sure if she was full of hope or fear. The face she saw in the mirror couldn't be hers. She saw her mother's deep brown eyes and blond hair. She shook her head, and the woman's head shook, too.

The woman in the mirror was not a grief nurse. Not anymore.

She turned away and knelt beside the discarded tokens of the family Karina had tried to drive into madness. Lynx picked up Eridanus's gold chain, bracing herself for the tang of fire. All she felt was cold metal. No flames at her back, no smoky cinnamon against her tongue. She realized why she felt blank, empty. She couldn't feel grief.

She took each token into her hands in turn, closing her eyes, reaching with her mind, but the dark tendrils were gone. When she tried to pull herself inside herself, there was nothing. No oak tree. Just a void. She had thought before that she was broken, but she knew now what it truly meant to be incomplete, a piece of you snapped away. If she wasn't a grief nurse, who was she? Her throat was raw and tight, but her eyes were dry. When she was certain that the tokens would give her nothing, she placed each one on the windowsill, like the sea glass she had lined up on her dresser.

What she feared had come true – her tree was gone, just as she had learned to love it. Now, she would have to learn to live without it.

Lynx stepped out into the hall. Not until the skylights above her shone in the colours of winter did she realize that she would never enter Sculptor's room again. She looked behind her at the shut door, the doorknob forged into the shape of an oakleaf.

Good riddance, she wanted to say, but she wouldn't have meant it. This house had made her who she was.

She continued down the hall until she reached the drawing room. The door was open, spilling golden light across the floor. She went to the threshold and peered inside.

Her heart jumped. They were there, all of them – Mr. Aster, Ms. Aster, Eridanus and even Crater. Mr. Aster and Eridanus stood beside the window, looking out. They spoke in low voices, heads bending toward one another, and Eridanus turned to his father and embraced him. Mr. Aster smiled.

Ms. Aster sat on the settee beside Crater. He was still Brightly dressed, hair combed back, cravat impeccably tied, but despite the weariness etched in his face, there seemed to be a light within him. A Brightness, maybe a vulnerability.

Lynx found that even though she was no longer a grief nurse, she was still aware of grief. She no longer saw it as a crow or a rose, but she felt its familiar presence. It was with the Asters, where it belonged.

There was movement and then the doorway darkened as someone stood at the threshold.

Orion. He saw her, and he took a small step back. She had never once seen him so surprised, but he did not give her away. He stepped forward, and she knew he meant to come with her, to help her off the island as he'd promised, but just as his mouth parted to speak, she shook her head. She no longer needed protection, not even Orion's. She smiled to let him know it would be all right. He studied her face for a moment then nodded once, and when she extended her hand, he took it without hesitation. Orion and Lynx smiled at one another. Then their hands fell away from one another and he closed the door.

The house was quiet. The dawn had not yet broken. In her room, she found a case, packed by Orion. He must have waited for her in the glasshouse and placed the case here when she hadn't arrived. He was prepared for anything.

She slipped out the door, savouring for a long moment the feeling of the handle in her palm.

Lynx reached the shore just as the sun began to creep across the horizon. The clouds were gone, and an umber light shone across the world. She picked her way across the island, toward where the ferry met the land.

As she stood on the wooden jetty, she watched the ferry rock and judder as it docked.

'Are you the only one then, miss?' the woman who stepped from the boat asked. She stood with one foot on the ferry, the other on the jetty, as she wound a rope around a piling.

Lynx nodded. She'd taken a hat but hadn't worn it. Her hands worried at its brim. The woman eyed her hair, suspicious, and Lynx found comfort in the familiar expression. When the woman offered her hand to let Lynx aboard, Lynx felt a thrill hemmed in sadness. She should be happy. All she'd ever wanted was to be someone else, and yet—

''Morning,' said a gruff, cheerful voice. It was the captain, wearing a worn cap, sporting a dark beard, heavy boots thudding onto the deck. 'Just yourself?'

'Yes,' said Lynx. 'I'm the last of the guests.'

He nodded, eyebrows flicking upwards. 'That's an unusual choice to wear your hair like that. Not something you see often around here.'

Lynx fought the impulse to lift her hair up and twist it away from her face. Her eyes were brown now, but her hair was still fair. Not white, but pale enough to draw attention.

Lynx looked back toward Mount Sorcha. All she could see was the sandy coast, the black rocks, and the forest beyond. 'I'm not one of them.'

'Ah, no, of course not,' said the captain. 'Well, welcome aboard.'

As the ferry moved away from the dock, rocking gently, water slapping against its sides, Lynx turned her back on the island she'd called home. Her hunger was gone, but she wasn't sated. She chewed her lip and watched the sea stretching out before her, waiting to catch a glimpse of a dark shape, a girl emerging from the waves.

She saw nothing but the sea.

As the ferry made its way across the bay, Lynx blinked away the raindrops that landed on her eyelashes. She didn't move into the lower cabin, and instead let the wind draw its cool fingers across her skin. She swallowed a hiccup of fear, the sinking feeling that this was it: she couldn't go back. Her fingers played with the buttons of her coat.

Even though they were still on the sea, she could taste the mainland in the air. Smoke and horse shit and too many bodies pressed together.

'That's us then,' said a voice. The captain stood on the deck behind her, and she realized that the ferry was already moored. It was tiny, compared to all the other boats bobbing in the water of the harbour.

'Thank you,' she said.

'Alright, miss. Good luck to you.'

Lynx picked up her case and stepped onto the dock. She felt small as she walked onto the mainland, the shouts of people, the clatter of hooves, the indelicate roar and bang of motorcars rattling around her. She'd forgotten how different it was at Mount Sorcha, how much it felt like another world, trapped in the past, all glittering colours and gold lights.

She was unable to resist the pull of a crowd forming along the harbour wall. She clutched her case and stood on her tiptoes to see above heads and hats. Everyone was watching something in the harbour, a dark shape sliding through the water. She heard the word 'whale' and caught a glimpse of a black body, a solitary dorsal fin.

'What's happening?' she asked the girl beside her, who was being half-hoisted up by a friend or a lover.

'There's a young whale trapped in the harbour,' the girl

shouted down to Lynx.

Just then the whale burst from the water, body thin and pointed like a blade of grass, underbelly a shimmering white. A spray of white rose all around her as she landed, and the crowd gasped. The whale twisted onto her side as she cut through the water and lifted a fin as if to wave. The crowd shifted in its excitement, and Lynx was forced to shuffle to catch a glimpse of her again. She found her, just as the whale shot a stream of water from her blowhole.

'She's playing,' Lynx said, breaking into a smile.

Someone shouted and then everyone moved again, drawn to the left, pulled along like magnets as the whale swam. Lynx stood, solitary in the crowd, clutching her case and her hat while the whale darted circles around the harbour, barely missing the moored boats, making them rock and sway as she swam past. Then, as if she'd known all along, as if she'd never been trapped at all, she leapt one more time from the water and shot away through the harbour's mouth.

The crowd roared in triumph. Lynx laughed and cheered with them. They had thought the whale trapped, but she was only playing. Already she was gone, home and free.

As she heard the sound of her own laugh fill her ears, a sound she hadn't heard in such a long time, the world seemed to drop away beneath her. She nearly dropped her case. She was rocked from joy to sadness, all in that single moment. She, too, was free, but she was not going home. She had no sea to welcome her. She closed her eyes, the sounds of the crowd a muted roar, and felt herself suspended, as if floating in deep water, blackness below her, and the hazy light of the surface far above.

She wanted to go home. She wanted the coloured lights of the winter wing to dance across her body, to sit on the cold floor of her room and have Andromeda read her fortune. She wanted to hear Sculptor's dreadful piano playing and Crater's incessant gossip and to have Eridanus confide in her. She wanted, more than anything, to taste grief again. In that moment, she felt as if she would do anything to get it all back. That she would swim across the bay, back to that island if that would take her back in time.

She let the grief – her own and no one else's – roll through her. She welcomed it and did not ask it to leave. Instinctively, she tried to go within herself, and when the bustle of the harbour fell away, she looked around her in shock. She stood on a hillside, much like her mother's grief. At her feet grew a tiny sapling, no bigger than the length of her hand, with three perfect green leaves. She dropped to her knees and brushed her fingertips against a leaf. It was soft and cool.

For the first time in her life, she truly had a choice.